Scott Schneider has masterfully written a novel that you will immediately identify with. Each character reminds you of someone you know, and you literally feel that you are either in the bleachers watching the game or inside the deep-seated controversies this family is facing. This is a must read book that perfectly illustrates the issues of forgiveness and redemption. Truly a Diamond in the rough!

—Michael Jankowski
Lead Pastor, The Harbor Church
Long Island, New York

In this novel, Scott has done a fascinating job of peeling back the many layers of one man's soul to reveal how the complexities of his life's experiences, both good and bad, impacted and impeded his relationships with other people, and even with God. I found myself continuously drawn to want to read more and more, and as I did, every chapter became my favorite! It's not a heavy read. In fact it's very delightful, but it carries a potent and clear message on the power of forgiveness. Don't be surprised to find bits and pieces of your own soul being peeled back as you go through its pages, and be prepared to have a little bit of transformation taking place in you as it does in Taylor Green, the book's main character .

—Rick Kraker
Founder and Director of People on Purpose, and one of the founding pastors of City Church, now Churchome, Seattle, Washington

DIAMOND
IN THE
ROUGH

A Journey toward Faith in the Midst of Struggle

W. Scott Schneider

WESTBOW
PRESS®
A DIVISION OF THOMAS NELSON
& ZONDERVAN

WestBow Press books may be ordered through booksellers or by contacting:

WestBow Press
A Division of Thomas Nelson & Zondervan
1663 Liberty Drive
Bloomington, IN 47403
www.westbowpress.com
1 (866) 928-1240

ISBN: 978-1-9736-9402-1 (sc)
ISBN: 978-1-9736-9404-5 (hc)
ISBN: 978-1-9736-9403-8 (e)

Library of Congress Control Number: 2020910700

Print information available on the last page.

WestBow Press rev. date: 6/25/2020

DEDICATION

I DEDICATE THIS BOOK TO MY WIFE, COLLEEN, AND OUR NOW-ADULT children: Lindsay, Ben, Dan and Jennie (and grandson Roman), Peter, Faith, and Heidi. You're the greatest gifts in my life.

I also would like to wholeheartedly thank some of my close friends: Kenny A., Anthony B., Bob B., Joe B., Lou C., Chris D., Mike J., John K., Brian L., Tom L., Liz M., Vinnie M., Tom M., Alan R., and Bob T. You're the best. There's literally no doubt about it.

And last but not least, I've got to give a shout out to Jordan P., from Selden Starbucks for both the endless cups of coffee and the smiling encouragement to "finish the book!" LOL!

Thanks, Jordan. Glad it's finally done.

FOREWORD

By Pastor Michael Jankowski

This is a gripping story of a man and his spiritual journey and a family who is in desperate need of wholeness and healing. In just a few short chapters, the author puts you right into the mind of Taylor Green; a man in crisis. Everything he knew and held dear is thrown into jeopardy and he is faced with the greatest personal and existential crossroad of his life; one that will define his very character and the future of his young family.

I have known Scott Schneider and have had the privilege of being his pastor and friend for nearly two decades. *A Diamond in the Rough* is the fruition of a vision that began many years ago to tell a story of redemption and forgiveness through genuine struggle.

This book will captivate your mind as you find yourself identifying with each of the characters in the story. May God bless you as read it and let it be a light for your soul.

Pastor Michael Jankowski
The Harbor Church
Long Island, New York

Prologue

"C'MON, SHEILA. FORTY DOLLARS!" HE DEMANDED.

"No!" she yelled back.

The sound of a man and woman arguing was easily heard from behind one of the paint-chipped apartment doors inside the dilapidated redbrick tenement building. The housing project sat in a seedy section of Columbus, Ohio, populated primarily by its own unenthused residents. Few others would prefer to live or even travel there, including the local police, whose conspicuous absence cultivated an already-lucrative economy for the street pharmacists and other low-level criminal enterprises that frequented the premises after dark. Though neighborhood familiarity and an unspoken curfew kept most permanent dwellers generally safe, the activities on the avenue corners and within the dingy alcoves of the four-building complex created an uneasiness for all, even those tucked behind their iron-barred windows and multi-locked doors.

It was an unseasonably hot evening in the spring of 1982, and the mixed sounds of rock, Motown, and the early stages of rap music permeated the quad. The interior stairs and common corridor leading to the apartment was dimly lit, but the faded colors and well-worn carpet runner could still be seen as it approached the bluish-gray steel door. Stale humid air, augmented by cigarette smoke residue, lingered within the hallway and made the atmosphere even more unpalatable to breathe. A thin vertical line of light edged the cracked opening, as if someone had just entered but didn't intend to stay.

Inside, a disheveled-looking man wearing a beat up army-green winter coat was standing in the middle of the room, stumbling in his speech and becoming more frustrated by the second. Except for a separate bedroom off to the side, the entire living space was contained within one modest area. A couch, coffee table, and upholstered chair were clustered together on one side, with an open kitchen set up on the other. The line in the floor between the hardwood and linoleum clumsily demarcated each room.

A large department store braided rug covered most of the scuffs and scratches the mom couldn't rub out with Murphy's Oil, though nothing unfortunately could hide the patches of dull gray that thanklessly emerged in the common areas of the kitchen, where the tiles had worn through. Two prior decades of traffic and neglect had taken their toll on the once-vibrant silver-speckled pattern, which could now only be noticed under the heaters or on the floor edges abutting the walls. Shadows of rust spots, painted over and then painted over again, were slowly winning the battle for the base boards and most of the other appliances in the apartment. The lady of the house had not given up, however. Everything that could be cleaned, patched, or covered was, and it made the place, at the very least, a well-cared-for and even cozy abode.

The mood was tense. At the small dinner table, an athletic-looking brown-haired boy remained seated in front of his half-consumed piece of homemade chocolate cake. It was his favorite, but he had stopped eating. He was still in his Little League uniform, which had been significantly dirtied by the game. A baseball trophy, clearly the subject of the celebration, sat in the center of the table for all to see, including his cute and chunky five-year-old sister. The two fixed their eyes on their mom, who stood defensively in front of the table, bravely facing their well-known but unwelcome intruder. Though she hated what was happening, she protected her children with the fierceness of a mother bear from yet another robbery of what could still be a good childhood memory for both of them. It would be over her dead body that anyone, including their father, would strip them of the small pocket of joy life was allowing in that moment.

Sheila Green was a thin, rail-like woman, who stood at about five seven, with shoulder- length, brunette hair, neatly pulled back in a bun. High heels and a pressed waitressing dress further dignified her stature; however, the years of combating an abusive, absentee husband while raising two children on her own had unkindly added lines to her face and leathered her skin well beyond what a woman of thirty-two should look like. Tonight her nemesis had surfaced again, intoxicated.

Unemployed and looking for money, the unkempt drifter would have stood at six four if hard living hadn't slumped his once-sturdy shoulders and Marine-like frame. Unfortunately, this present condition never stopped him from operating under the false sense of authority he genuinely believed he was entitled to over his estranged, little family.

He ordered her again. "I'll pay you back next week. C'mon!" he said, taking another intimidating step toward her.

"I don't have it, Robert. You need to leave!" she yelled back while maintaining her ground and pointing toward the door.

"Oh no?" the bully shouted, challenging her again.

Knowing she was far too responsible not to have some cash in the house in case of an emergency, he glanced at the large dresser against the wall adjacent to the pullout couch. Topped with a jewelry box and other womanly paraphernalia, it subtly gave away that the space doubled as her bedroom at night and probably contained what he was looking for.

He headed there as she feverishly pursued him from behind. With all the strength and courage she could muster, she grabbed him as he reached the bureau.

"Don't you dare!" she shrieked, desperately needing to hold onto the little money she had sitting in the top drawer.

Half shocked by his former wife's apparent, though fragile, strength and confidence, the now-infuriated drunk answered with a sloppily executed military maneuver, breaking her grip and slamming her against the adjacent wall.

"You lyin' to me, Sheila!" he yelled again, now directly in her face. His features began to monstrously distort as the spittle sprayed her cheeks.

Momentarily traumatized, she couldn't respond.

"Daddy!" screamed the frightened little girl.

Simultaneously, the boy wedged himself between the struggling adults to try to protect his mother. Then, with one surprisingly gigantic heave, he shoved his father hard at the waist.

The force propelled the man into a backward stumble, which ended with his tripping on the leg of the kitchen table behind him and crashing to the floor.

A quiet hush thickened the air between them, leaving all participants awkwardly frozen in an atmosphere where time felt like it was standing still. While it may have been strangely calm in that moment, the three members of the tiny household who resided there knew better and remained on their side of the room, bracing themselves for what they innately anticipated would be the storm of their lives.

The bully paused a minute before picking himself off the ground. He was visibly shaken. After briefly gathering his wits again, he grabbed the kid-sized baseball bat he'd spotted leaning against the adjacent wall. The room became frightfully silent as he stood motionlessly, seemingly plotting his next move while the others remained fearfully still, waiting for what that might be.

In truth, the ever-decreasing and lonely world of Robert Green was becoming even smaller as his half-hungover, half-drunken senses desperately grasped for a way to stop the downward spiral that now defined his existence. Though beaten by life and the consequences of bad decisions, the square-jawed, tough-talking boozer was still strong enough to overpower the women he'd deserted and unfortunately coward enough to do it. She was the only one left he could push around or at least intimidate to underwrite his next binge. But now it appeared that even his hold on that was beginning to falter. What's more, a new enemy had arisen.

The once-childlike, admiring eyes of his son were now riveting into his with a brewing hatred that was becoming bigger than both of them. Robert could feel himself falling, not from without but from within as his scattered and enraged thoughts grasped for a way to regain control of the last of those who feared him, people who, but for his lost battle with alcohol, should have been his family.

"*Think, Robert, think!*" he commanded himself, nervously fidgeting with the bat. His eyes caught the trophy that had fallen off the table and now lay on the floor before him. Though spotted with ketchup and some fresh patches of cake icing, it had survived the crash and was still in one piece. He glared at his now-formidable-looking twelve-year-old son.

"Think ya big now, do ya?" he goaded, pointing to the trophy with the bat. "Think you can push your old man around, huh, boy?"

The young man didn't respond but remained stock still in front of his mom. He continued to stare back at the would-be predator. The silence was deafening.

"Here's what I think!" his dad yelled, lifting the bat before violently cracking it down hard on the sparkling-though-delicate ornament.

The three stood in shock, watching the metallic little hitter shatter between the barrel of the bat and the floor. The impact instantly transformed the once-praiseworthy symbol into a hundred unidentifiable bits of plastic, now strewn across the linoleum.

The bully didn't stop there but became more encouraged with each sustaining blow as he feverishly smashed the item again and again, splintering its wooden base and bending the silvery steel seraphim beyond recognition. The boy's face winced with each painful swing, but he stayed in front of his mother as if to ensure the assault would go no farther than the trophy. After the final wallop, a fatigued Robert Green, bat still in hand, stared back at each of them with a twisted look of satisfaction that he had just crushed their rebellion and restored order over his little fiefdom. The victims remained motionless.

Narrowing his eyes and squaring his jaw, he surveyed the room again, reveling in the uneasy quiet his actions had just created. His problem, however, was what to do now. No one else was talking, not even to each other. They were just looking at him as his mind began to ping-pong between embarrassment and exasperation, struggling for a next move. Sensing he should quit while he was ahead, he slammed down the bat and strode out the door of the apartment.

As his steps clunked down the tenement stairs, the little girl ran into the awaiting arms of her mother, who collapsed back into the couch, holding her. Calming her hysteria, the relieved mom gently stroked her daughter's hair, relaxing them both. Her son, however, walked straight to where his bat lay amid the hopeless rubble of his championship trophy. He cautiously lifted it off the floor and slowly rotated the lumber in his hands, inspecting it for damage. Noticing a fatal crack down the center of what had always been his most prized possession, the young man appeared dangerously contemplative. He turned to his mother for an answer, though the look in his eyes journeyed far beyond where she was sitting.

"He broke my bat, Mom … he broke my bat," he quietly stated.

"Taylor … Taylor," his mother beckoned from the couch with the arm that wasn't holding his sister.

Her son, however, remained silent and aloof, caressing the bat and gazing at the aftermath of what had just been destroyed.

Chapter 1

"Okay! Remember, we got only one out. Hold close to the bag and be ready to tag up!" the coach shouted to the runner on third.

He turned and gave a quick word to the batter behind him, who was heading to the plate. His tone lowered slightly as that of a father to a son. "Put it in the outfield, and we win. Okay, kid? In the air or on the ground, just make contact and punch it out there," he instructed, confident it would get done.

Weekday evenings in late spring had baseball in the air, and the Little League game was at the bottom of its last inning with the score tied at 3–3. There was one out with a man on third, and coming up to bat was the stocky blond kid the coach had just talked to.

Wearing his blue-and-white uniform adorned with patches of dirt on his pants, the twelve-year-old Skip Green strode to the plate with both the purpose and poise of a major leaguer. The deep-blue, short-sleeved shirt proudly displayed the Rivermont Ambulance emblem on the front, with the number five on the back. Though only about four feet, ten inches tall, the right-handed slugger was determined as he briefly stopped just before the batter's box to set his stance and take a couple of hard and level practice swings. He dug himself in and carefully scoped out the field position before confidently gazing at the awaiting pitcher, a long, gangly youth in a similarly styled red-and-white uniform.

Skip's father, Taylor Green, crouched behind the on-deck circle just outside the dugout paralleling the third baseline, the place he typically coached from when his team was at bat. From there he could quietly observe the whole field as well as any repositioning by his opponents. He focused on his son, who was taking his stance in the batter's box.

Though Taylor was thirty-eight years old and still cutting a tall, lanky figure, the stiffness in his legs and lower back reminded him that he was crowding forty. He wore a deep-blue baseball cap, and his matching coach's jacket was unzipped and hung down loosely. Underneath it was a white, button-down business shirt with a dark-blue, conservatively designed tie. It was knotted about one and a half inches below his slightly opened collar. His navy-blue suit pants, once pressed and pristine for court earlier in the day, were now smattered with the dust kicked up by the game, which unashamedly covered his wing-tipped dress shoes as well. He didn't care though.

With a clipboard resting in his right hand, Taylor used his left for a bullhorn to bark instructions and pep talk to his players. So far it was business as usual. He had already read the field position and was in the process of signaling both the batter and the runner at third what they needed to do—all with a precision that made him infamous with pretty much all the opposing coaches. He didn't apologize for this reputation but rather thrived on it, enjoying the thrill of the competition and even his own notoriety.

After receiving a friendly pat on the shoulder from the third-base coach, another volunteer dad, whose shirt sleeves and ironed khakis evidenced that he'd come straight from work too, the speedster at third readied himself for a dash to home when the time was right. Suddenly, the opposing coach bounded out of his dugout and up to the first baseline. He was much younger than Taylor—somewhere in his late twenties and wearing a red Rivermont Building Supply team hat along with a hooded sweatshirt, beat-up blue jeans, and well-broken-in work boots. Handsome and deliberate, the stocky young man had the look of a former athlete who hadn't left his playing days completely behind and needed to win a little more than he should have. With his hands cupped around his lips, he barked his own set of commands. The pitcher delayed in starting his windup.

"Okay, cleanup hitter up! Everybody back!" he nervously cautioned. "There's only one out. Watch the tag up! Outfielders, throw straight home! Infield, don't let anything through. And look to third first!"

Taylor smirked to himself, knowing his overzealous opponent had already overstepped his bounds by crossing into the first baseline. He eyeballed the teenage umpire to reprimand his adversary, which the kid did, uncomfortably waving the slightly embarrassed young man back. In a quick retreat, the coach backpedaled, briefly glancing toward the captivated parents on their side of the diamond before striding over to his place just outside the dugout.

Taylor grinned again over the tension getting the best of the guy, but as he did, he quietly observed their third baseman frantically backing up with the rest of their infield. This was a mistake, a tactical error on their coach's part. He should have kept that kid up to cover a potential bunt and squeeze play, which was exactly what Taylor was now signaling. He deftly flashed his third-base coach the sign by making a fist with his left hand and pumping it down once from behind his clipboard. The instruction was nonchalantly passed on to the player, who continued to face forward while keeping his eyes on home. Taylor simultaneously sent a message to his son to bunt toward third base, where the opposition was now hopelessly out of position.

With the third baseman too far back to make the play, it would be up to the pitcher, a left-handed kid who would have to reach across his body to barehand the ball and throw it home. He'd never be able to do it in time, Taylor wisely thought. A right-hander maybe, but a lefty never, especially if Skip puts the ball on the baseline just inside the chalk like his dad knew he could.

"Punch it out. Punch it out" came Taylor's coded deception in a low but clear tone. Only his players knew it really meant the opposite.

3

The other team, however, continued to take the bait, believing the slugger was looking to put the ball into the outfield.

Skip's eye contact with the pitcher remained unbroken as his father's voice echoed from behind him amid the background chatter of the bleacher fans. Taylor was proud but not surprised that his son had already loosened his grip on the bat handle to ready himself to bunt. There was no one else he wanted at the plate in a moment like this. He just hoped Skip could make contact before the other coach noticed the gap in front of third and corrected it. Taylor figured they had one pitch, maybe two, if they were lucky, but Skip would certainly try to tap the first one if he could.

The crowd became silent as the pitcher wound up. In came a predictable fastball, high and just a little outside, intended to catch Skip fishing. The runner at third was already on the move as Skip responsively laid down a perfect slow-dribbling bunt up the third-base line toward his oncoming teammate. Skip barreled down to first as the tension burst with the roar of the fans from each team.

By the time the sluggish grounder completed its roll about ten feet down the line, the runner was already passing it at a furious pace. The third baseman rushed in but was a good fifteen feet behind the play, while the astonished pitcher awkwardly tried to field the ball as well. Lumbering down from the mound, he made it there first and spastically backhanded the ball toward his heavily padded teammate standing in front of home. However, the baffled expression on the catcher's face portrayed the obvious reality the pitcher knew, even before he released the throw: the runner had already crossed the plate, and the game was over.

Receiving the ball into his thickly cushioned glove, the catcher turned toward his coach with a look of bewilderment. He had no idea what to do with the baseball stuck in his mitt or how the other team had scored so easily. The coach didn't say a word but merely waved him and his teammates in. With heads bowed, they all began quietly trotting off the field and filing into the shelter of their dugout. They appeared both confused and disappointed as each young man settled into his place along the bench. Some were angry and started to grumble before the coach and his assistant quickly calmed things down. Though silent, the players looked to them for an answer as to why they had lost to a team that, but for one or two kids, was far less talented than they were.

Truth be told, the boys didn't know what had gone wrong, but their parents probably did. The coach hadn't been paying attention when he allowed the third baseman to drop back with everybody else. Though this is generally a good idea with a power hitter up, it's an absolute blunder when there's a runner on third. If his boys hadn't figured that out yet, they would in due time.

The coach glanced over at the pandemonium across the way and shook his head in disgust. They were in the playoffs now, and his team, the better team, wasn't. Scuffing his work boot into the dusty ground, he couldn't disguise his frustration over being so clearly outfoxed.

"My fault, fellas" was all he could say as he stood in front of the dugout and addressed his guys.

But the eyes of the boyish faces staring back at him wanted more than that as they looked into his for an answer as to why they had literally had no chance of preventing the game-winning run. Occasional gleams of disappointment from some of the parents flickered toward the fledgling young coach as well, causing him to look down at the ground to avoid eye contact. He couldn't offer them much either, and his fragile ego was definitely not prepared to discuss his mental error any more than it had to—especially with this crowd.

He took a brief gaze down the right-field line before adjusting his cap and turning back to his players. "You're a great team, and it was a pleasure coaching you guys. It really was," he said again as they continued to sit pensively on the bench. "Look forward to seeing you all out here next year," he ended, patting each on top of his head before releasing them to their parents.

The players dejectedly shuffled out of the dugout and into the consoling hugs and handshakes of their families and other supporters waiting just outside the entranceway. As they departed, the coach busied himself with collecting and loading the equipment into the duffel bag. Assistance came from one of the more merciful parents on his team, an older gentleman who with his son helped gather up the scattered helmets, bats, balls, and empty water bottles still littering the dugout floor. Though the coach couldn't wait to get out of there, he quietly appreciated their friendship.

"Thanks, Terry," he said.

"James played a great game … they all did," he added, nodding to Terry's son.

Shoving another helmet into the canvas bag, he began to think aloud. "Our guys hit the ball, got on base." His voice slightly trailed. "Just couldn't close the door." He sighed in frustration.

Still crouched, both men gazed over at Taylor Green, who was sitting and talking with his team on the other side of the field.

"Congratulations, guys. You did it." Taylor high-fived them. "You're in the playoffs now. Are you ready to step it up?" he added more seriously, making individual eye contact with everyone in the group. "This is where the men are separated from the boys. Does anyone know what that means?"

"We try harder," answered the wiry kid who'd scored.

"We do that too. We do that too," Taylor encouragingly agreed, smiling back at the young man, whose looks and speed reminded him of a future Ricky Henderson.

"But what it really means is this," he continued, now kneeling in the middle of them. "When boys are out there, they belong to their coach or their dad or their mom," he said, now captivating the attention of even the adults gathered loosely behind them.

"But when men are playing this game," he said, pointing to the field, "they belong to each other, and really to no one else. They play together. And it's theirs to win or theirs to lose. Think about that," he said, allowing a slight contemplative pause, "and I'll see you all at practice tomorrow," he added with a grin, shuffling them off.

The winners continued to celebrate as their parents struggled to tear away each hero and head toward the parking lot. Across the way, the other coach subtly nodded to himself in agreement with what Taylor had said.

"He knows the game, my friend," Terry gently acknowledged along with the still- smarting young man. "The man knows baseball."

CHAPTER 2

"PRACTICE AT FOUR THIRTY, FIELD THREE! BE HERE EARLY. OKAY, parents?" Taylor yelled to the departing crew. Though observing their nods, he repeated the time again for the sake of clarity.

Assisted by his five-year-old son, Taylor began to gather the equipment in the on-deck cage adjoining the dugout. Nathan was his youngest, slight in stature and somewhat small for his age. The brown hair, freckles on his nose, shorts, and colored T-shirt made him a typical-looking little boy. However his tender disposition, which Taylor insisted he'd gotten from being with his mother too much, overly concerned his father. Though he wasn't like his rough-and-tumble older brother, Skip, Nathan thrived on being in his dad's presence, even if that meant sitting in a dugout for two hours and watching other kids play.

After saying goodbye to the last of his buddies, Skip burst in and jumped his father from behind. He stubbornly attached himself to Taylor, clenching his forearms with an intensity that demanded a struggle.

The field was now empty. In the distance Taylor could see his oldest son, Tim, walking toward them from the outfield as he and Skip continued to wrestle. Tim was fourteen, tall, and a little bony for his age. Like his dad, he parted his medium-length brown hair to the side.

"The last of the three opposites." Taylor chuckled to himself, noting the sharp contrast between Skip's rugged and unpredictable disposition and the reserved and disarming nature of his oldest boy. Tim played for the school's junior high team and was in uniform, carrying his mitt, jacket, and backpack loaded with books over his shoulder. Taylor gave him a welcoming smile and tried to decipher how he had done from the look on his face. However, he could see that the young teen was in no mood to discuss his game or put up with any of his little brother's energetic displays.

"How'd you do?" Taylor asked.

"We lost four to two," Tim said dismissively.

"Oh," his father responded, hoping for more details.

None came as Taylor felt himself becoming short of breath and a little distracted with Skip's relentless wrestling.

"Oh well. Did you play second?" he asked, somehow managing to get out a further, more sympathetic, inquiry.

"Yeah," Tim wearily replied.

"How'd you do at the plate?"

"One for three with a walk," he answered, regripping the heavy knapsack rather than resting it on the ground.

"That's all right," his father said. "Did you make contact each time?"

"Yes, Dad. I hit the ball. Can we go now?" Tim blurted out in frustration.

"Tim! We won!" Skip broke in. "We beat Building Supply!" he added, clenching his father's arms from behind as Taylor playfully shook him just enough to challenge the hold.

"Yes, indeed. We pulled it out in the end," Taylor said, turning his head back to him. "But besides that beautiful bunt and Jesse's speed, tell me why that run came in so easy."

"Because the third baseman didn't have a clue," Skip bragged, though his father wanted a specific answer.

Their horse playing winded down as Taylor leaned backward to allow Skip's feet to touch the ground. The boy released himself and walked around to see Tim and continue their conversation.

Looking at Skip, Taylor asked again, "But where was he playing?"

Skip's eyes narrowed while they quietly gazed up at his dad's. Taylor could tell the wheels were turning and offered a little help. "Okay, champ. Tie game, bottom of the seventh, man on third, one out," he said, patting him on the head.

"Right-handed power hitter at the plate with a *left*-handed pitcher," Taylor said. "How do you set your field in that situation?"

Skip had the answer, and after giving a slightly cocky glance to his older brother, he confidently responded, "I bring my third baseman up and tight to the bag for anything coming down the line. Because my pitcher's a lefty, I'd expect the hitter to bunt toward third to make it hard for him to cross over and make the bare-handed play, which is why I'd have the third baseman there. The rest of my infield would be playing in the middle, not out, because the play might be to home." He grinned at his father, appearing fully satisfied with his conclusion.

Taylor was impressed but as usual extended the challenge. "Still righty batter ... what if it's hit hard between third and short?"

"My shortstop would already be shifted slightly to the left because my third baseman was on the bag. Play to home," Skip quickly said.

"Okay," Taylor conceded. "What about a ground ball up the middle?"

"How hard?" Skip said.

"A shot," Taylor answered.

Not falling for it, Skip smiled. "No change, Dad. It's up to the pitcher. Even if short was in regular position, the guy on third is going home. They'd never get the ball there anyway. It's a hit with a man on third. It's over."

Taylor stepped back, pleasantly surprised by his son's insight. "Oh yeah? How about a slow dribbler straight to short? Easy play, but now your guy's way out of position, professor," he teased.

"Power hitters don't dribble balls in the infield, Dad," Skip replied. "Besides, you gotta play percentages, don't ya?" he added, stoically reminding his father that he was no kid when it came to America's game.

Taylor took another step back in feigned awe. Skip ignored the patronizing at first before giving it back. "Good judgment and calculated risks win ball games," he playfully mimicked. "And always remember, Son, baseball is a thinking man's game," he added, lowering his voice and pointing his finger at his dad in further imitation.

Tim shot a quick glance to his father that it was beyond time for the teen to get home, eat, and deal with the mountain of homework contained in the now-heavier pile of books he was carrying. Taylor gave his eldest an acknowledging smile before messing up Skip's hair and poking his stomach. He was indeed proud of his tenacious little protégé, who clearly was on track to exceed him in what they both held dear.

CHAPTER 3

PAULA GLANCED AT THE CLOCK AS SHE HURRIEDLY BEGAN PUTTING dinner on the table. Her husband was gonna be late again.

"Shar, can you take care of this?" she asked, looking down at the papers and other odds and ends on the L-shaped kitchen counter.

"Sure," her teenager answered just before a soft jingle sounded on her mother's phone. Paula eyed the screen; it was Tim texting her back that they had won and were packing up. Taylor's cell, of course, was still off. Though they had a little time before the dinner reservation, the restaurant would be packed on a Friday night. Her face was noticeably tense.

Thirty-six years of age, with an olive skin complexion and northern Italian blonde hair, Paula stood about five six and weighed 125 pounds or so. Her hazel eyes and peppy, attractive smile cleverly disguised the tough Queens girl who resided beneath but was more than capable of surfacing when pushed. Wearing dress pants, a white blouse, and low heels, she was ready to go out for the evening. Taylor was cutting it close as usual.

Without breaking her stride, Paula glanced at the time again as she quickly delivered another hot platter of food to the table. From there she peeked into the living room for a moment and gave it a brief scan. Hardwood floors and tasteful early-American furnishings marked the decor, which flowed throughout most of the first level of the house. The foyer wasn't as organized as she wanted it to be, with excess jackets and sweatshirts piled on the coat hooks, and shoes and sneakers strewn throughout the doorway area, but she'd have to live with that for now. Having to pick up the three or four empty cups sitting on the coffee table, without coasters, irritated her as well as she swiftly returned to the kitchen to get dinner squared away. Helping out, Sharon cut into her mother's speedy rhythm by offloading the cups and putting them in the sink. She was slightly taller than her mom and had a medium build and her father's brown eyes. Wearing jeans and an oversized sweatshirt, her long brown hair had been thrown into a ponytail.

"You look nice, Ma. Where're you going?"

"Your father and I are going out tonight," Paula answered, heading to the oven.

"Really? Where?" Sharon responded with a slight tone of surprise.

"Seaman's Wharf."

"Oh, that's good."

"And maybe even a show," Paula tentatively added, looking into the oven rather than at Sharon.

"Oh really? What?"

"*Fiddler on the Roof*," Paula answered, continuing to avoid eye contact. "They're doing it at the Playhouse."

"The musical?" Sharon asked with a look of disbelief.

"The musical," her mother affirmed.

"That's not gonna work."

"Your father happens to love classics, for your information."

"Pfft," Sharon retorted, raising her eyes. "It's as crazy as him going dancing," she added under her breath as she turned to bring a plate of baby carrots to the table.

"He danced when we were in college," Paula noted lightheartedly, though not letting the last comment go.

"That's because he had to," her daughter tersely replied.

Paula didn't appreciate the remark, and her eyes declared as much as Sharon returned to the counter to get more food. Without skipping a beat, she motioned for the teen to get the rest of the plates to the table.

CHAPTER 4

TAYLOR CONTINUED PACKING THE REST OF THE EQUIPMENT INTO the duffel bag. Skip, however, grabbed the last bat before it went into the heavy canvas sack and sauntered to the plate.

"Throw me some pitches," he pleaded.

"Come on, Skip," Taylor rebuffed, holding open the bag and motioning with his head to put the bat in.

"Please?" Skip pressed with added drama.

Relenting to his son's determination, Taylor acquiesced. "Okay, but when it's time to go, we go. No whining. Agreed?"

Skip nodded, happily starting to toss the remaining stray balls up to the pitcher's mound, where his father was now heading, quickly fastening his own mitt along the way.

"Tim, throw on the gear and catch?" he asked apologetically to his eldest, who somehow knew he'd be enlisted. "Just for a few minutes?"

Tim raised his eyes and groaned with a look of exasperation; it was his way of reminding his dad that he'd heard this before and he hated catching. He reluctantly began donning the shin guards and pads.

"Nathan!" Taylor declared to his youngest, who was still playing in the dugout. "Get your glove on and take left center field. Just throw the balls back in to Daddy."

The little guy obediently ran to the outfield, while Tim finished adjusting his facemask and clipping on the last of the catching equipment. Skip was already in his stance, taking practice swings.

Gathering a glove full of balls, Taylor approached the rubber and began to closely examine his son's stance. Skip brought his bat back into position and slowly rotated it in a tight circle over his shoulder. All was silent.

Taylor didn't wind up right away. Standing on the mound, he continued to scrutinize his son's stance, looking at every inch of his positioning without even noticing his readiness to swing. After an extended pause, Tim sighed, a gesture his father ignored.

"C'mon, Dad! I got three hits today!" Skip cried.

Undeterred, Taylor maintained his focus and continued to peruse the batting stance with a studious eye. Though he would never admit it aloud, Skip was his pride and joy. He was strong, athletic, and extremely feisty. In addition, he had marvelous eye/hand coordination like his father and a deep drive to win anything he was involved in. However, unlike his dad, Skip had someone behind him to both give and guide him in everything he needed to be the best.

Taylor thrived on his son having that advantage and was more than willing to do all he could in the development of Skip's abilities. Nor did he mind the oversized ego being cultivated alongside it. It was worth it to Taylor, as was his son's being an intensely sore loser. Though Paula never tolerated that behavior, her husband saw it as more of a healthy, competitive spirit rather than anything negative, so he only disciplined it superficially.

"My sore losers will beat your good sports every time," he would say, chuckling to his wife. He was probably right, too, though he was equally aware of how much of a hands-on mom she was when it came to how her kids acted in public. The sudden yank of their hair or clench of an ear could attest to that.

"Looks good, Skip, but that right foot of yours is sticking a little too far behind you. Bring it in and bend your knee just a little bit more," Taylor said without taking his eyes off his son's lower body.

The private lesson had obviously begun.

Skip reluctantly obeyed, exhaling a slight groan for only Tim to hear. "Does it always gotta be perfect?" he muttered.

"Yup," his older brother confirmed sympathetically.

"It feels a little awkward right now, but it will give you greater range and more power in your swing," their dad added from the pitcher's mound on high. Taylor straightened and made eye contact with Skip. "It'll also give you a better launch angle. Don't worry. You'll get used to it. Have I ever steered you wrong?"

"No," his son grudgingly huffed.

Taylor delayed a moment more to look at something else.

"Really, Dad?" Tim challenged, impatiently shaking his head.

"C'mon, Tim," his father warned. It annoyed him to no end when his oldest broke in like that. He glanced back at Skip before beginning his wind up. "Ready?"

Skip nodded.

"Remember what I told you about the curve ball. Don't commit too early. Watch it coming in."

From the outfield Nathan commenced a teasing chatter, which lightened things up for the other three. One pitch was followed by another, and in moments, all four began their common fun fantasy of playing in the World Series. A longtime Met fan, Taylor fell into his familiar role of pitcher Jake DeGrom. Skip, of course, loved the Mets too and assumed the place of former slugger David Wright as he stroked about ten to fifteen balls into the outfield over the next several minutes.

Taylor wrapped it up with a final pitch. At that, Skip smashed a blazing line drive into left center, exactly where Nathan was playing. Taylor quickly turned, hoping his little guy was out of harm's way as the ball took its first hard bounce only ten feet or so in front of him. Much to his dad's amazement, Nathan actually charged the ball before dropping down to one knee to block it from getting by him. He then caught it like it was a matter of routine and returned the ball back to his father.

"Nathan! That was perfect! Who taught you to field like that?" he yelled to him while glancing back at Skip and Tim, assuming it was them.

"I don't know," Nathan sheepishly shrugged. He was visibly embarrassed by the surprise and boisterous attention of his father.

A delighted Taylor gave another commending look to the boys in appreciation for what they'd done with their little brother.

"It's Mom," the two awkwardly admitted, unable to take the credit.

Taylor shook his head in disbelief, seemingly needing to hear it again. However, before they could, the vibration of his cell phone reminded him he was late.

"Let's go! I gotta be home and out the door again in fifteen minutes!" he bellowed to his crew. The four scurried to pick everything up before funneling through the gate next to the dugout.

"Where you goin' tonight, Dad?" Tim asked.

"Got a meeting," Taylor answered with a sigh.

"Again?" Skip said.

"Yeah, again," his father said, hustling them toward the parking lot and trying to pick up the pace. "By the way, guys, they should have had the pitcher throw either low or further outside to prevent that kind of bunt or at least make it harder," he offered as a final thought.

"Yeah," Skip and Nathan agreed while Tim obstinately rolled his eyes as he lugged his backpack from behind.

"Dad, do you think I'll get a baseball scholarship like you?" Skip wondered aloud.

"Skip, you can get anything you want if you try hard enough," Taylor said, glancing back at all three as the now-tranquil ball field slowly diminished behind them in the dusk.

CHAPTER 5

TAYLOR PULLED THE MINIVAN INTO THE DRIVEWAY, AND THE BOYS piled out and hurried into the house. The two-story cedar-shingled colonial with attached garage was located in an upper- to middle-class development just north of the downtown area.

Comparable with the neighborhood, the lawn and landscaping were fairly well kept, with stockade fencing around the Greens' larger-than-normal backyard.

Shouts of "We won" and chatter about the game flooded the house as the hungry brood began to take their places at the table. Taylor unloaded his clipboard, scorebooks, and other coach-related paperwork on the counter. After removing his cap, he relaxed in a heap into his chair at the head of the table. He looked at the drawing Nathan had just brought him and was having a brief conversation about school.

Paula greeted him with a kiss and began hastily dishing out the food. Taylor could see she was aggravated again, probably over his being a little late. *She doesn't understand what it takes sometimes for a dad to do right by his kids*, he indignantly thought before passing the paper back to Nathan. Hopefully one day she would.

"Mom, did the new neighbors move in?" Tim asked, handing her his plate.

"Matter of fact, they did. They're a very nice young couple. He's a police officer right here in town, and they have a little boy and a baby girl," Paula said.

"How do you know that already?" Sharon asked

"I walked over and welcomed them, the way a neighbor ought to," Paula said.

"Oh no," Tim moaned.

Reaching for his clipboard, Tim's remark wasn't lost on Taylor either. He well knew what Tim was talking about.

"You didn't get religious on them, did you, Mom?" Sharon asked in a half-accusing, half- pleading manner.

"Not yet," Taylor grumbled without lifting his eyes from what he was reading.

"Please!" Sharon dramatically continued before her mother could answer. Raising her eyes to the others, she lightheartedly put her arm around Paula. "Another invasion of the body snatchers. God help our neighbors."

They all laughed as even Paula offered a patronizing chuckle at the inside joke before changing the subject. "How was the game?" she asked, directing her question to Taylor.

"They played great. Skip bunted, and Jesse scored on an awesome squeeze play. Could you please grab me a plate? I gotta be out of here in seven minutes. I've gotta—"

"We're going out tonight," Paula countered.

Taylor returned a blank look. Her uncompromising stare, however, reminded him that they must've had other plans. Taking a step back, Paula held out her arms so he might notice the obvious; she was dressed to the nines and ready for a date. Her stylishly fitting white blouse, dark slacks, and tastefully applied makeup no doubt highlighted the romantic evening she was looking forward too.

"You're kidding!" she said, leaving him another opportunity to remember.

Taylor still didn't, though by his expression he was definitely trying. "What did you plan, Paula?" came his uninspired response coupled with an inference that he was never informed.

The kids grew quiet as the tension thickened between their

parents. This irritated Taylor even more. Though he had probably forgotten, he was looking like the uncaring dad again.

He lifted his hands in surrender. "I can't tonight, Paula. I got a lawyer's thing. I thought I told you. I'm sorry. I really am," he added, now ducking her stare. "Pass the chicken please," he said, looking at Sharon.

She coldly forwarded him the platter.

After a pregnant pause and her husband's avoided eye contact while he served himself, Paula strode to their bedroom at the other side of the house. Taylor ignored her reaction and began to eat, sheepishly glancing at everyone around the table. Finally Sharon stood up and assumed her mother's role of doling out the rest of the food. Though the awkward exchange between their parents hadn't distracted her younger siblings from chattering and devouring their meal, she remained icily quiet after finishing her task and sitting down. Taylor was annoyed as well but mistakenly challenged his daughter's demeanor with a quizzical look.

"Really, Dad?" she said in response.

"It's something I have to go to, Sharon. I'm secretary this year," Taylor said, mostly for the benefit of her brothers to hear too. "You may be a lawyer someday, Shar. You'll understand then," he added, taking in another forkful of mashed potatoes.

Sharon just looked at her father before shaking her head in disgust.

"Watch it, young lady," Taylor cautioned, making sure she stayed on the proper side of the respect line.

Though she stubbornly obeyed, she stood up, exited the table, and went upstairs to her bedroom, leaving her supper behind and Taylor momentarily speechless. She'd gotten the last word, even if it cost her her dinner. She was her father's daughter for sure.

"Unbelievable," Taylor said to himself, loudly enough for her to hear as he got up and headed for his bedroom to somehow smooth things over.

His usual method in these situations was to justify his missing their event while at the same time offering a guarantee that he'd make it up later. Palatable substitutes for the future ran through his mind as he approached the door. He hoped one or two of them would work in a hurry because he had to get going.

Paula stood in front of her mirror, angrily taking off her earrings as Taylor walked in. She continued to look into the mirror after he began to speak. The glass reflected both of them.

"Paula, listen. We can do this again. It totally slipped—"

"This was the 'again'!" his wife cut in, undoing the other earring and almost yanking it away.

"Paula, this is one of those things I have to do. Judges go. Other lawyers go. It's my job. I have to go," he offered apologetically.

"Really? You *really* have to be there?" Her fiery eyes pierced his as she turned to look at him directly. "Taylor, what is it?" she said after a pause that clearly made only him uncomfortable.

"It's a mistake, Paula. That's all it is," he said, shaking his head defensively like the matter was being blown out of proportion. "I can't all of a sudden not go—"

"And I can't beg you to spend time with me, okay, Taylor," she snapped back, though now looking deflated as she turned toward her dresser.

"Oh, c'mon, Paula. For cryin' out—"

"Because it doesn't work!" she shot back again back without turning around.

"Oh, here we go!" Taylor exclaimed, turning his eyes toward the mirror as he began to fix his tie. *How can she be so obtuse about my job?* he thought, still shaking his head. Without it they wouldn't have the house, the cars, or any of the nicer things they do. And he had no problem doing what he had to do to provide them. How could she not see that?

"I work hard, make good money, and try to do the right thing," he said while rushing to gather his things.

Paula didn't respond but continued putting the rest of her jewelry away.

"That's not enough though," he muttered while walking into his closet, hoping to get away with the last jab. Returning to the bedroom door, he saw her now standing there, waiting for him.

"It's not enough for you either, Taylor," she coolly affirmed, demanding eye contact for the rest of the discussion.

"Nice shot, Paula," he poignantly replied. Jutting out his hand for the doorknob, he felt hers already covering it as she remained there, facing him.

"Oh no you don't, Taylor Green! Don't you dare!" she cried, wanting to get the conversation back on point.

Taylor, however, was clearly too hot for that. "This is where it goes. This is where it always goes, doesn't it, Paula?" he spouted, his voice rising by the word. "The marriage isn't important enough, and I've proven that, haven't I, Paula?"

"No, Taylor," Paula said as calmly as she could.

"Yes, Paula. Which is why you said what you said. This is what you do," he added defensively.

At that she closed her eyes and lifted her hand in stop fashion in front of her husband's chest, a telltale sign she was extremely angry but trying to keep control. "That's not where I'm going, Taylor Green. And you know that. I'm talking about now," she said, looking him squarely in the face and speaking in a low but deep tone that was determined to arrest the toxic direction their exchange had just taken. "And that's where you and I are, Taylor. In the now," she quietly finished.

Though the pain on her face remained, Taylor could see Paula's eyes begin to soften and search his like she was looking inside him for something she couldn't find. In the past he had jokingly referred to this stare as her "x-ray vision," but in truth it always made him uneasy as he sought to avoid this becoming another one of those moments.

"Well, 'now' is when I have to go, Paula," he replied, negotiating his hand to open the door behind her. He carefully escaped eye contact as she stiffly let him pass.

I obviously can't be everything she wants me to be, Taylor frustratingly thought while striding down the hallway. *But it'd be nice if one day she'd be happy with who I was,* he added while exiting the house.

Moments later Paula, now clad in her sweats, emerged from the bedroom to rejoin her family. Down the corridor she could see Sharon was standing stoically at the entrance to the kitchen, waiting for her.

"Why do you put up with that?" the teen demanded, as if entitled to an explanation.

"Let's get some ice cream. Can you pick it up?" Paula replied. She was too tired to fight with anyone.

Raising her eyes and shaking her head in disdain, Sharon grabbed the keys and stomped through the back door without a word.

CHAPTER 6

THE RED LIGHTS FLASHED FOR ONLY A SECOND OR TWO, PROVIDING all it took for Nathan and Skip to unload off the mid-sized yellow bus, which had stopped in front of their house. Paula grinned as Nathan ran over to greet her. Still in her blue nursing scrubs and white sneakers, with her picture ID dangling loosely around her neck, she had just gotten home herself.

The boys' shirttails were hanging out as their backpacks bounced over one shoulder. Paula smiled again amid their chatter, knowing they could hardly wait to drop them on the foyer floor inside and have a snack.

After the school bus departed, she noticed a short distance down the road that a woman was pushing a baby carriage with a young boy playfully leading the way. As they approached, she recognized they were her new neighbors and cheerfully waved at them. Seeing Evette alone with just her baby and little guy reminded Paula of how lonely it could be trying to do motherhood away from family and friends. Rivermont was miles from the tight-knit Queens community she'd grown up in, and Paula well knew it had taken a lot of adjusting. She shepherded her reluctant boys over to introduce them.

Corey, the rambunctious, young kindergartner, reached the Green property well ahead of his mom. He was big for a five-and-a-half-year-old, slightly chunky, and he had a crew cut that was stylishly squared off at the top. Due to his size and enthusiastic personality, he was a little clumsy but very friendly as he encountered his new potential playmates with innocence and excitement.

"Well, hello, Corey. Have you met my boys?" Paula said with an endearing smile.

As always Skip was uncomfortable with meeting new people and glanced away. Nathan, however, responded without reservation. Paula gently pulled her overly shy son closer as Evette arrived with the carriage.

The Johnsons were an African-American family now living in a predominantly white neighborhood. Though Paula was very social anyway, she wanted to make doubly sure their neighbors felt welcome in their new residence. She extended her hand to Evette as she arrived with her baby.

"How ya doin', Evette?"

"Good, Paula, thanks," she answered, smiling at the boys.

"This is Nathan and Skip," Paula said, turning to them in expectation that they would say hello.

Nathan did. Skip only mumbled, provoking a stern glance from his mother that he wasn't too cool to respond. Skip's entrance into adolescence had become quite bumpy between him and his mom, and the instant exchange was another reminder of that.

"Skip?" she said in a reprimanding tone.

He sheepishly slipped out a "Hello."

Evette warmly extended her hand to them. "Evette Johnson. I'm pleased to meet you boys," she said. Then, relieving Skip of the negative attention, she turned to her own son. "In our old neighborhood, Corey had no one to play with his age, and let me tell you, he is so excited now," she said with a grin.

Her kind and approachable disposition was comforting to Paula. Evette looked about twenty-eight and stood at approximately five seven. She was dressed casually in jeans, sandals, and a spring jacket. Though slightly overweight, which Paula attributed to her recent pregnancy, Evette appeared secure and unpretentious about herself, a trait that was even more attractive.

"Mom!" Corey defensively piped up.

Paula could see that now two of the boys were embarrassed, which sparked smiles from both adults. Looking at the baby and then at her boys, she drew attention to who was in the carriage.

"And this is Rose." Evette smiled.

"Where did you deliver her?" Paula asked.

"Hanson Memorial. That's where my OB was."

"Oh," Paula acknowledged impressively. "I work over at Pinecrest. In the ER. How old is she?" Paula asked, turning back to the baby.

"About three months." Evette smiled again, proudly looking at her daughter as well.

"She's so cute," Paula remarked as she glanced over at her sons, who clearly weren't yet baby lovers. "Nathan and Skip have a big brother, Tim, and a big sister, Sharon. Skip and Tim spend a lot of time at the ball field with their father this time of year."

"Me too!" Nathan indignantly added.

Paula gave her youngest a smile, affectionately squeezing his shoulders. She looked back at Evette. "My husband's name is Taylor."

"The lawyer?" Evette asked.

"Uh-huh," Paula said, leaning back over the carriage and taking in the baby again.

"My husband, Robert's, a police officer, and I think he knows your husband," Evette said. "Isn't he also involved with the school?"

"The school board, Little League, the bar association—you name it, Daddy's in the middle of it," Paula joked, looking at Nathan.

"Why don't you come in for a cup of coffee? I just got off work and could use a little caffeine boost myself," Paula said, motioning that they all go in.

"Sure," Evette answered. She peeked into the carriage in hopes her Rose would remain asleep for the visit.

Paula directed the boys to take Corey into the backyard and play while she got them all a snack.

Entering through the front, they retreated onto the large rear deck, which extended off the kitchen and overlooked a deep, open backyard. Paula quickly scanned the immediate area to make sure it was presentable.

Handsome outdoor furniture was augmented by colorful flowers and potted plants, which bordered the railing on all three sides. Their fragrance was as vivacious as the purple, red, and white colors Paula had carefully chosen to further beautify her often-used outdoor refuge.

Aside from some basic shrubbery and a few maple trees on either side, the backyard itself, however, was predominantly open as it stretched to where it bordered the horse farm a considerable distance away. Wood-posted fencing separated the farm from the back-end property line, which ran along the entire block of homes, including Evette and Robert's place next door. To the left of the deck was a homemade backstop, modeled after those found on ball fields in the 1920s and 30s. Constructed of wood rather than chain-link fence, it faced toward the horse field, where an assortment of tennis and rubber-coated hardballs could be seen sprinkling both the Greens' backyard and even over the fence and onto the farm property.

Paula never let the boys retrieve the balls from there unless the horses were secured in their stable or Taylor was with them. In truth, she couldn't stand the sight of baseballs from her yard sitting on someone else's property, so she often grudgingly slipped through the fence herself and tossed them back over. Though dodging the minefield of horse manure patties in her nursing sneakers was definitely below her paygrade and ridiculously beyond the comfort zone of a city girl, waiting for her husband to take care of it on the weekends wasn't worth it to her either. So she just did it.

The oversized backstop told a story as well, which she anticipated having to explain to her new neighbor sooner or later. It was almost eighteen feet high at its peak and sat only about ten feet off the back of the house, completely blocking the view of the downstairs bathroom and guest bedroom. The regulation pitcher's mound and batter's box were set up exactly forty-six feet apart. The bases, however, were slightly less than the standard sixty feet, only because shortening the distance was necessary to stay within the confines of their yard. A smaller, makeshift pitching mound was situated about thirty feet in front of home plate to accommodate Nathan, the T-baller in the family.

Though Taylor had tried to convince her that the majesty alone of this reduced-size baseball field more than compensated for the oversized backstop, Paula was never totally sold on it. However, his argument that it protected the house from the foul balls and errant pitches that occurred with regularity made it easier to live with. Though just barely. Deep down Paula was also mindful of where her husband had grown up—a tenement without even a backyard, let alone a place to play the game of his dreams. That was what really gave Taylor the mileage he needed to build the aberration Evette was now looking at.

Though Taylor had never asked for it, his childhood evoked huge amounts of sympathy and compassion from his wife, who, coming from a large and loving Italian family, couldn't fathom what it was like to grow up the way he had. Unfortunately, this perspective started to lopside their relationship the more she acquiesced to Taylor's continual sacrifice of their time together, all in the name of family and future. As a result, the moment-by-moment or even day-to-day interest in the person of Paula Green gradually eroded to where it was now, seventeen years later, pretty much absent from her husband's side of their conversation. This left Paula mixed with resentment and the sinking feeling that Taylor simply didn't enjoy her company the way he used to. While she didn't believe he would ever leave her, she couldn't deny that if attention was like oxygen to a marriage, she was slowly suffocating.

"Everything but the stands and concession." Evette chuckled, jarring her host back to the present.

"Let me get the coffee," Paula said. She returned with two steaming cups as Evette continued to squint to view the details of the miniature stadium.

Leaning over and resting their elbows on the railing, both

women observed their sons, who were starting to play. As Skip tried to pitch to Corey, it was apparent he didn't know even the basics of how to swing a bat, let alone hit a baseball. Nathan did his best to patiently instruct the ambitious little boy on choking up and waiting on the ball, but it was to no avail.

Evette looked discouraged. "He wants to play so bad, but his father works the night tour and takes as much overtime as he can get. We need it, especially now," she said, pursing her lips as she watched her son struggle.

"Well, he's certainly welcome to come over and jump in when they're playing," Paula said comfortingly. "They wouldn't mind helping him at all."

"I appreciate that," Evette said, still looking at her son.

Her eyes moved on and quietly toured the rest of the yard. Looking toward the back of the property, she became curious about what appeared to be numerous baseball gloves hanging from strings across the uppermost cable of the horse fence. She used her hand as a visor to further observe that the pockets of the mitts were turned inside out as they dangled individually under the heated sunlight.

"What's that out there?" she asked.

Placing her hand on her forehead to block the sun, Paula looked on with her, though she knew what she saw. "Mitts," she said after a brief pause.

"Oh," Evette replied with a puzzled look.

"They're the baseball gloves from my husband's Little League team," Paula said, a little embarrassed about having to explain Taylor's obsession. "He soaks each one in his homemade secret formula, then sun-dries them until they're perfectly broken in," she said, continuing to look at the horse fence to avoid eye contact with her new friend.

"I see." Evette softly smiled.

"It's crazy," Paula said with a smirk that gave them both permission to laugh.

CHAPTER 7

BURKE, ARONSON & GREEN WAS THE ONLY LAW FIRM TAYLOR KNEW, and he was extremely proud of it. It occupied a freshly converted Victorian home, which was nicely landscaped and sat in a well-kept section of Rivermont's business district. The interior was classically furnished and decorated, starting with the polished wood-floored waiting room, which opened into three offices, a small library, and a secretarial area toward the back. Up the authentic center-hall staircase were more offices and professional work areas.

In the midst of the hectic atmosphere, with phones ringing, printers humming, and people busy about their tasks, Taylor strategically placed himself behind one entire side of the large glass-topped table located in the conference room. It was a small- to mid-sized practice, and as a partner and main litigator there, he liked to be both accessible and in the middle of whatever was going on.

The table was covered with legal pads and papers separated into distinct piles along each side. His telephone, the very wellspring of any law office, was strategically situated in the middle, while the computer keyboard was just to his left. It was hooked up to a large screen, tastefully mounted on the wall adjacent to the conference room table. Taylor had pushed all the other chairs against the built-in bookcases that lined the room so he could comfortably roll his chair from pile to pile and multitask. Though he had returned from court only moments before, he was already going full throttle with his jacket off, sleeves rolled up, and tie slightly loosened around his collar.

Taylor thrived on the pressure of a busy practice and didn't mind the reputation of being intolerant and overly demanding at times. In fact, he saw it as an indication that things were getting done and people were reaching their potential. He barked instructions to Marge, his secretary, who sat in the space between Taylor's actual office and what she commonly referred to as his "control room." This was where he spent about 90 percent of his time. She barked back.

Marge Bryant was a fairly stout woman in her midsixties with medium-length gray hair and a welcoming smile. Though a chain smoker with an arid sense of humor, she maintained a highly professional appearance and demeanor when clients were about. Intuitively brilliant, Marge nonetheless tended to verbalize her moment-to-moment frustrations with sharp adjectives and inaudible mutterings Taylor had learned to ignore a long time ago. Nor was she above snapping at her boss or tossing pencils when words wouldn't cut it. But Marge more than earned that in Taylor's mind. Her loyalty could never be doubted, and her wit and ready laugh always lightened his day.

Marge had been Taylor's secretary since he entered the firm fifteen years ago as a junior associate, fresh out of law school. Though he had often displayed far more zeal than wisdom in those days, Marge, unlike many others, keenly perceived that under the young man's arrogance and apparent insensitivity beat the heart of a lion, whose courage and cleverly disguised care for others were worth protecting.

Employing her skills as an accomplished legal secretary, she flawlessly covered for Taylor's freshman mistakes. No one noticed that more than Taylor, and as the years went forward, the unspoken yet steadfast support they faithfully extended each other welded a bond of trust few mothers and sons even shared.

His office mom was no doubt a part of what fueled Taylor's meteoric rise to partner in the firm as well as his becoming one of the community's most sought-after attorneys. Taylor deeply appreciated her for that, but to those who didn't know better, the abrasiveness and continuous sharp exchanges that characterized their daily operation made the working environment appear stressful. However, in truth, they had come to have a depth of communication that matched the flow and precision of a well-choreographed ballet. Marge also had an innate ability to appropriately handle each of the many interruptions that came with a law practice while at the same time accomplishing various tasks at once, often without even bothering Taylor.

A client was standing in the conference room while Taylor was on the phone with another. He waved him in.

"Don't forget the closing this Thursday. The bank wants it at their place," Marge said, her voice slightly raised from the other room.

Taylor heard without responding. "The permits are coming. The lease is okay," he said into the phone.

"You should be opening by next week."

Without looking up, he cupped his hand over the receiver and yelled to Marge, "Eleven or—"

"Two," Marge said.

Taylor motioned to the paperwork on the table for the client to sign as Marge strode in with the balance of it. She then quickly packaged everything for him before he took the sealed manila envelopes and mouthed a goodbye to both of them.

"Tom Saunders called about his will ... and his son got arrested again," she said, glancing down the hall to make sure the other client had left.

"Drunk driving?" Taylor asked, looking up at Marge while cupping the phone again.

"How'd you guess?" she said with a chuckle.

Another client waved while he walked by the conference room door as Taylor cupped the phone again.

"Every time that kid gets arrested, we have two things to do: get him out of jail and cut another chunk from his inheritance,"

Taylor said with a laugh for only Marge to hear. "If that kid ever knew how much money he's lost since he first got busted, he'd really start drinking."

"A sobering thought," she replied as she headed out to her desk. Taylor swayed back into his phone conversation.

Moments later Marge reentered the room with Vin Russo, Taylor's accountant and fellow school board member. A jovial, longtime buddy of Taylor's, Vinnie was about forty-five and balding; he had a dark beard and slight potbelly. He was dressed casually as usual and hand-motioned for Taylor's attention.

"School board meeting tonight. Members at six," he mouthed in a hushed tone.

"Tonight?" a surprised Taylor whispered back.

Vinnie nodded before waving goodbye to the others and heading out.

A now-harried Taylor got off the phone. "What's the time, Marge?" he yelled out the doorway toward where he knew she was sitting.

"Ten to four," she answered.

"Shoot!" he said, standing up. "I told the boys I'd meet them at the field today. Where's my stuff?" he yelled to both Marge and himself.

Spotting his gym bag on the floor next to one of the chairs, he grabbed it and scampered into the adjoining bathroom to change. Just after he closed the door, he heard Russell, a fairly new associate attorney, barge into the conference room.

Though Marge tried to stave him off, it sounded to Taylor like he was, as usual, in desperate need of his boss's guidance. A tall and slender but gawky young man of about twenty-six, Russell had a fair complexion and stylishly short auburn hair. It was never in place, however, due to his nervous energy and frequent clutching of the top of his forehead.

Taylor liked the kid; he smirked to himself as he listened to his less patient secretary try to get rid of him. Fresh out of law school, Russell was uncompromising in his drive to be a success and to do a thorough job with whatever he was given. This ambition impressed Taylor, who refused to see him as the absent-minded klutz his partners raised their eyes at but instead as one who walked in a parallel universe, sometimes seeing what others didn't, though often hampered by a lack of self-confidence and clumsy social skills.

Everything was a crisis to Russell, and this tendency opened him up to constant office teasing and even occasional chiding from Taylor himself.

"Can't hold your hand all the time, Russell!" he shouted when the questions became too much. Unfortunately for the young lawyer, shame and embarrassment were still viewed as valuable tools of instruction by the partner who'd hired him. Having been trained by it himself under the hand of some of the most cantankerous judges, Taylor steadfastly believed this mode of correction served as the very crucible in which good trial attorneys were formed both inside the courtroom and out. He equally knew that it would take a fair amount of "sink-or-swim" experiences before Russell would possess the ability to handle the diverse challenges of a litigation practice; and this was sounding like another one of those messy occasions.

"Mr. Green!" Russell exclaimed, looking about the room.

"Taylor, Russell. Taylor," he said from behind the bathroom door, trying to defuse him.

"Okay," Russell responded, fidgeting with a page of what he'd been reading. He still was unable to call his boss by his first name.

Marge giggled from behind her desk as the young man respectfully waited. Taylor hurriedly emerged in jeans and a sweatshirt, and seeing Russell pacing the conference room floor, he calmly held up his hand, stopping him midsentence.

"Any calls, Marge?" Taylor asked, turning his head to his secretary.

"Nope. All clear," she answered.

Looking back at Russell but with his arm still extended, he sat

34

down and put on his beat-up pair of baseball cleats over his stocking feet.

"Russell, can this wait?" he asked in a tone that was confident it could.

Marge was now standing at the doorway, grinning. Russell didn't respond at first but nervously started shuffling through the papers he'd been clutching. "Well, it—"

"Can it wait for tomorrow?" Taylor politely repeated, heading off his associate's attempt to say something Taylor knew would be more than a yes or no answer.

"It can wait," he reluctantly admitted with a sigh before glancing down at the papers again.

"Great." Taylor smiled in approval.

"We made it through another day," he added with a pat on Russell's shoulder on his way out and a wave to a still-smiling Marge.

CHAPTER 8

BATTING PRACTICE AT THE TOWN FIELD WAS AN IMPORTANT AND uniformly intimate time Taylor and his boys shared during an otherwise-busy baseball season. By tradition the batters proceeded in age order, with Nathan leading off.

"Okay, killer, you're up," Taylor said.

With the confidence of a pro, Nathan took a few practice cuts, hammered the plate with his small aluminum bat, and assumed his stance. Tim was behind the plate, catching while Skip took shortstop, the usual place his little brother hit the ball.

"Okay, who's up?" Taylor asked, as was the custom.

"Thurman Munson!" Nathan exclaimed.

"Thurman Munson's not playing anymore. He died in a plane crash!" Skip shouted from the field, trying to make Nathan feel stupid.

"I know!" Nathan defiantly shot back, though Taylor could tell he was embarrassed.

"Since he was your favorite hitter, he's always Thurman Munson," Tim explained to his father, rolling his eyes.

"No!" an exasperated Nathan shouted again, growing more upset.

Interrupting what could have become World War III, Taylor moved the conversation forward. "Okay, listen," he said, turning around to Skip and then back to Tim and Nathan. "Nathan can be

Thurman Munson. He was a great hitter, and so are you," he added, looking directly at his little boy.

Taylor pulled a dollar out of his back pocket and held it up to him. "But can Thurman Munson get on base?" Taylor said as he moved back to the top of the pitching mound and waved Skip over to cover first.

"Okay, no more kids' stuff, Thurm. See if you can get it by me," he said before going into an overly dramatized windup and lobbing it in.

Eyeing Skip's movement across the infield, Nathan answered with a beautiful bunt down the third-base line and dashed for first. Hysteria broke out as both Taylor and Tim began to charge the ball. Taylor subtly waved him off, bare-handed the ball, and threw it toward first, making sure it sailed well above Nathan's head. Unfortunately, it also went too high for Skip's outstretched glove; Nathan made it in safely and started to jump up and down on the bag in jubilation. Taylor lumbered over to congratulate him while extracting the dollar from his jacket pocket.

"Gimme five, Thurm! Nice bunt! Have you been practicing that?" Taylor added, a little confused as to how he could on his own.

"Mom plays with him at home," Tim answered.

"Really?" Taylor responded, sincerely surprised that his wife would get that involved in something he had always handled since they first started having kids. Paula's primary concern was always their schoolwork, and though it was hard for him to picture her bunting a baseball, he was more than happy with the results.

"And all this time I thought I was married to a nurse," he said, proudly turning back to Nathan with a grin.

"Uh-huh," a slightly blushing Nathan admitted. "Mom says following God is like running around the bases in a baseball game," he added, quizzically looking at his father for confirmation.

"Well, it certainly worked well for you, Son," Taylor quickly replied, cautiously sidestepping the issue. His wife's habit of importing a religious angle to everything in life was annoying enough, but he'd never thought he'd have to deal with it here.

There's always a catch in that business, he frustratingly reminded himself.

An awkward pause emerged as Nathan remained silent, innocently looking at his father and waiting for a more complete response.

"It's kind of a game they have, Dad," Tim said apologetically to break the tension.

"A dumb game!" Skip added.

"Do you know what the bases are, Daddy?" Nathan asked, unknowingly pushing the issue again.

Taylor wished his little guy knew how to avoid this topic the way his older siblings did, but Paula's game certainly didn't help. Like it or not, he would have to muddle through the religion lesson as best he could.

"I'm sure I have an idea about it, Nate," he answered. "And I think you're really hitting the ball well too," he added, subtly trying to change the subject again.

"Okay, what base am I on?" Nathan cheerfully teased.

"First," Taylor answered.

"Dad!" an indignant Nathan complained, thinking he was being patronized.

"Okay, let me guess … first base? … going to church!" Taylor kidded, though hoping he stumbled onto the right answer.

"No!" the little boy retorted.

"I give up," Taylor said, holding up his hands in admitted ignorance.

"Believe in God," Nathan reminded his father, assuming that he'd simply forgotten.

Not knowing what to say, Taylor glanced over in Skip's direction and noticed he was turned toward right field and had thrown the ball straight up and high in the air to catch it. Seeing this as well, an astute Nathan bolted to steal second, which was within the rules of their game. Getting over on his obnoxious big brother would be an added bonus as another burst of pandemonium broke out, with Tim flying after him, his catcher equipment rattling along the way, while he yelled for Skip to get him the ball. Skip impatiently waited for the towering throw to land in his awaiting glove so he could pick off his wise-guy little brother. It was a respect thing now that charged the intensity. Nor would either of the older boys want to deal with their father's relentless jabs at being shown up by their youngest sibling.

Unfortunately, that would be the case as Nathan dove safely into second a step or two ahead of Tim and well before Skip's throw. Taylor was impressed again with the quick thinking on the little guy's part. He shook his head in disbelief, but with the smile of a proud father, he jogged over to give him another high five.

Smirking toward Skip, Nathan dusted off his pants and looked up to his dad again with the inevitable next question.

"What's—?"

"Go to church!" Taylor interrupted with a chuckle, now feeling okay with any game that would make his son a better ballplayer. *Besides, it's got to be the right answer by this time*, he thought.

"O for two." Tim sighed under his breath toward Skip before arcing the ball back to him.

Skip's eyes bulged in anticipation of what his gutsy little brother was going to do with that, which was confirmed as Nathan jetted to third immediately upon Tim's release of the ball. Now Tim was the one caught sleeping at the switch as he found himself behind a whizzing Nathan en route to another open base.

"Tim!" Skip yelled, wanting to get his attention to whip the ball back so he could make the tag.

His big brother, however, decided to try to get ahead of Nathan first, though he was still about ten feet behind him. With Nathan nearing the bag, Tim had closed the gap enough to hold out his mitt just over the boy's unprotected head for Skip to deliver the ball. Though Skip was pretty accurate, it was too close for Taylor, who motioned him to hold off as a frustrated Skip flopped down his arm with the ball still in hand. Nathan slid in, safe again.

Taylor started to trot from second to offer congratulations as Nathan stood on third, patting himself off in the businesslike fashion of a mature ballplayer. He turned his head to catch his father's coming but held up his hand to stop him. Taylor smiled over the little guy's brazenness. He had his brothers by the tail in one game and his dad in another, and Taylor could see he was enjoying it.

"Can't go unless you know, Dad," he said with a grin.

Playing along, Taylor dropped his hands and looked at the other boys for help. He was so proud of his kid's speed and baseball acumen that it made even the Bible lesson worth it. He waited for an answer.

Though Tim left him hanging, Taylor heard something from behind.

"Faith that—"

"You can't tell him!" Nathan shouted back at Skip, who now stood at second a few feet behind their father.

"Shut up, Nathan!" Skip warned, pointing at him with the hand holding the ball. "Dad doesn't need your dumb game!"

An exasperated Nathan started to yell back, "It's—"

"Hold it!" Taylor interjected, stopping the mercury which was rising between them, especially in Skip. "Guys, guys," he said again, motioning with his hands for everybody to calm down and gather round him for a moment. As they did, Skip's anger toward his little brother continued to escalate.

"Dad already knows about all this!" he snapped, giving him a quick shove.

Nathan was about to push back, but both were stopped as Taylor put himself between them. He crouched down and backed them a little farther apart. Skip was clearly flustered, and the overly matched Nathan was battling back tears.

Taylor knew what was at the bottom of this issue, however, and it wasn't Nathan. His only crime was being too innocent to realize he was dancing on the tip of an iceberg that had quietly resided between his parents since before he was born. Taylor stood back up, but, bending over with his hands on his knees, maintained eye level with his confused little boy.

"Son, I know I don't go to church, but I think it's good that you guys do," he said with sincerity. "And when you're adults, you'll be able to make your own decisions about that and a whole lot of other things."

"But do you believe in God, Dad?" Nathan asked.

The question visibly angered Skip again, necessitating that Taylor put his hand on his shoulder to keep him in check. Tim, however, seemed just as curious as Nathan.

"Of course I believe in God, Son," Taylor said after a short pause. "Maybe not like Mom," he added, "but I think any faith that helps you to be a better person is a good one, Nathan. And you're a good little guy." He smiled, messing up his hair again. "And I'm sure God understands that people believe in him in different ways."

Taylor hoped that that answer would pacify things and peacefully end the discussion, though he knew it was bound to come up again with a kid like Nathan. Deep down, Taylor was never comfortable with how narrow and uncompromising Paula's views were and that their kids were growing up the same way. In his own defense, it was Paula who had changed, not him. However, by the same token, Taylor secretly believed it was his affair about ten years before that probably triggered her becoming so religious. So he had only himself to blame.

She never pushed it on him though, he thought to himself, and but for moments like these, their disagreement in that area was manageable for everybody.

"What's your way, Daddy?" Nathan asked again, pulling his father back in.

"Well, your dad's not that religious, Son, that's all. But I don't think there's anything wrong with it," he quickly added, wishing he had never gotten into this conversation.

"What's 'religion'?" Nathan asked, looking up at his dad with a puzzled look.

"What's religion?" Taylor sighed, repeating the question to buy himself some time. "Religion is the way people believe, Nate, whether it be in God or in something else. Anyway, it's got nothing to do with baseball," Taylor added, roughing up his son's hair again.

"What's Jesus's religion?" Nathan probed, now more inquisitive.

Taylor stood back up and put his hands on his hips, realizing the little guy wasn't going away until he got it all out of his father.

"Well, your mother's really the expert on that, Nate, but I do know he was a great man who lived a couple of thousand years ago and taught a lot of people about God and about how to be a good person and all that. After he died, people started a religion about him called Christianity, which is what you probably could say was his religion," Taylor concluded, again hoping this would end the discussion.

Not so, unfortunately.

"Mom said he rose again and that we can still talk to him," Nathan answered, looking up at his dad again for agreement.

"He doesn't talk to you, Nathan!" Skip defensively piped in.

Taylor was relieved by the interruption, but he placed his palm on Skip's chest to stave off another fight.

"He does too!" Nathan cried.

"When? I never heard him!" Skip snapped back, giving Taylor a look that he had this.

"Mommy says God talks to your heart," Nathan stammered. His voice was now cracking.

Tim placed his hands on Nathan's shoulders and gently pulled him a little more away.

"Hold on. Hold on," Taylor commanded them both. "That's enough about religion for one day. Who God is talking to, I don't know. But I do know he's not playing baseball, and at this hour neither are we," Taylor said, corralling them off the field.

Though the atmosphere was still tense between them, Skip and his little brother reluctantly complied.

Taylor strode toward the parking lot slightly ahead of the boys. He was glad that the conversation was over, but Nathan's words were agitating and reminded him of why he couldn't stomach going to Paula's church in the first place. *It's a big world out there,* he thought in frustration. *And if history has taught us anything, it only gets smaller and more dangerous when the religious stuff goes too far.*

It's already alienated my wife from me, he thought again as he glanced back to make sure the boys were close behind him. And he knew that sooner or later, it was going to confuse their kids too.

Looks like it already has, he angrily realized as he upped his pace to the car.

CHAPTER 9

"TELL MOM I'LL BE BACK AT EIGHT," HE BARKED FROM HIS SIDE window.

Making it home in record time, Taylor remained behind the wheel, hustling the boys along. He was already late for his meeting. "And do your homework!" he added.

Scurrying into the house for dinner, they acknowledged their father's words as he started backing out of the driveway.

Taylor quickly navigated through the familiar neighborhood streets and began heading down Houghton Avenue, one of the main thoroughfares in town. He was late, and unfortunately the two-lane highway connecting downtown to the local suburbs was still busy with traffic. Traveling a good twenty miles an hour over the thirty-mile-an-hour speed limit, he went around cars whenever he could, undaunted by the spring drizzle now slickening the road. Meanwhile, Paula and the kids were eating supper, laughing, and joking around the table.

Taylor strained to look through the windshield as other commuters and the new falling rain continued to hinder his progress. Hastily approaching a slow driver immediately ahead of him, he impatiently began to tailgate. The other car signaled a right turn and moved about halfway into the shoulder. However, rather than making the turn, it unexpectedly braked. Taylor reflexively turned to the left to avoid a rear-end collision, causing his vehicle to lose traction and spin sideways into the opposite lane of traffic.

Before he could see it coming, an oncoming SUV broadsided his compact car. The impact propelled him sideways in what felt like a slow, suspended motion; in his mind's eye, he was still moving forward, but his body and everything around him ominously turned in a direction he couldn't take hold of. It was almost hypnotic until the floating-like feeling abruptly ended with the slam of his driver's side door colliding squarely against an unforgiving utility pole. Taylor felt his head plunge back against his seat amid a showering of glass and the exploding sound of what was undoubtedly his airbag.

Chapter 10

Tubes, wires, and IVs riddled the bandage-covered man Paula knew to be her husband. He was barely recognizable, lying motionlessly in the intensive care unit of the hospital she worked in. Standing at his bedside, she maintained a careful watch of the monitors designed to keep a person alive as their beeps and buzzes continued in the steady harmony she was well familiar with. It had taken rescuers almost thirty-five minutes to extract him from the tiny Ford Focus, which was still hopelessly curled around the iron stanchion it had careened into. They had to cut through the roof, she recalled being told while she sat in a blur in the OR waiting room. Hours before she'd tried to answer the police officer's question about where she wanted the vehicle towed. She didn't know. Her mind went blank, and she felt almost hollow. That would be something Taylor would know.

Paula resecured the connections on her husband's bruised and almost completely discolored body, making sure everything was properly functioning. He was still in a deep sleep from the anesthesia. Her friend Pam, an operating room nurse fresh from Taylor's surgery, strode in to check on him. She was still in her scrubs and cap, and she noticed Paula had just finished the job she came in to do.

Lean and hardworking, the well-seasoned OR nurse was about five seven and had her normally shoulder-length brunette hair tucked up in her cap. She stood next to Paula with her hands on her hips, looking on with her colleague.

"All fixed up?" Pam asked, being as positive as she could.

"Yup," Paula responded without taking her eyes off Taylor.

She turned to Pam. "What's the news?" she asked, searching her friend's face for what she desperately hoped was a good report.

Pam's normally businesslike expression and indomitably cool Irish eyes began to melt as she looked back at Paula. Before she could answer, the surgeon himself entered the room to follow up with his patient. Dr. Robert Goodman was a distinguished-looking, older gentleman; he was tall, slim, and in his mid-sixties. His graying hair was short and combed to the side. Like Pam, he was still in operating room garb, though his cap was pulled down and clinging to the back of his neck. Hearing what was said, he cut into the conversation.

"The news is that Taylor's alive, Paula, which is a miracle in itself," he said as sensitively as he could.

As the doctor was still speaking, Paula turned around to the window, where blackened darkness permitted only a reflection back on her husband's body laying lifelessly still under heavy medication. Her eyes began to well up as she waited for the inevitable report.

The doctor walked over and took her hand. "He's gonna know who you are, Paula. He's gonna know your kids, and he's going to have his mind," he said, warmly squeezing her palm.

Tears began to roll down her cheeks as she anticipated what the surgeon was about to say next. She already knew what it was. "Where is he paralyzed, Bob?" she asked, turning to Taylor.

"From the waist down," the doctor said with a sigh. "The impact severed his spine at about L-4."

The reality of actually hearing the words said imploded within her as she tried to maintain her composure. Thoughts of her husband not being able to hustle through the front door, wrestle with the kids, or even rake leaves on a Saturday afternoon flooded through her mind. *He'll never be able to stand next to me*, was her last thought before being enveloped in Pam's warm embrace. They both began to weep.

"Hold on, girl. It's gonna be okay," came her coworker's sisterly encouragement.

"I don't know how he's gonna handle this," Paula said in a whispered cry as the two continued to tightly hug.

Loosening her grip after another moment or two, Paula gently patted her friend that she was okay, at least for now. Though it took some convincing, Pam and the doctor finally left to clean up, and Paula found herself alone in the room again. She turned back toward Taylor and exhaled for what felt like the first time since getting the call that he was in the hospital about seven hours before. It was going on two a.m., and but for the background beeps and buzzes of the monitors, the twelfth floor was peacefully quiet as Paula sat on the wide but cold marble windowsill, gazing out over the town and deep into the evening horizon.

She still couldn't fathom how quickly and devastatingly things had just changed. In fact, the whole scene seemed almost surreal, and she found herself silently pleading to God that this was just a bad dream and that she would get to wake up, and it would all be normal again.

As she quietly rested her head against the thick glass, her tired, tear-filled eyes searched for comfort as they drifted into the night sky.

CHAPTER II

"LA SPEZIA, THREE HOURS ..."

Edguard Pierre Definiuně glanced out the train window at a countryside that was getting greener by the second under an alluring, pastel-blue Italian sky. It was the summer of 1919, and World War I was finally over. The rolling hills were dotted with livestock again, and the villages, now full and thriving with commerce, were no longer afraid to sport the beautiful colors of the life within them.

Edguard smiled at each passing clothesline blossoming with apparel and the hundreds of harmless travelers, who flooded the dirt and pebble roads. Most of the ride was in country though, and it was the endless procession of family farms that got to Edguard the most. They created a patchwork of the peaceful life he well knew the events of the last decade had violently ripped from them.

Sitting back against the bench seat of the sparsely populated passenger train, he noted that most of the other French soldiers had already returned to their home country. Not Eddie though. The orphan-turned-infantry-sergeant wasn't going back to France. There was no family, no job, and certainly no debt he owed to his country anymore. He had fought bravely and saved enough of his comrades to earn himself the French Medal of Honor, a badge his command was still waiting for an address to mail it to. He had none yet, but he was fast on his way to getting one.

With a load of francs in his pocket and his dream of becoming a fisherman less than a hundred miles away, Eddie Definiunē (pronounced Def-in-ee-yoon) was loving life again.

In truth, the twenty-five-year-old had seen more of the underside of humanity than anyone would care to. For the soldiers, the Great War wasn't political or ideological at all. It was five years of brutal conflict fought man to man, inch by inch, and trench by trench. Eddie's unit had been stationed in Northern Italy to help save their border from Austrian invasion; it was a battle they had been losing by the day, underscored by the devastating onslaught at Caporretto. More men died than lived in that one.

Eddie was a survivor though, which was perhaps the only good thing about growing up an orphan. He knew how to teach others to fight too, which proved to be a game changer for the not-so-little band of French soldiers who had come to trust him.

"Ya can't care about your own lives anymore, fellas," he would bark to his petrified command. "We gotta take theirs first, or we're never gettin' outta here."

He wasn't always proud of that advice, but it worked, and probably a lot more young men had made it back than would have without Eddie. Now it was his turn, he quietly reminded himself. And unlike the others, Eddie Definiunē had to find that place he couldn't wait to call home.

"La Spezia?" He halted in Italian that actually wasn't bad.

"La Spezia," the elderly conductor said with a smile, stopping in the aisle and enunciating it properly for him. "Three hours," the kindly gentleman answered again, motioning with his fingers.

"Paolo, get back from that dock!" yelled his mother from a second-floor window.

Marie Canderale had moved into her parents' apartment atop the small harborside fish market they owned about six months before. She was there because her husband, Joseph, was one of the thousands who had died in the bloody war, leaving her and their three young children without many options. Unfortunately, being a widow in your twenties wasn't that uncommon in those days, though it never remedied the devastating loneliness of missing her other half.

When the spring of 1920 eventually broke through, it brought better business to her father and more stability for her little guys: Joseph, Paolo, and Salvatore. All were quite rambunctious and under the age of seven. It had been almost two years since they lost their dad, and they were finally getting comfortable with their new surroundings. Having the run of Grandpa's market helped, and at times they even got to venture out to the docks with him, where he negotiated with the commercial fishermen.

One was a polite young man from France, whose friendliness toward the community and obvious passion for the sea had brought him the respect of even the other captains. Marie's parents' open admiration and routine comments about Edguard's being single and "kind of handsome" were annoying to her. She had absolutely no interest in trying to replace her husband and avoided even the slightest eye contact with him.

He noticed her immediately though.

"Is Marie here?" he bashfully inquired while doing business with her father.

She never was though, which frustrated her dad, who also subtly glanced about the area, looking for her. Unbeknownst to both of them, Marie often watched the whole thing.

Like clockwork she found something that needed attention in their apartment upstairs as soon as she saw Eddie's boat pulling in, usually at half past four. From there she secretly observed him dock and then transact business with her father. As other young women fawned over him, Marie laughed when he looked for her. Her excitement over watching him, however, was quickly paralleled by her guilt over wanting to. This went on for months.

Finally, on a day when her father needed her on the dock, she knew contact with the captivating Frenchman was inevitable. Her quiet return of a smile was all Edguard needed, and the courtship was on.

Whether it was the compassion in Marie's eyes that gave Eddie hope for the deeper things in life or whether he was just plain smitten with her, he didn't know, but the once lonely and battle-torn young soldier found himself forever bringing gifts and doing all he could to spend time with his first and only sweetheart. This soon graduated to long walks along the Mediterranean, where Marie listened to him dream of a life she never thought would come to her again. Though it certainly wasn't a fairy tale that got her and Eddie together, it wound up feeling just as sweet when her soon-to-be husband wasted no time in convincing her to marry him. He adopted the boys immediately thereafter, and by 1930 the Definiunẽs added two more to the brood.

Marie was pretty much running her dad's fish market by then, and her husband had two boats going. By 1935, however, Europe grew ugly again. Smelling another war, Edguard made no bones about getting his family out of what had become fascist Italy and over to France. From there he decided to leave the continent entirely.

With the savings from their business and the sale of his boats, Eddie was able to find enough friends and bribe enough people at the French consulate to immigrate his family into the United States in 1936, where they landed smack-dab in the middle of the Great Depression. Ellis Island took the accent from Edguard's last name, but he gained Jamaica Queens and a life without war, at least not in his own backyard.

Though he was inches from being broke, Eddie was still a scrapper and went straight into what he knew. Before long he and his junior partners, sons Joseph and Paolo, had a fish store of their own on Archer Avenue. Two years later, Joseph, then twenty-four, met and married Lillian, and they had three boys: John in 1940, Robert in 1943, and Joseph Jr. in 1947.

The fish market thrived and expanded; however, Joe Jr., Joe's son and now one of Edguard's many grandsons, opted to pursue an education, putting himself through community college at night. By 1967, at the age of twenty, the young man had a full-time job in management in the appliance industry. It was at that time that he married Dorothy ("Dot"), literally the girl next door and the love of his life, who had become a stewardess for American Airlines. The two worked hard together so he could complete his four-year degree in the evenings.

Finally in 1970, with cap, gown, and certificate in hand, Joseph Jr. became the first Definiunẽ college graduate. He was already a father by then, and by 1974 he bought his own store and had two more children, making it a daughter and two sons. Though he wasn't working in the family business, his father, Joseph, was indeed very proud, as was his grandfather, a now eighty-year-old Edguard.

The couple further pursued the American dream by moving out to the suburb of Bayside, where they did what it took to put their kids through Catholic school and hopefully college thereafter. Though "Big Joe" or "Joe D.," as his friends called him, had nothing against any of his offspring doing what they wanted to do, it was over his dead body that they weren't getting their degree first, starting with his princess, who now found herself far from home, at State University at Albany, embarking on a career in nursing.

"I'll take it medium with a little milk, please" came the polite request at the university café.

"Is that cawfee from New Yawk?" mimicked a sarcastic male voice from about ten people back in line.

The Queens girl reflexively turned to eye her offender. He only laughed, which was immediately followed by the supportive guffaws of his obnoxious cohorts. As far as she was concerned, they were the ones with the accent, not her.

Ignoring the immaturity, she turned back to her friends. "Who's that?" she demanded.

"Taylor Green," one of them said, blushing.

She looked back. He was still grinning at her and then chuckled patronizingly when she glared in disapproval. A mortified Paula

Definiuně grabbed her coffee and strode toward the exit as quickly and tactfully as she could. Her friends reluctantly followed.

Pushing down hard on the metal cross bar, which opened the door, she mistakenly glanced back, only to be caught again by the awaiting smile of that cocky, presumptuous, and yes, attractive upperclassman.

"Paula?"

"Paula?"

"Paula, cawfee?" came the wake-up caress of the morning nurse's hand on her shoulder.

It was already six a.m. Thankfully her sister-in-law was at the house, getting the kids out. The steam and welcoming aroma of the coffee started to take her out of her fog as she briefly sipped it and looked over at her still-deeply-sedated husband.

CHAPTER 12

THE BOYS FRANTICALLY COLLECTED THEIR BACKPACKS BEFORE heading out to catch the bus. Paula pushed everyone along, making sure all had eaten, were properly dressed, and had what they needed for the day. Skip was noticeably quiet as he mechanically gathered his books and other items. Like his siblings, he was eager to see their father, but also extremely concerned about the paralysis.

"Can we go and see Dad tonight?" Tim asked. "It's been five days."

"Yeah! I want to see Daddy," Nathan joined in.

"I told you last night," Paula said. "Daddy's on a lot of medications right now, and there's a lot going on with—"

"Are they fixing his legs?" Skip excitedly cut in before she could finish her sentence.

Paula's face strained. Telling her kids their father wasn't going to walk again was a conversation she already should have had. But how could she when she hadn't had it with her husband yet? Taylor wouldn't let her, and the distress she'd seen in his eyes more than convinced her not to push it right now.

She ignored Skip's question and continued. "He's not ready for visitors yet." She looked down at him and placed her hand on top of his head. "They're doing everything they can, honey."

"Jeff Harding's dad will be coaching for Daddy tonight ... This is the big one, isn't it?" Paula said, changing the subject.

Skip nodded in cautious anticipation of what his mother was

about to say next. He hadn't played since his father's accident, and Paula saw no indication that that was going to change. However, she gently held him back while his brothers went out the door so they could finish their conversation alone.

"Mr. Harding said if you don't feel like playing tonight, he totally understands, but he'd love to have you in the lineup. What do you think?"

"I don't know." Skip shrugged despondently.

"They'll be videotaping the game for Daddy," Paula coaxed, trying to encourage him.

"All right," he relented.

"But can we see Dad after?" he asked, pepping up again.

"That's a little late, honey. Daddy gets tired." She softly smiled. "Maybe we'll call him."

"What about tomorrow?" Skip persisted. "It's Saturday. How 'bout I go with you then?"

"We'll see. We'll see," Paula replied, hustling him out the door.

CHAPTER 13

SITTING SLIGHTLY PROPPED UP IN HIS BED, TAYLOR TOOK A SECOND sip of his coffee. This was the first time in three days he'd felt clearheaded. Out his window he could see the morning sun shining over the tops of the trees. If he wasn't paralyzed, he'd say it was beautiful. But it wasn't. Nothing was.

The scurry of activity outside his door told him the hospital's day shift was coming on. It was their busiest time, with doctors, nurses, techs, and medical students flooding the hallways and making regular stops to do whatever they did. He hated that time of day, largely because the increased attention he received served as a continual reminder of why he was there.

Paula had called the night before and told him the kids won the championship. She was upbeat as usual, filling the empty airspace of their conversation with every detail of the game, especially Skip's play. Taylor did his level best to sound happy about it, though he certainly wasn't ready to see anyone yet. He still wrestled with what to say to them when he did. Thankfully he was no longer in intensive care but alone in a single room. He had an IV posted on one side of his bed, infusing mostly fluids and pain medication, and on the other side was a clicker for the television. With all the strength he could muster, he pushed downward on his arms, lifted himself up at almost a ninety-degree angle, and attempted to move his legs.

He glanced at the open doorway from time to time to make sure no one was watching as he continued trying what was obviously a futile exercise to everyone but him. He couldn't get any portion of his lower body to so much as flinch, despite giving it every ounce of energy and emotion he had. Suddenly, his straining was interrupted by the familiar sound of his son Skip's voice approaching amid the friendly chatter down the hall. Taylor could hear the nurses welcome the boy like a celebrity as the discussion regarding the game he'd won filled the corridor. Apparently Skip had a bat signed by the players and was about to present it to his father. Taylor wasn't ready for this though. He just wasn't ready, and his wife knew that.

As their footsteps neared the room, he quickly slumped back down in the bed, pretending to be in a deep sleep. Paula's voice could be heard inquiring with her colleagues about his morning and whether he was eating all right. From their station the staff nurses answered positively shortly before she and Skip entered the room.

Paula gently rubbed Taylor's shoulder as their son, with bat in hand, eagerly waited for him to wake up. The shaking became subtly more firm as Taylor refused to respond. Paula's eyes darted to the instrument readings and IV connections. They were all normal. Noticing an open, folded-over *Sports Illustrated* magazine on the table next to the bed, she calmly continued to shrug and cajole her husband to open his eyes.

"Why won't he wake up?" Skip nervously asked.

"It's okay, Skip. Daddy's fine," his mother said.

"He may have been up a little too late last night. That's all."

The knowing squeeze or two Taylor felt on the back of his neck told him his wife was aware of what was going on; however, he still didn't respond.

An attending nurse could be heard entering the room. Similar to Paula, she quickly viewed the monitors and discreetly checked Taylor's pulse. She then shot her colleague a look that confirmed their patient was faking, but for the sake of the little boy, she covered for him.

"Some of the medicine your daddy's been taking makes him very sleepy, Skip. He'll be okay in a little bit," she said. "How about we all go down to the cafeteria for a soda?" she added, glancing at Paula.

"Good idea. Let's give Daddy a break," Paula replied.

Before leaving, Skip gently slid the bat under Taylor's arm and against his side. He gazed at his dad for an extended moment before his mom quietly ushered him out. The sound of their chatter slowly faded away as they exited down the hallway toward the elevators.

Hoping the coast was clear, Taylor squinted an eye. The room was empty. He propped his body up again and reached for the folded magazine next to his bed. Just as he began to focus on his article, Paula deftly entered through the open doorway, awkwardly surprising him. Taylor, however, refused to acknowledge that he'd been caught and was, in fact, offended by her sneaky return. He angrily ignored her while still trying to read. The tension beneath the prolonged pause began to build as Paula continued to stare at him from the foot of his bed.

"Taylor what are you doing?" she demanded as calmly as she could.

"I'm reading, Paula," he flatly answered.

With righteous indignance, his eyes remained fixed on the article, while her gaze quietly sat on him. After a few moments, he couldn't hold out any longer and slapped down the magazine in frustration. "Why did you bring him here?" he bristled.

"Because he's your son!" she snapped back, though her face appeared painfully fragmented.

"You should have just called me first," Taylor responded, slightly deflated.

"It wouldn't have mattered," Paula answered. She was right. "They've been waiting all week, and they're all downstairs, Taylor. They need to see you."

Taylor glanced down at the baseball bat.

"They won it for you. I have it on video," she said, trying to cheer him up.

"That's good, Paula," he dryly acknowledged. Why she thought a ball game or anything else would matter at a time like this was beyond him.

"That's all?" she asked.

"I don't know if you noticed, but I am paralyzed right now," Taylor tersely replied, pounding his lifeless legs with his fists. "I'm kind of preoccupied," he added sarcastically.

"You're not paralyzed, Taylor. Your legs are," she said.

"Oh, that's all!" Taylor said, not having any of it. "It's just that I'll never walk. I'm sorry," he chided, slapping up the magazine again to supposedly go back to his reading.

"I didn't mean it that way, Taylor. You know that," she conceded with frustration.

"Well, I won't be going to court anymore. That's for sure," he declared, still looking at the article.

"Why not?" she challenged again.

"Because I don't do that," he sternly affirmed.

"So, what are you going to do, Taylor?"

He shook his head. "Have no idea, Paula. But I'm not having people feel sorry for me. That's for sure. And I'm not going to wheel myself around a baseball field either. So you need to back off right now until I figure things out, okay? Does that make sense?" he harshly added, looking up from the magazine to further cement his point.

"It does, Taylor," Paula acknowledged after a pause. "But we're also grateful you're alive." She sighed. "A lot of people are."

"So I can live like this?" Taylor mused. "Ask them if they want to change places, Paula," he added cynically.

Paula didn't respond.

Taking notice that his last remark had silenced her, he continued with his tirade. "I'm not going to pretend that everything's all right, Paula. It's not all right! And I don't want cards. I don't want prayers. I don't want visitors. And I certainly don't want advice … from anyone," he mumbled under his breath.

"What *do* you want, Taylor?" she quietly asked, reluctantly open to his direction.

"I want someone to tell me how I can walk again, Paula," Taylor candidly stated after a pause. "And if no one can tell me that, I don't know what I want. At least not right now."

The comment remained unanswered. Instead she briefly looked into his eyes before peering out the window for another moment or two. "All right, Taylor," she capitulated, hastily putting on her coat and grabbing her things to leave.

"What are you doing?" he protested.

"I'm going downstairs to get your kids and take them home," she said without looking back.

As she reached for her pocketbook on the adjacent chair, he could see she was fiercely holding back tears.

"Call us when you're ready," she added, striding out of the room.

Hearing her footsteps quickly pass the nursing desk en route to the elevator, Taylor noticed that there was no touching base or having conversations with staff the way she customarily did after her visits. Though he knew her leaving was all his doing, for some strange reason it was still upsetting, and he began feeling uncomfortably alone.

He sat up and coldly stared into the blankness of his now-empty room. Firmly gripping the handle of the bat Skip had tucked next to him, he flung it hard against the wall, splitting the lumber before it noisily clanged against the tiled hospital floor. The echo traveled outside his door and followed Paula as she continued resolutely down the hall.

Chapter 14

THE SLIGHTLY BENT RED METAL FLAG DANGLED FROM THE BOTTOM of the family mailbox. It had been broken for weeks, and neither Paula nor the boys could figure out how to fix it. Glimpsing it through the dining room window, Taylor realized it would probably be up to him, though he still hadn't mustered the ambition to go out and look at it yet.

It had been nine months since his accident, and just about everything outside had noticeably declined. Taylor's own meticulous handiwork was what used to provide the outdoor landscaping touches; however, since those chores had been relegated to his overworked wife and adolescent children, paint had started to chip on the trim, bushes had become overgrown, and the flower gardens were in a bad need of weeding.

A long, wooden handicap ramp now sloped down and connected the front porch to the driveway. This was the most conspicuous change to the Green home within the last year, and Taylor despised looking at it, just as he hated seeing the numerous other ramps and features that hadn't been needed a short time before.

His eyes turned to his secretary, Marge, who had just pulled up in her maroon four-door Malibu. She exited the car, opened the rear door, and began to remove a load of files from the back seat to bring into the house. As usual, she was dressed in professional attire, including high heels, as she struggled to balance the heavy Redwell files and close the car door. Taylor then heard the slap of the front screen door and watched Paula jog down the ramp to help her. Marge appreciated this as the two began to converse like the old friends they were.

"How's it going, Marge?" Paula asked, grabbing some files out of her hands.

"Not getting any younger. That's for sure," Marge said, though still bearing the grin of the trooper she was.

They rested the materials on the hood of her car so they could talk. Paula was still in her uniform, having just gotten off from work.

Taylor remained sitting in his wheelchair inside, looking at both of them through a narrow opening between the dining room window curtains. *Life had certainly changed for those two as well*, he reflected bitterly.

Except for telephone contact with his firm and only necessary client interaction, Taylor had pretty much kept himself off the grid since coming home.

"The office doing okay?" Paula asked.

"Hectic as usual, but we're holding our own," Marge replied. "Jack's picked up all the court work, and they've got Russell into things way over his head," she said with a laugh, though Paula knew she didn't really think it was funny. "We need your husband back." She sighed.

Quietly shaking her head, Paula just shrugged. She felt bad for Marge and the others.

"How's things around here?" Marge asked after a brief pause.

Paula's forlorn expression gave it away as she gazed into the distance. Even Taylor could see that his depression had taken a toll on her, though she was trying to keep her spirits up.

"We're doin' okay," she said. "I'm putting in a lot of overtime at the hospital, and Shar and Tim have had to really pitch in at home with the boys."

"Skip doing any better?" Marge asked, her voice dropping an octave, showing her concern.

"It's hard to tell," Paula answered. "He still doesn't really talk.

Kind of withdrawn from his friends at school. Won't play ball this season." Her voice trailed off.

"Really?" Marge noted in surprise.

"He kicked and screamed when I tried to bring him to counseling," Paula answered.

"Stubborn as a mule. Just like his father," Marge added, shaking her head with a slight smile to lighten things up again.

"Absolutely," Paula admitted, joining the mood. "He won't learn to drive yet, but I'm still working on it," she said, motioning with her head toward the house and Taylor. "He goes to physical therapy three times a week. He's trying to get his upper body stronger, but that's about it."

"Still doesn't want to come to the office?" Marge hopefully asked.

"Nope."

"Hardheaded as he is, I really miss him." Marge sighed again.

The sound of a jet plane flying high overhead briefly caught their attention. They both relaxed against the side of Marge's car and took a moment to watch it peacefully traverse a quiet, blue sky.

Noticing that Paula was occupied with Marge, Taylor closed the bedroom door, reached into his closet, and pulled out two canes. He tightly gripped both with each hand, braced himself, and steadily pulled his body upright out of the wheelchair. With his unfeeling legs and feet dangling below, he bravely held himself up between the canes and attempted to move forward, one side of his body at a time.

After months of secretly practicing this exercise, he could actually balance himself on the canes and turn and pull each side of his lower body a step or two without falling. It took every ounce of his upper body strength to get that far, however, as he gritted his teeth to maintain that position.

Getting his legs to somehow begin to move again or at least to balance him enough so he wouldn't have to spend all his time sitting in a chair seemed like the only desire he had left in life, but it was a burning one, consuming every thought for the future. *I have to walk again,* he insisted to himself, even if only partially. He could will it.

He pushed forward, and after dragging his lower body four or five agonizing steps, he flopped himself on his back at the foot of the bed, exhausted. He lay there for a few moments, and after catching his breath, he grabbed one of the canes and held it across his chest in a bench press position. Five steps in nine months of backbreaking work was hardly progress, he thought, as he angrily hurled the cane across the bedroom floor. His eyes tightly closed while he placed the palms of his hands on his sweat-beaded forehead in anguish. Another failed effort.

Outside Paula was still looking up at the sky with her arms folded across her chest.

"Might be a long time before he comes back to the office, Marge," she said.

"I know," Marge conceded, looking at the sky with her. "Does he still want out of the partnership?"

"Uh-huh," Paula answered. After a moment she looked back at Marge and gave the latest update on Taylor. "He'll work at home, do a little research on his computer, and make enough for us to get by. But that's as much practicing law as he's gonna do. He doesn't like to leave the house for work or anything else." Paula sighed, knowing that this wasn't news to his secretary.

"Yeah, I know, but I guess after all this time, I'm just surprised," Marge answered, sounding a little discouraged. "He really loved his job. I figured sooner or later he'd come roaring back like always."

Paula reached over and put a consoling arm around her old friend. "He's still pretty mad at the world right now, Marge. What he loved to do he can't do anymore. No more walking into court or running around the ball fields with his kids. He can't do anything the way he used to, so he won't do it at all. But he's still inside there, Margie," Paula declared after a thoughtful pause. "That hardheaded man you work for is still in there," she added with a squeeze and a gentle shake, giving both of them a last boost of hope to hold onto.

They took a prolonged embrace before getting interrupted by the buzzing of Marge's cell phone. Paula picked the files up off the hood to let her go.

"Call me if you need anything," Marge offered, getting into her car.

"Thanks, Marge," Paula answered.

"You hang in there, girl!" came a motherly yell as Marge hung her head out the window while backing down the driveway.

"Will do!" Paula shouted back.

Balancing the files in one hand, she reached for the front screen door handle with the other.

Taylor heard her coming and had already put himself back in his wheelchair and rolled into the kitchen.

Chapter 15

The maple trees were beginning to bud as their branches stretched high across one border of his backyard. Taylor's eyes were closed, however, and with his head tilted back, he tried to relax with the help of a cold beer tucked in his right hand.

It was early afternoon, and as he preferred, he was home by himself, sitting on the deck. Donning a baseball cap, a blue pullover fleece, khaki pants, and Docksiders, Taylor could feel the weather finally warming up again. Gentle breezes complemented the placid sound of softly chirping birds. This restful welcome of spring, however, was suddenly interrupted by the slam of the Johnsons' back door and Corey's excited hollering, filling half the neighborhood. His mother had apparently agreed to play ball with him, and he was taking full advantage of the opportunity.

Jarred out of his siesta but remaining as inconspicuous as possible, Taylor wheeled himself across the deck to where he could peek into the Johnsons' backyard. Corey had gathered his bat and as many balls as he could in what appeared to be the beginnings of a sandlot-style batting practice, something that had been commonplace at the Green home before his accident. The sight of them starting to play gently lured Taylor's mind into a quiet tranquility, whereby he momentarily forgot that he couldn't walk anymore.

He wasn't thinking; he was just imbibing the smells, colors, and sounds of all that spring had once been to him. His serenity, however, was cut short after a minute or two by Corey's obvious struggle at the plate. The little guy couldn't hit even the easiest underhand pitches his mom awkwardly served. This resulted in moans of discouragement that resonated throughout the backyard, causing Evette to caution him not to wake up his napping little sister.

Taylor continued to silently spectate the game from his deck, muttering under his breath his disappointment with Evette's inability to correct her son's flawed batting stance and swing. Corey's knees weren't bent, he didn't choke up, and he rested his bat on the back of his shoulder, which caused a downward rather than level swing. He was also markedly late in getting the bat around for each pitch, further evidence that the kid had no idea how to hit a baseball. Nor was there a hint that his mother knew either.

Taylor could hardly bear watching anymore, and in a voice slightly raised, which he hoped couldn't be traced, he barked a basic but much-needed instruction into the adjoining yard.

"Choke up on the bat!" he yelled.

He watched his unsolicited advice land with a thud between Corey and his mom.

Startled, they both turned in surprise and looked toward him. However, he'd already secreted his head below the deck hedging, where he remained undetected. After a further pause, Evette resumed the game. She probably thought it was one of the boys yelling from a bedroom window, Taylor assumed.

He continued to watch but with a little more caution than before. Thankfully, Corey was now choking up on the bat and within moments made solid contact with the ball, sending it into the Greens' yard. Taylor's eyes followed it with pride as it landed parallel with the deck and bounced slightly beyond.

Corey and his mom were ecstatic as the kid jubilantly chased the ball to marvel at how far he'd hit it. However, before he got there, Taylor quietly scooted his wheelchair through the open sliding door, discreetly closing it behind him. He had no idea why he was hiding from a five-year-old, but he undoubtedly wanted to. Rolling himself behind the adjacent kitchen counter, he was safely out of view. He could hear the tapping of the little boy's footsteps as they scampered up the ramp as well as his mother's distant protests behind him. Suddenly there was silence. Then a faint knocking on the sliding glass door. Taylor remained motionless, wondering whether the kid had seen him. Hopefully he hadn't.

The bounding steps of Corey's mom converged on where the knocking was coming from, and their muffled voices confirmed she was scolding him. Taylor felt bad for the kid and a little silly that he was just sitting there in the dark only a few feet away. But he wasn't going to move.

"Why doesn't Mr. Sticks answer, Mommy?" an inquisitive Corey asked in a voice loud enough for Taylor to hear.

"He needs his rest, Corey," Evette answered. "And stop calling him 'Mr. Sticks.' His name is Mr. Green."

The sound of their steps trailing away was the last Taylor could hear of them. Though he had no idea why the kid had called him that, he was relieved they were gone. He'd have to be more careful in the future, he thought, as he peeked through the kitchen window at the two walking hand in hand back to their yard.

CHAPTER 16

WALKING ON CANES WAS DOABLE, AT LEAST FOR SHORT SPURTS, HE said to himself as he attempted to navigate across the deck again. It was early afternoon, way before the kids got home, and Taylor's hands were locked on the two canes he used covertly for just that purpose. With his gray sweats and sneakers on, he was ready to go to work again.

The sleeves of his sweatshirt were pulled up and exposed the powerful wrists and forearms that enabled him to tightly grip the canes and balance himself in a standing position. A quick view of the setup illustrated the goal of walking on his canes to the other side, where another chair awaited him. The idea was to condition his upper body to lift and balance himself to move forward and swing his legs under him step by step.

Regardless of how irrational such thinking would be for other people, especially his wife, Taylor knew the task was possible for him and that his willpower could actually pull it off. How good he would get at it, he didn't know, but for the short term he'd settle for ambulating in an upright position, at least across his deck, without falling. Nobody needed to see this exercise either, he purposed within himself, and after a furtive side-to-side glance, he started from his usual standing position and exerted the first step with his right-hand cane. The strain within his upper torso was as intense as the determination on his face; he pushed out a groan with each slow pull of his body, with legs in tow, one side forward at a time.

Rotating from right to left, Taylor made it to about the middle of the deck. He then took a breather, reset, and pushed his upper body up high on the canes again so his legs could rest directly beneath him before moving forward again. He'd already safely taken about six strenuous steps, and he stabbed his right cane forward to begin the next one. As he did so, up popped a kid's head from just below the floor level of the deck.

"Hi, Mr. Sticks!" Corey chirped.

A startled Taylor reflexively turned, causing a complete loss of balance, which sent him crashing down on the deck surface. Both canes went flying, and the sight and sound of the impact horrified Corey, who now stared at what looked like a lifeless grown man pasted to the wooden floor.

Fortunately, it appeared far worse than it actually was. Taylor slowly propped himself up by his elbows to catch a view of the little intruder peering at him from a few short feet away. Corey's face looked frozen.

"What are you doing here?" barked a frustrated Taylor.

Half in shock, Corey remained speechless but was about to burst into tears. Taylor quickly composed himself, holding up his hand as a sign of peace, and tried to keep him from crying.

"It's okay. It's not your fault," a now-embarrassed Taylor consoled. "You surprised me. That's all."

Those words seemed to calm Corey down.

"I'm sorry, Mr. Sticks," he said.

Checking himself for injuries and whether anything had broken due to his fall, Taylor sat up against a nearby wall. His mind raced for a way to handle the kid's discovery as he wiped the sweat off his brow with the back of his forearm and caught his breath. "Why do you call me that?" he asked with a sigh, still recuperating.

Corey innocently pointed to the canes with a look that said the name should be self-explanatory.

"Because you're always walking on those two sticks," he answered. "Why are you always trying to walk?"

"I was just exercising," Taylor scoffed in denial. "And I really don't do it that much," he added, hoping to downplay the whole ordeal.

"Oh, I see you out here every day, Mr. Sticks," Corey indignantly replied. His knowing smile said he wasn't as gullible as Taylor thought.

"From where?" Taylor asked, now concerned about what the talkative five-year-old knew.

"From my room," Corey answered matter-of-factly. He pointed up at the neighboring second-floor window, which overlooked their location.

"I thought you went to school," Taylor retorted, frustrated that he'd been seen.

"I go to school!" Corey piped up.

"When do you get home?" Taylor asked a little more calmly. It was clear that challenging the little guy wasn't a good idea.

"Lunchtime," he answered.

"You're in kindergarten," Taylor muttered to himself as it dawned on him.

Corey nodded as Taylor folded his arms across his chest, uncertain what to do next.

"My daddy drinks that beer too," Corey observed, pointing to the sweaty, half-filled can by Taylor's wheelchair.

"Oh," Taylor acknowledged. He was sorry the kid had seen it.

"My mom says too much beer is no good for you, Mr. Sticks," he added.

The concern in Corey's eyes took Taylor aback a little bit. He seemed pretty attentive for a five-year-old and surprisingly not as annoying as people generally were to Taylor these days.

"She's right," Taylor replied, looking over to see whether anyone else was in Corey's backyard. Thankfully no one was there.

"Did you tell your mom I've been drinking beer too?" he asked, feeling that everything was probably out of the bag by now.

"No," Corey patently said.

"Oh." Taylor tiredly exhaled. After a momentary pause, he looked back at the boy and sighed. "What do you need, Corey?"

"Nothin'," Corey said, but Taylor could see he was a little disappointed that his new adult friend no longer wanted his company. "Want me to help you get up?" Corey offered.

Taylor respectfully declined but then noticed that one of his canes had gone off the deck and was somewhere in the abutting bushes. He pointed to it, and Corey brought it up the steps to him. While up on the deck, the little guy took a complete view of the overgrown baseball field in the Greens' backyard.

He perked up. "Do you know how to play baseball, Mr. Sticks?"

"A little," an exhausted Taylor replied, still trying to keep the conversation short.

"Would you teach me?"

"I don't play, Corey," Taylor bluntly responded, impatiently reaching for the other cane and looking for a place on the railing where he could hoist himself up again. He needed to put the canes away and get himself back into the wheelchair before Paula or anyone else got home.

"I think you better get back to your mom, okay, Corey?" he instructed.

The boy reluctantly obeyed, though along the way he periodically turned back and looked at Taylor before reaching his back door.

CHAPTER 17

PAULA CLEARED THE LAST OF THE DINNER DISHES WHILE TAYLOR sat in his wheelchair at the head of the table, peering out the sliding glass doors. The view of the backyard was still light enough to see. His brief moment of placidity was interrupted, however, as Paula dropped a piece of mail on the table in front of him. Seeing it was from the school, Taylor noticed his son trying to ease himself out of the room while the others were still cleaning up. His mother quickly corralled him.

"Skip's report card came in the mail today," Paula announced to Taylor, waiting for him to look at it.

He reluctantly read what it said, which was in substance that Skip was failing most of his subjects and hadn't done his homework. Taylor could feel the chill of his wife's eyes on the top of his head as he further reviewed the information. He hoped to find at least one or two redeeming qualities in there somewhere, but there weren't any. Paula's continued silence served as a stiff reminder of how she'd been telling him about this problem since his accident and that he too even saw how Skip couldn't care less about school.

Though Taylor kept his eyes on the paper to appear interested, it was becoming apparent that his chosen path of quietly remaining aloof for the last ten months, preoccupied with either feeling sorry for himself or trying to walk, was coming to home to roost. Sure, he wished his kid could adapt and do better, but quite frankly Taylor was questioning the point of a lot of things himself. His struggle with this perspective certainly wasn't something he was proud of, but it was real nonetheless. He also well knew that such thinking would never fly with someone like his wife, so to avoid a useless conflict, he would go through the motions as best he could.

Perusing the document again, he noticed Skip was just as uncomfortable as he was. Neither wanted to discuss the delinquencies, but it was obvious Paula wasn't going to let them get away with that. Though she always chose her battles, Taylor could sense that unfortunately this was gonna be one of those picks.

"Look at the absences," she said to both of them.

"Has he been sick a lot?" Taylor gingerly responded without looking up.

"You know he hasn't," Paula curtly answered.

Noticing that the report didn't bother his dad that much, Skip tried to capitalize.

"Junior high is—"

"We're not discussing what junior high is anymore, Skip," his mother sharply interrupted, jutting the palm of her hand inches from his mouth in an explicit direction that he close it immediately.

"What about junior high?" Taylor quipped, obviously looking for an out for each of them.

"Oh, you're interested!" Paula snapped sarcastically.

Though an annoyed Taylor stood down, he could see that his wife was already bent on driving the situation to crisis. "Junior high is the school your son has been attending this year, Taylor. And I use the term *attending* loosely!" she exclaimed, picking up the card and slapping it in an even tempo against her other hand.

As she was doing this, she walked around behind Skip as if presenting him to his father. He was clearly uneasy, though a new defiance emerged in his countenance that differed poignantly from the jovial boy his dad had once known. Taylor could see Skip was using his father's apathy to manipulate his way past serious consequences, which deep down Taylor knew he was too depressed to do anything about anyway. *What kind of pep talk can I give that won't sound as hollow as the speaker himself?* Taylor wondered as he groped for a way to deal with a situation he'd been in denial about and had subtly escaped confronting for the last ten months. It was his hypocrisy that was paralyzing him now, and he was sure his son could see that too.

Clenching Skip's triceps from behind, Paula had him face Taylor, holding them both captive. She started to do his talking as well.

"I got new friends I won't tell anyone about. Dad. And I'm barely passing, which is pretty good since I don't go to school that much either, Dad," she further mimicked.

Turning her head to Skip, she was clearly unafraid to go fact by fact with him. "I can't tell you everything your son has been doing, Taylor, but I know a lot more than he thinks," she said, shaking him a little bit. Taylor remained frozen in his chair.

"Dad, I'll do better next term. I will," Skip roguishly insisted.

Taylor knew he was looking for the quick out they both wanted. Unfortunately, so did Paula.

"That's not what we're talking about, Skip!" she harshly interjected.

Closing his eyes to avoid further confrontation, Taylor lifted his hands in surrender. Things got quiet.

"Skip, go to school and do your homework. Okay?" he mildly declared, hoping that if nothing else, his mother's riding would force him to do better. "And listen to your mother," he added after a pause, as if it should pacify her and conclude the conversation.

"No! Listen to your father!" she jabbed, directing her fiery eyes back at him.

"I just told him to do his homework!" Taylor howled. "What do you want me to do?" he added, holding out his arms in his own defense.

"Forget it!" a disgusted Paula shot back, waving him off as she strode to the sink to finish the dishes. "Go to bed, Skip!" she commanded, giving him a look that said though his father may not, she certainly would be keeping the upper hand in his life. He swiftly disappeared upstairs.

Taylor turned to look out the sliding glass doors, primarily to avoid eye contact with his wife. "You're making too much of this, Paula," he said in an effort of reconciliation, knowing she was fuming right now.

"Can't do it by myself anymore, Taylor," she answered matter-of-factly, still washing the pots and looking out the window over the sink.

"I know," Taylor said. He hoped his brief words of comfort would suffice.

"Really?" she replied in disbelief. "Do you have any idea what he's been up to this year, Taylor?"

Continuing to peer outside, he didn't respond.

"Didn't think so," she confirmed after an awkward pause. Placing the two or three pots she had just dried into the lower cabinets, she moved to another subject. "The coach from school called last night."

"Uh-huh," Taylor acknowledged.

"Can't get Skip to go out for the team. Says he's been trying to talk to you," she added with a tone of accusation that this information was probably true.

She remained pretty angry as she hastily packed the rest of the plates into the dishwasher.

"He doesn't want to play," Taylor curtly replied, still looking out the sliding glass door.

"Since when?" Paula shot back, looking at Taylor and demanding eye contact.

"Since he's not a little kid anymore, Paula," Taylor retorted.

"And you talked to him about that?" she challenged.

Taylor could hear in her voice that she was fed up. But so was he. It was kind of difficult to be the greatest father right now. Kinda tough to be a lot of things.

"There's nothing to talk about," he answered, returning his gaze outside.

Drying her hands with the dishtowel and hanging it up, she walked around the counter and headed over to Taylor. "Why he's not playing anymore? There's nothing to talk about?" she challenged again but in a calmer and more deliberate manner.

Taylor glanced up at her for a brief moment but then looked back outside. Unfortunately, the sky was now dark, leaving only his reflection in the blackened glass and Paula staring at him from behind. He wasn't up for this battle, but he obviously didn't have much choice.

"It's been a rough year for everybody, Paula. I can't work. I can't walk. I obviously can't play baseball, and I—"

"—can't be a father anymore," she cut in, now with a tone that said she was sick of her husband's self-pity.

Offended, Taylor pulled open the sliding door and forcefully pushed down on the wheels of his chair, propelling himself out to the deck. Paula left him alone and went to check on Nathan and the others.

He closed the door behind him and for the next ten minutes or so tried to clear his head. Life in the abyss between what should matter and why it didn't, wasn't something he enjoyed thinking about, much less trying to explain to someone like Paula, who would never understand anyway.

The cool night air felt better as he closed his eyes and tilted his head back. His rest, however, was soon jarred by the slam of the Johnsons' side door. Taylor could see Robert, still in uniform, striding toward his car to leave. The door opened again, and Evette emerged, holding the baby with Corey in tow, clutching her leg.

"Evette, don't even start with me!" Robert cautioned in a voice low enough to avoid embarrassment from his relatively new neighbors.

Evette appeared upset. "I didn't start anything. Where are you going?" Her face crumpled.

Robert turned his head again to see whether anyone was

watching. Though Taylor was, he was hidden behind the hedge that abutted his deck.

Robert quickly closed the door of his car and started to back out before Evette could finish her next sentence. Taylor witnessed Corey again, who now stood in the driveway with his mom as his father's headlights withdrew from their little family. The confused youngster stayed and watched his dad's car dart down the street as his mother stormed back into the house. Turning around, she called for him to come in behind her. After a moment or two and another round of Evette's demands that he come inside, the visibly stunned young man sheepishly complied.

Taylor's eyes couldn't help following him through the closing screen door. His gaze remained fixed there for an additional minute or so before he turned his chair back toward the horse farm.

Staring into the now-quiet night air, he closed his eyes again, fighting to get some peace.

Chapter 18

Corey jumped off the bus and sprinted up the steps of the porch and through the front door, shirttail hanging and backpack swinging. Evette saw him coming as he entered the foyer and sauntered through the center hallway, heading for the kitchen in the rear of their home. She had already taken out cookies and a drink for his after-school snack. True to form, Corey couldn't stop chattering about his day, even when his mother pointed him upstairs to change into his playclothes.

While up there, he took his customary glance through the bedroom window over to his neighbor's deck. Surprisingly, Mr. Green wasn't there. Corey shrugged it off and resumed changing before dashing down the stairs to his awaiting cookies.

"Mom, can you pitch me some balls today?" he asked, half expecting a negative response.

"Not today, honey, but there's somebody in the back who would like to play with you," she offered with a slight smile.

Thinking it was one of the Green boys, Corey immediately grabbed his mitt and darted for the door without even touching his snack. Evette chuckled, raising her eyes at how the cookies were abandoned so easily. That was a first.

Corey rounded the corner only to see a man with a baseball cap on, sitting in a wheelchair in the middle of the yard. The picture was confusing to him. No kids were there at all, and as he drew closer, he noticed Mr. Green was also wearing sweats and a well-worn catcher's glove on his right hand. A mesh bag full of baseballs was tied to one side of his chair, while a Little League bat, Corey's size, was tucked in the other.

"Hey, Mr. Sticks!" Corey yelled as he excitedly tried to grab it.

Taylor held him off but couldn't help returning a smile in response to the enthusiasm.

"Hold on. Hold on. Here's the deal," Taylor said, looking eye to eye with Corey to ensure his attention. "I'll teach you to play, but you have to make me a promise, okay?"

Corey settled down and skeptically looked at Taylor, thinking that raking leaves or some other adult-type condition was about to be imposed. Taylor looked around to make sure nobody was watching and leaned closer. "You can't tell anybody about me trying to walk, okay?"

"Deal." Corey grinned.

That was easy enough, Taylor thought, holding out his hand for a handshake. "And it's Mr. Green, Corey. Not Mr. Sticks, okay?"

"Okay," Corey agreed, though his attention was more toward pulling out the bat than anything else. Before handing it over, Taylor focused him on some basic instruction. He carefully positioned himself in his chair and slowly swung the bat in perfect form while Corey watched. From there he set him back about forty feet or so and threw a varied set of ground and fly balls, followed by an occasional soft-line drive.

Out of necessity Taylor moved them to his backyard so he could situate himself in front of his backstop, while he struggled to catch the many errant returns from a kid who had never been taught how to throw either. This problem, coupled with Taylor's inability to get to a ball more than an arm's length away, made for an extremely frustrating afternoon, but he pushed through it. Hopefully, in a few weeks he would progress enough with his walking to use his canes or crutches whenever he wanted and at least be a little more independent. Sure, it was crazy and, realistically speaking, probably ridiculous. No one would ever help him in the way he needed, but what did they know? *What does anyone know?* he thought while he overstretched his body again for a ball that lofted just out of reach.

Corey retrieved the bad throws Taylor couldn't get to and spent most of the afternoon doing so. His instructor meanwhile had to patiently sit and wait, which was never exactly his strong suit. After about an hour, Taylor had enough, and they quit for the day, well before anybody in the family got home. A happy Corey scampered back to his house, while Taylor secreted their equipment under his deck, second-guessing whether the price of the kid's silence was going to be worth it.

Chapter 19

Weeks passed, and the arrangement actually took a turn for the better. Taylor continued his exercises in peace, and Corey could now hit, field, and even throw with a modicum of accuracy. Interestingly, their alliance soon evolved into a partnership, with Corey scooting over early to Taylor's deck to assist him before they played. It bought time for both of them, and though Taylor would have rather done his walking alone, Corey, being the bright and sensitive young man he was, quickly grasped what his middle-aged friend was trying to accomplish and assisted him in each of his homemade routines. Taylor appreciated that and was relieved that the kid was too young to question the rationale of what they were doing. Nor was he aware of its dangers.

Whether it was steadying one of the canes at a crucial time, bracing an arm, or stopping a fall before it started, Corey became well adept at protecting his coach. More importantly, he shared Taylor's belief that he could someday ambulate fully upright again and maybe even walk, a hope Taylor privately harbored since his accident. Corey also began to push Taylor to stay up on the canes longer, to take that extra step and try again after he began to lose confidence.

Following a fairly grueling afternoon session, the two took a break on Taylor's deck. Taylor was showing Corey how to hold the baseball to throw a curve while they intermittently sipped their iced teas. He was also sadly aware that his little friend's father had moved out of the house and had been living someplace else for the last month or so. Corey hadn't said anything to him, but Taylor could sense how important it was that his dad see how well he could play now, probably as much as Taylor wanted to walk again. Taylor also noticed a genuine passion for the game developing in Corey and that the kid's enthusiasm was even sneaking up on him as well.

"Now you put your fingers here, and as you throw, turn your wrist like this." Taylor demonstrated, keeping his eyes on what he was doing.

"How do you know so much about baseball, Mr. Green?" Corey asked.

"Oh, I don't know." Taylor sighed, remembering what it used to be like to play.

"Did your dad teach you ?"

"No, he didn't, Corey," Taylor stoically replied. Still studying his grip on the ball, he knew he wouldn't be able to answer the barrage of questions that were undoubtedly about to come, but he'd keep it as brief as possible.

"Did he die?" Corey asked with eyes wide in innocent curiosity.

"Not till much later," Taylor answered.

"Did he work a lot?" Corey asked again.

"No, he definitely didn't do that." Taylor chuckled, gazing out at the backyard. "He just moved away," Taylor added, desiring to end the conversation.

"Where did he go?" Corey asked sympathetically.

Taylor didn't answer at first but looked back at his mitt and started tossing the ball back and forth into it, reflecting on the question. It was something he himself had wondered about his whole life.

"I don't know, Cor," was all he could say to his little friend.

"Oh," Corey said.

Taylor could see Corey was a little taken aback by the comment and starting to feel bad. "It's hard to remember, Corey. I was pretty young when he left," he added, trying to lighten things up for both of them.

"Oh." Corey sighed again as Taylor resumed gripping the ball and tossing it into his glove. "How about your mom?"

"I still had my mom, Cor," Taylor said. "She had to work a lot to take care of me and my little sister though. Definitely didn't have time for baseball," he offered with a slight chuckle. "But she was a good mom."

"My dad works a lot too," Corey confided. "He doesn't ever want to be poor."

Turning and looking out at the field, he squinted while peering into the distance.

Taylor just listened.

"He watches baseball on TV. He says they make too much money for just playing a game," Corey said, now looking at Taylor to see whether he agreed.

Taylor nodded with a soft smile. "Your dad may be right. But that's how I got to college." He chuckled.

"How?" Corey asked.

"Playing baseball. Tell your daddy that," Taylor said with a grin, smacking the ball into his glove again. "I owe a lot to this game," he added solemnly.

"What position did you play?" Corey asked.

"Pitcher and sometimes even catcher," Taylor answered, looking back at Corey while displaying the catcher's mitt he'd been wearing.

"I bet you were real good, Mr. Green," Corey bragged with a boisterous smile.

Taylor chuckled again. "Well, I was 'pretty' good, Corey."

Taylor stared out at the field, letting his mind temporarily declutter into the simplicity of his playing days. After a moment or two, he pulled himself out of it and gently tapped Corey on the head with his glove. "Time to go, my friend. I'll see ya tomorrow."

Corey nodded and waved as he headed down the ramp. "See ya later, Mr. Green."

While Corey passed through the Green backyard and into his own, Taylor noticed they had forgotten to put the canes and baseball gloves away. There were also a few balls sprinkled across their little infield that hadn't been cleaned up either. However, before he could yell over to Corey, he heard the clack of the front door and Paula's cheerful "I'm home!"

Taylor panicked. The mitts and balls without their kids around could never be adequately explained to someone like Paula. Nor would evidence of him trying to walk on his own go well with her either. The science was on his wife's side, and so was the sanity. Though Taylor was keenly aware of that, he also knew that without that possibility, he might lose his.

His mind raced about what to do. He could toss his mitt over the railing and into the bushes, but what about the canes leaning against the other side of the deck? It was too late anyway; Paula was already opening the sliding glass door and calling his name.

Taylor tilted his face toward the sun to appear to be sunbathing in hopes she wouldn't notice either the canes or the mitt he'd just dropped to the floor on the opposite side of his wheelchair. Maybe she'd go back in the house and change or something.

Sitting in his chair, soaked with sweat, he could hear her footsteps approaching. Taylor kept his eyes closed, feigning an afternoon siesta, though he could feel her standing next to him.

"Taylor?" she probed, sounding concerned.

"Hmm?" Taylor hummed in a pretend half sleep.

She gently shook his shoulders. "Taylor, you're soaked. What's going on?"

He opened his eyes and tried to appear groggy, squinting back at her like she'd awoken him.

"What's the matter, Paula?" he asked innocently as he wiped his eyes with the back of his forearm. "Was getting some sun, must have dozed off," he added before she could say anything.

Paula surveyed the area around him with that all-familiar suspicious look in her eyes, undoubtedly noticing both the canes and his catcher's mitt. However, she surprisingly didn't say anything but moved on to another subject.

"It's a gorgeous day out, isn't it?" she said.

"It really is," Taylor replied, cautiously enjoying the small talk.

She walked back into the house to get dinner started, leaving the sliding door open behind her. Taylor's relief was short lived, however, as she began to talk through the screen of the open kitchen window above the sink.

"Nathan will be home soon. He has his first practice today. Why don't you go with him?" she suggested with a little push.

That woman never misses a thing, a now-irritated Taylor reminded himself. "You know I'm not getting involved this season," he yelled toward the window, glad that they couldn't see each other.

"Well, you had your mitt out. I just thought—"

"Don't start, Paula, please," he said, bristling. "Playing around with a baseball doesn't mean I'm ready to get involved. I already told you we'll see next year," he added, cautioning her to put the matter to rest.

"All right. Forget I even said it. Just stay home the rest of your life," she chirped from deeper inside the kitchen.

"Maybe I will, Paula!" he barked back, angrily wheeling himself in through the sliding door.

Paula was now standing over the sink, drying her hands with the dishtowel. She didn't appear intimidated in the least, which bothered Taylor even more.

"I guess it was more about you than about them," she stated plainly.

"Seriously, Paula?" a highly offended Taylor cried, barely able to keep from boiling over.

"This much, Taylor," the feisty city girl volleyed back, displaying a quarter-inch gap between her thumb and index finger to illustrate her point. "This much for them," she pressed again, "would certainly go a long way."

Taylor didn't respond as Paula calmly walked into the pantry.

Of course, he wanted to give more to his kids. He just couldn't right now.

"Heaven knows they need it," she added under her breath, not really caring whether he heard it as she pulled some items off the shelves for dinner.

"Sorry I'm not movin' fast enough for ya, Paula," he shot back. "And I guess heaven knew they needed this too, huh?" he jabbed again, opening his hands and staring down at his chair.

There was no response other than the sound of shuffling cans and packages before she re-emerged into the kitchen. "So this is what it's about?" she asked, looking at Taylor while she unloaded everything on the counter.

"You brought it up, Paula," Taylor smugly replied. "But allow me to say, as respectfully as I can, that whoever it is you're talking about would owe me a lot more than he gave me if he existed. So let's just give this God of yours the benefit of the doubt and understand that he doesn't, at least not in the real world, which is where we all live. Fair enough?"

"No," Paula answered plainly, lightly tossing a sauté pan on the stove and getting the burner going.

"No?" Taylor chided, belittling her again.

"No, I don't agree, Taylor," she said. "And I won't be cross-examined by you either."

"They call it the engine of truth, Paula," Taylor challenged.

"Oh really. Who says that?" she volleyed back, casually poking her head into the fridge to retrieve something.

"People in my profession, Paula. People who live by reason."

"Then why don't you go back to your profession and do it, Taylor?" she replied without missing a beat.

"Can't argue with me on this, can you, Paula?"

"You're right. I can't."

Her nonchalance frustrated Taylor even more as he turned to head back out to the deck, but before he could pull the slider open, the doorbell rang. It was too early for the kids to be coming home from school, and Taylor certainly wasn't expecting anyone.

Suddenly Paula's eyes grew wide. "It's Tuesday!" she said.

Taylor's face was still blank.

"Some friends were gonna stop over. I totally forgot!" Paula's hands cupped her cheeks.

Taylor wasn't happy either. He hated company, and on those rare occasions when it couldn't be avoided, he set himself up with work in his home office or something else out of the way. "Come on, Paula!" he moaned, critically shaking his head to say she should have had her act together.

He knew she despised that tone, but he had no problem adding to the stress that was already noticeable on her face. She quickly scanned the kitchen and dinette area, prioritizing what needed to be done while collecting some loose glasses off the table and heading to the front door.

"Hi, guys. Come on in," she welcomed.

The women entered and began to sit down and relax at the kitchen table. Paula started making the coffee, while Taylor had slipped out to the deck before he could be seen.

Carol and Marianne had known the Greens for a long time. Carol was in her fifties and lived with her husband a few doors down. Her kids had all grown up and were on their own. She was taller and dressed more formally than the other woman.

Carol was always a little too prim and proper for Taylor, and he avoided her as much as possible, even before his accident. Her stiff demeanor and sometimes judgmental attitude had earned her the "Church Lady" nickname he'd bestowed on her years before. No one necessarily disagreed.

However, Taylor equally couldn't deny that beneath Carol's dry and opinionated surface beat the heart of a well-intentioned person, which he grudgingly surmised was why Paula and her friends tolerated her. She was also the one who had organized the complete dinners that had been brought over to their family for a month or so after his accident, while Paula had been staying with him at the hospital. Taylor had to give her credit for that, though the two remained strong-willed, highly vocal people who were never going to see eye to eye. For Paula's sake, however, they did make efforts to negotiate around each other when they had to.

Marianne, on the other hand, was a contemporary of Paula's and a fairly close friend. She was about Paula's height and had dark-brown hair that was a little over shoulder length. Like Paula, Marianne worked full-time and had kids about the same age. She was a little on the bubbly side for Taylor, but he could see that, at the very least, she kept his wife's spirits up. This was a positive he reckoned was worth putting up with. Even now the tone of their conversation and unpretentious interaction made it easy to sense that the two were very comfortable with each other as Marianne jumped in to help.

Joanne Woods was new to the group. She was about thirty years old with short reddish-blonde hair and a fair complexion. Her husband, Steve, was a minister who had just recently taken the job at Paula's church after their other one retired. Though they had been in town about a month or two, they were still in the process of situating their elementary-age kids in school and getting acclimated. Joanne's runner-like stature stood at about five seven, and, similar to Marianne, she was casually dressed.

"How's it going?" Paula cheerfully asked, looking at Joanne.

"We're still kinda moving in. But it's been good," she said with a smile.

"Just give me a minute," Paula added, hastily removing the last of the random books, paper, and junk mail off the table.

"What do you like, Joanne? Regular or decaf?"

"Regular would be great," she replied.

"Regular for me too, Paula. I need a little boost for the afternoon," Marianne chimed in.

"Carol?"

"Same," she said.

"Where's Taylor?" Marianne asked.

"He's out there," Paula answered, motioning to the deck.

"Bein' a grump today?" she asked.

Paula held out her hand, tilting it slightly from one side to the other in the traditionally Italian "menza-menza" fashion, something her friend quickly understood.

"So, what've you guys been up to?" Paula asked the group, changing the subject.

"I had a day off and gave Joanne the grand tour of Rivermont." Marianne chuckled. "We did Tanger Mall and had lunch at Applebee's."

Paula nodded and, after placing the mugs on the table, headed toward the deck. "Be with you in a sec," she said, opening the sliding glass door.

Marianne's glance followed her as Carol raised her eyebrows. Joanne passively ignored the gesture and attempted to break the tension by starting another conversation. "So how long have you and Paula known each other?" she asked, turning to Marianne.

"About five years or so," Marianne answered, politely turning back to Joanne but still appearing distracted.

"Oh," Joanne acknowledged.

"Our kids played on teams together. That kind of stuff. We met and became friends," Marianne added, periodically glancing out at the deck.

"This is rude. Come in and say hello," Paula insisted.

Taylor remained reclined in his wheelchair in the far corner. He was trying to relax and get some sun out of sight. He had absolutely no intention of going in.

"They're your friends, Paula," he answered without opening his eyes. "I'm in no mood for anybody right now."

Paula wasn't leaving.

"Carol here?" Taylor asked, hoping the threat of a confrontation would fend off his wife.

"Yes," Paula answered in a tone that her presence was still no excuse not to go in.

"Paula, let me ask you something," he challenged, though his eyes remained obnoxiously closed. "Do ya really want to be where she's going?" he said sarcastically, referring to their shared religious beliefs.

Hearing the slam of the sliding door, Taylor chuckled.

Paula strode back into the kitchen. As she did, Joanne sensed the tension and offered some relief. "If this is a bad time, Paula, we can—"

"Oh no. It's okay," Paula answered, cutting her off. "We'll be fine."

Just then, Taylor wheeled himself through the sliding door and nodded hello to everyone.

Given that Paula had made it obvious he was out there, he figured he'd have to make a brief appearance to avoid looking antisocial.

"Joanne Woods, this is my husband, Taylor," Paula said. "Her husband, Steve, pastors at our church."

"Hi, Joanne," Taylor said warmly, extending his hand.

"Nice to meet you, Taylor," Joanne responded in kind.

Taylor looked over to Carol, who he noticed was forcing a fake smile, typical of her ever-present dissatisfaction with him. Though Taylor couldn't care less about whether she or anyone else liked him, the message that he didn't measure up set his insides off like a time bomb.

The tension thickened.

"Hello, Carol!" Taylor said with disingenuous excitement. He knew that being addressed in such a flamboyant manner would annoy her.

"Hello, Taylor," Carol flatly replied.

"Taylor!" Paula warned.

"All right, all right." He chuckled, politely retreating. He definitely wasn't interested in getting into it with Paula again and calmly turned to Joanne. "If you don't already know, Joanne, I don't go to church. I hope that doesn't offend you," he stated plainly but respectfully.

"Not at all, Taylor," she replied.

"Well, it deeply offends my friend Carol over here," he said with a smirk, taking another shot at her as she sat at the opposite end of the table.

"I'm not the one you should worry about offending, Taylor," Carol snapped back.

"Oh, really?" Taylor challenged.

"Taylor!" Paula intervened again from behind the counter, but Carol's stare only egged him on.

"Wait a minute, Paula. I'd like to ask Carol something. Honestly," he said, turning to her.

Though Paula was mortified, there was nothing she could do at that point, knowing her husband was undoubtedly about to test her friend with the same unanswerable questions she herself had been battling with ever since his accident.

Looking at Carol but periodically glancing at Joanne, Taylor was implicitly challenging the newcomer as well. "Now, Carol, forget about how you feel about me and that in your book I probably had this coming. But how could a loving God allow this to happen to her," he charged, tapping the armrests of his wheelchair and motioning to Paula, "or our family or anyone else for that matter? Honestly?"

"Is that a serious question?" Carol retorted.

"Um-hmm." Taylor nodded confidently.

"Okay." She nodded back, reaching down into her bag, which sat next to her chair. After fumbling around for a few seconds, she pulled out a small Bible and began flipping through the pages. Taylor raised his eyes and shook his head as Carol smugly continued to do what she was doing without looking up.

"It's all in here, Taylor, if you ever—"

"Carol," Joanne quietly interrupted, cutting her off while leaning over and nonchalantly placing her hand on Carol's forearm. Carol's shoulders tightened at the touch, and she looked as surprised as Taylor was. "Why don't we just talk?" Joanne said.

Turning his attention to her, Taylor had no immediate words to say. No one else did either, which only increased the awkwardness now hovering over their gathering. As the silence continued, Taylor noticed Paula was leaning over the counter, resting her elbows on its surface, and staring at Joanne. However, Paula's expression appeared more curious than concerned. So did Marianne's.

"I think what Carol was trying to say is that life's not fair. And it's not," Joanne added, turning to Taylor.

The statement piqued Taylor's interest, and though Carol struggled to suppress her embarrassment, Paula and Marianne noticeably shared his intrigue with their guest.

"Taylor, we don't know each other yet, and I didn't have the accident you did, so I honestly don't know what you're going through and probably never will," Joanne admitted, carrying her words as cautiously as possible.

Her eyes narrowed and lips tightened as she spoke, which, along with her tone, showed to Taylor a willingness to display her vulnerability with this subject rather than the superficial self-assurance he would have expected from someone in her position. He continued to listen.

"Just like I can't make sense of why this happened to you or your family or even pretend to know how to find God in it," she added sympathetically.

Taylor waited for the "but" followed by a typical religious cliché or some life-coaching advice. However, it never came. He nodded as an implicit invitation that she go on.

"The best I can do is offer you my belief that God exists and that he will show himself to you, even in this, Taylor. But I think it's a journey only you can take." Joanne sighed after a reflective pause. "And no one else can," she added as if to remind herself and the others of whose road this really belonged to.

Taylor was slightly taken aback, given that her statements neither challenged nor necessarily agreed with what he'd said. Nobody else was saying anything either.

After another moment passed, Paula broke the silence. "Sorry you got hit with this, Joanne," she said apologetically.

"No, no, it's okay," she replied. "I appreciate your husband's candor," she said, looking over at Taylor.

He nodded back, acknowledging the comment as he turned his wheelchair toward the sliding glass doors. "Thank you too, Joanne," he said. "That's refreshing to hear. And if what you believe helps you live your life better, I honestly think that's good. How that answers why people like myself and millions of others were never given even a chance at a good life or being all we could be is your issue. But what I believe, and certainly what I can't deny seeing, is that the life we have is our own, Joanne, and neither fairness nor even love is ever guaranteed for any one of us. And if at the end of the line there is a God, like you all say, then, all things considered, I don't think I've done so bad. But I also understand that I don't have all the answers in that category," he bluntly affirmed, glancing at Carol and the others. "And neither does anyone else," he added as he went back through the door.

Chapter 20

"C'mon, Mom!" Nathan yelled from the front seat of the van as it sat in the driveway.

Paula ran out of the house with her extra-large pocketbook dangling from her shoulder. Though stressed with the usual list of other responsibilities she had going on, she didn't want to be late for his first day of practice.

"Where's Skip?" she asked as they were hastily backing out.

Nathan stayed silent.

"Why didn't he come home on the bus today?"

"He said he was getting extra help," Nathan replied.

Paula looked at him suspiciously. He definitely wasn't doing that.

"That's what he told me," Nathan quipped, defending himself.

"Where was he when he told you that?" she asked.

"Out by the bus, okay?"

"Did he have his jacket on?"

"I think so," Nathan answered.

Meanwhile, in a depressed section downtown, two or three adolescents were milling around in an abandoned alley. Secreted in the back were Skip and some of his friends, smoking pot and hanging out behind a beat-up dumpster. A police car pulled down the alley, and Skip furtively took his last puff before joining his fleeing comrades as they scaled the chain-link fence directly behind them. The two officers exited their vehicle but declined a foot pursuit given that the boys were already over the fence and vanishing into another industrial area.

Paula pulled her minivan into the park. The area was already bustling with activity as players, coaches, and parents scurried to their respective fields to practice. Maintenance people were also out and about, beginning preparations for opening day, which was only in a couple of weeks.

A man in his early thirties wearing a fairly beat-up hoodie, gym shorts, and high-top sneakers was seen in the distance, carrying a large duffel bag full of bats, balls, and other baseball equipment. The size and weight of the bag caused an awkward stride as he headed to a field with a boy about Nathan's age.

Seeing Steve Woods dressed as he was and in this setting surprised Paula a bit as she jogged to keep up with Nathan. Apparently they were all going in the same direction as Nathan caught up to Steve and his son.

"Pastor?" Paula asked, coming up behind him.

He turned around. Standing approximately six one and weighing about two hundred pounds, Steve Woods was kind of on the husky side. His medium-length brown hair was roughly tucked under a baseball cap representing the team he coached. He seemed harried as he lugged the duffel bag while struggling to keep pace with the boys, who were now even farther ahead of him. They finally made it to the area of the assigned fields.

"What team you on, Brian?" Nathan excitedly asked Steve's son.

"The Cubs. My dad's the coach," Brian proudly volunteered.

"Assistant coach," his father corrected with a tone that he may have gotten himself roped into something more involved than he thought.

Joanne, with their three-year-old daughter in tow, joined them. Carrying a bag filled with coloring books and other activities in one hand, she had her now-too-tired-to-walk toddler by the other.

"How about you?" Brian asked, continuing his conversation with Nathan.

"The Yankees. My dad used to coach," Nathan answered, his voice dropping a little.

"And I hear he's the best coach in the league, Nathan," Steve added, gently mussing the kid's cap. "I bet he'll be back after he takes a little break this year," Steve assured him, trying to keep Nathan's spirits up.

Paula smiled in agreement, putting her arm around Nathan's shoulder and jostling him. "Looks like your team's getting ready to practice, kid. Go ahead over," she said, gently pushing him along.

"What about our team?" Brian asked his father.

Steve surveyed the area and noticed that the team scheduled before them was still on the field. "Bri, why don't you get our guys throwing and catching over there while they finish?" he said, pointing to an area where the rest of their team was congregating.

Brian sprinted to them while Steve and Paula walked over to a four-foot-high chain-link fence that adjoined the practice field. Joanne was already there, situating her daughter so she would hopefully stay occupied while her mother watched practice.

Unloading the heavy bag off his shoulder and plopping it down at the base of the fence, Steve looked on with Paula as her eyes followed her little son jogging to his field. It would be his first season without his father being down there, and though she was holding the tears in, she felt herself becoming emotional.

"Listen, we can swing over and drop Nathan home tonight after practice if you want," he offered.

"No, it's okay."

"Really, it's no problem," Joanne said again.

"You sure?" Paula asked, looking at both of them. Though she'd always been reluctant to impose on anyone, she was behind schedule and could use the help today.

"Not a problem at all," Steve confirmed.

Paula looked over to make sure Nathan's coach was at the field. However, before leaving, she rested her elbows on the top of the fence to watch him for another moment or two. She then turned to

Joanne, who was standing next to her, also looking on. "How you recovering from my husband?" she asked, somewhat embarrassed.

"Oh, I'm fine." Joanne chuckled. "That stuff doesn't bother me."

"That's good." Paula sighed. She hoped it was true. The last thing she wanted was another person intimidated by Taylor.

Steve leaned over and comfortably placed his forearms on top of the fence as well. Maintenance men, busy with their rakes, shovels, and other tools, dotted each field, beautifying its details. "They really go all out in this town," he observed.

"They certainly do," Paula said.

"Your husband's a legend down here, isn't he?" he said, scanning the multitude of activity.

"Yeah," she acknowledged, slightly smiling. "This game was everything to him."

"Did he play in college?" Joanne asked, turning to look at Paula.

"He did," she said. "He was good too."

Joanne nodded warmly.

"That's where I met him," Paula added after a pause. She looked back at the field, seemingly pulled into a distant memory. "I don't think he'll ever stop missing the game," she said, turning her head slightly to the side so Joanne couldn't see the unexpected tears beginning to well in her eyes.

"Is he coming down for opening day?" Joanne asked after offering her a tissue she'd pulled out of her bag.

"No," Paula answered soberly. She briefly patted her eyes with the tissue before folding it up.

The conversation paused for another moment or two.

"Talking about it makes it worse," Paula confided, finally breaking the silence. "I can't seem to help him anymore."

"You *are* helping him, Paula," Joanne said, continuing to look out at the field with her.

"No, I'm not," Paula frankly replied. "I'm not," she said again with even more resolution. "And the way things are falling apart,

I'm pretty confused myself," she let slip out, a little surprised by her own candor.

Joanne had no response, though Paula could tell she was thinking about it. Steve remained hunched over the top of the fence on the other side of his wife, apparently just listening.

"Sorry," Paula said after a moment or two.

"You got nothing to be sorry for, Paula," Joanne replied.

They both continued to gaze out over the field.

"Having all the answers is not what our faith is about anyway." Joanne sighed like she was talking to herself too. "And neither is being right all the time," she reflected.

After another pause, Steve leaned over so he could look at Paula. "Sometimes I think just loving someone is the most powerful answer of all, Paula. You're already doing that, so nothing else really matters," he consoled.

Though their words sounded nice, the emotion over it not working for her or anyone else in her family began to unexpectedly bubble up in Paula again. "Well, it doesn't seem to be enough," she blurted. Her eyes were now tearing heavily.

Upset at losing her composure, she turned and gave a brief wave as she strode toward the parking lot, wiping her cheeks with the folded tissue along the way.

Joanne followed as Steve remained leaning over the fence, staring into the distance as the other team began to filter off his field.

CHAPTER 21

THE FRONT DOOR FLEW OPEN, AND NATHAN DASHED IN WHILE THE dinner dishes were being cleared. Behind him Steve waited in the doorway to confirm delivery of their son. Before he could leave the table, Taylor noticed that the sound of the door had already brought his wife out from behind the sink to greet whoever it was who had taken their kid home. *Hopefully it won't be too long of an ordeal,* he thought.

"What's for dinner?" Nathan asked as he approached the kitchen counter.

"Chicken," Tim informed his little brother with a smirk.

"Ohh." Nathan moaned, seeing it was accompanied by potatoes and broccoli, all required eating by their mother.

"I'm sorry. Practice ran a little late," Taylor heard a man call from the door.

Thankfully it didn't sound like he was coming in.

"It's okay. We're used to it," Paula replied, now at the door, thanking him. "Come on in and meet my husband," she insisted.

Though Taylor had carefully kept himself out of the line of vision from the front doorway area, it was to no avail. His wife returned with Steve awkwardly in tow.

"Taylor, this is Steve Woods, Joanne's husband. Steve, my husband, Taylor," she said as the two shook hands.

"I hear you're coachin'," Taylor offered in congratulatory fashion.

"Trying to," Steve answered with a chuckle. "Unlike Nathan, most of the kids his age need a lot of work on the fundamentals."

"Perfection through repetition." Taylor smiled back.

Their conversation got interrupted when a knock was heard against the open front door. Then there was a familiar voice. It was Vin Russo.

Knowing how bold and gregarious his friend could be, Taylor became uneasy as Vinnie entered the group dynamic to inevitably discuss the poker game they had on for that evening. As predicted, he started to blab before meeting everyone or understanding who they were.

"We're a little light tonight," he said to Taylor, sounding concerned that they wouldn't be able to go forward. "Ray and Ira want to play, but Joe can't, and I can't get ahold of Rich. You wanna go with just four?"

"Sure, no problem," Taylor quickly responded, hoping it would quench any further conversation. Vinnie nodded and extended his hand to introduce himself to Steve before anyone else could. "Vin Russo. How are you?" he said with a grin and a hearty handshake.

"Steve Woods," Steve replied with a smile.

Thinking Steve was just a regular guy, Taylor feared Vinnie would seize the opportunity to fill another poker seat. *The man makes me uncomfortable enough*, Taylor thought. *And I certainly don't want to get into a sticky discussion about our game.*

"Nathan's baseball coach?" Vinnie noted, eyeing Steve's cap as he turned to Taylor.

"Not really—" Taylor began to say, subtly trying to head off his gambling buddy.

No such luck with Vinnie.

"You want to play?" he suggested to Steve, outing Taylor from the conversation.

"Sure," Steve responded, surprising everyone except Vinnie.

Taylor could see Paula was holding back a laugh while he

struggled to figure out how to back Steve out of a fairly high-stakes poker game without embarrassing anyone.

"Ten dollar ante. No loans. No limits. No crybabies." Vinnie grinned, benignly reciting the house rules to the new guy.

"It's okay, Steve. You don't—" Taylor started to say.

"It's no problem, Taylor." Steve nodded back without a flinch. "What time?" he asked, first looking at Vinnie, then at Paula, who was starting to go into shock.

She waved her hands defensively in a manner indicating she had no part in it. "I won't be here," she added, further absolving herself.

Seeing Steve smile, Taylor was relieved the reverend was obviously joking. He chuckled to himself and played along to have some fun with Vinnie. "Seven thirty, Father," Taylor said to Steve, knowing how vexed this would make his born and raised Catholic friend.

"But it's okay if you can't make it," he added, smirking at Vinnie, who looked to Paula for help.

"Father?" he asked her.

"Your fire insurance just went way up, Vin!" a laughing Taylor chided before she could answer.

Ignoring Taylor, he looked at Steve apologetically. "I'm so sorry, Father. I didn't know."

"Steve. Call me Steve," he said with a grin, calmly correcting the now-red-faced Vinnie.

"Don't worry about it." Steve laughed again, patting Vin on the triceps in assurance that everything was okay.

"You didn't have your collar," a still-embarrassed Vinnie tried to explain, motioning to his neck, where he would've expected to see one.

"In my church we don't wear collars," Steve said, still chuckling.

"I guess they gamble though." Taylor smirked toward his wife.

Paula glared back. She clearly wasn't receiving the humor.

Steve, however, smiled at the comment as Taylor waited for him to finish the prank and tell Vinnie he was kidding. Steve didn't say anything though, and as the pregnant pause continued to hover, Taylor began to feel as uncomfortable as everybody else.

"You're kidding, right?" Paula finally said, trying to break the tension. "They play for real money," she clarified a little more seriously now.

"I get it. It's not bingo." Steve smiled back, looking over at Taylor. "Sounds like fun, gambling with you guys," he added before nonchalantly heading for the door and waving goodbye to everyone.

"Was that a challenge?" Vinnic said, now looking at Taylor.

"Can I bring anything?" Steve called from the front door.

"No, we have everything," Paula answered.

All three shared a quizzical look as the front screen door slapped behind him.

"Now you can take someone else's money for a change," Vinnie quipped to Taylor.

Paula shot dagger eyes at her husband for a guarantee that this wouldn't occur. Though Taylor enjoyed how awkward this situation was for his wife, he found himself becoming increasingly uneasy with the whole thing the more he thought about it.

How could they have an enjoyable game with a guy like Steve? They certainly weren't gonna take his money. And protecting him would screw up the way they played against each other. It was beginning to look like a lost evening for Taylor, which frustrated him even more.

"Don't look at me. I didn't invite him," he said, holding up his hands defensively against Paula's condemning stare.

Vinnie wasn't helping matters either, smiling and shaking his head in disbelief. "Cards, beer, inappropriate humor …," he mused. "Think we can Instagram our game tonight?" He continued to tease.

"Don't you dare, Vinnie!" Paula snapped, striding past both of them on her way to the deck with a potted plant she'd just watered.

"Don't worry about it, Paula. No Instagramming, no jokes, and we won't take your friend's money either. I promise," he said with a playful grin.

Paula never turned around, though Taylor knew she was probably relieved by what Vinnie had said. Unfortunately, this guy's presence pretty much ruined one of the few things Taylor still enjoyed doing with his friends. He could only hope that after this game, it would be the end of it. If on the off chance it wasn't and Steve asked to come back again, Taylor had already rehearsed polite ways to decline such a request by either saying they were full or otherwise explaining that the game was actually meant to stay between old friends. He was a lawyer; he was good at that kind of stuff. He hoped it wouldn't come to that, however.

CHAPTER 22

"DEALER'S CALL. LET'S GIVE IT TO STEVE FIRST," TAYLOR ANNOUNCED, opening the first round.

It was about eight o'clock at night, and the dining room table was meticulously configured with poker chips, popcorn, and bottles of beer and soda as each of the guys bought their tokens from Vinnie, the designated banker. Taylor had set the table up himself as well as the hard, though routine, start time. Playing were Ray, Ira, Vinnie, Steve, and obviously the host.

Taylor sat at the head of the table, his usual place, while Ray and Ira were to his left. Vinnie and Steve were seated on the right. After about ten minutes of introductions and small talk, Taylor had the game underway. He didn't like chitchat before poker. To him it was either one or the other. His friends, however, didn't always feel the same way. Taylor tolerated the conversation as best he could, for the sake of the game.

Ray was one of his contemporaries. He had a pretty successful industrial air-conditioning business and was a long-time client. Whether it involved company matters or buying real estate, Taylor always handled Ray's legal affairs.

Ira was older and more distinguished than anyone at the table. An attorney as well, he had been a mentor to Taylor for almost two decades. Before the accident, Taylor had loved watching his friend on trial, often sending Russell to observe too.

"Good afternoon, Dr. Smith. I'm Ira Felzen." The bow-tied

grandfatherly looking gentleman would smile. That was usually the first and only comfort a witness experienced with Ira before being utterly devastated on cross-examination. What Taylor always found remarkable about his mentor was that he did it all without insult or offense but rather with a self-studied mastery of the topic that was often superior to even the experts he faced. "Cases aren't won in the courtroom, Taylor," Ira would say, "but at your dining room table during the wee hours of the night."

Preparation was indeed the hallmark of any litigator's success, and with Ira's help, Taylor had learned that well. The majority of their time, however, was spent inside the courtroom. In fact, it was Ira who insisted that the true trial lawyer would rather have his head handed to him in court than sit in the office doing paperwork. Taylor agreed, and they both ran that way, often bouncing ideas and techniques off each other when either was on trial. This was also why it so grieved Ira that his friend still refused to return.

Ira was smoking his pipe as he scrutinized his first hand of cards; his bifocals and short, gray hair encircled a balding top that enhanced his scholarly appearance. While Ray tended to be lighthearted, Ira was more cerebral in both manner and demeanor.

Paula went out as she routinely did on game nights, and the kids were in bed or otherwise occupied upstairs. Taylor knew his wife's discomfort with the card game wasn't really a religious thing but a concern with friends taking what she viewed as significant amounts of money from each other, supposedly for fun.

He remembered excitedly surprising her years before with an extra $1,100 while their family was on vacation at the Outer Banks in North Carolina. Though he'd tried to say he saved the money, Paula knew better and pulled out of him that it had come from the infamous card game. She insisted on giving the money back, which obviously frustrated Taylor and led to yet another vacation-spoiling argument. As often occurred with their marital disputes, the initial disagreement was quickly reduced to mutual self-pity, with Taylor then accusing Paula of never being happy.

Needless to say, Taylor kept his poker winnings to himself after that trip, and he certainly never divulged when he lost. How he'd gotten the funds to play now was something Paula neither knew nor seemed to care to know, which Taylor figured was probably because the card game was one of the few activities he'd resumed after his accident. It was certainly competitive, however. And though no one was going to lose their house at that game, you could certainly lose your shirt, a fact Taylor knew still bothered Paula.

"Now remember, no prayin'!" Vinnie joked as he looked over at Steve with a wink.

"Why not?" Steve smiled, playing along.

"Because it's cheating." Vinnie chuckled.

Taylor and Vin were very close, having known each other since Taylor first moved into town. Vinnie and his wife had two teenagers and lived only a few blocks away. He was also Taylor's accountant, with an office in downtown Rivermont near Taylor's.

Vinnie was a well-intentioned, community-minded man, who had a jovial sense of humor and was extremely easy to talk to. He even got himself to church with his family "at least twice but definitely no less than once a month," he'd proclaim. Taylor called them "fire insurance payments to avoid hell" and chided his friend even more when his churchgoing got in the way of Sunday golf outings or other activities he wanted Vinnie for. Always the good sport, Vinnie playfully ignored the comments, and when push came to shove, he was always there for Taylor. Taylor knew that, and Vinnie was one of the few people he hadn't withdrawn from, though their kidding remained relentless.

"How long have you been here in Rivermont, Reverend?" Ira respectfully asked.

"Steve." The newcomer smiled, licensing Ira to be informal. "My wife and I moved here about two months ago."

"Where from?" Ira asked.

"Michigan originally, then New York," Steve replied.

"Minister—" Ray fumbled, attempting to be friendly.

"Steve." He chuckled again as he began to organize his cards.

"Steve! Steve! His name is Steve!" an irritated Taylor interjected.

Though he was just as uncomfortable with a guy like Steve at the table, he wanted to keep things to cards and move the game forward. He hoped his friends would get that too.

"Okay, Taylor," Ray replied, trying to defuse his friend. "I was just asking what church he's from."

"Paula's church," Taylor curtly responded. "Now can we play cards?"

Ray backed off, raising his eyes to the others for a little levity before returning them to the hand he was dealt. Much to their host's relief, the game was finally launched.

As the hours flashed by, everyone, including Taylor, lightened up and joked throughout each round. Thankfully Steve knew how to play, so the betting could proceed as it normally did. In fact, Taylor and Steve were ahead as the game started to wind down.

It was late, and the room was now dark, except for the saloon-style lamp hanging over the table. In cone-like fashion, it illuminated only the card game and its players.

"Last hand," Ira announced as he passed the deck to Steve.

Shuffling the cards in a relaxed manner, the newcomer paused in apparent contemplation of what the final contest should be. A healthy pile of chips sat in front of both him and Taylor, with Taylor having slightly more. Ira was a little ahead, while the other two were just barely alive, each needing a big win to break even. Taylor could feel the tension thicken as the players anted up. Though the game was a little unnerving, this was where he loved to live. Other than Ira, everyone had skin in this one. Two people wanted to win, while two others needed to. The wise sage, however, would let the deal determine his longevity in this last hand as he'd always done in the past.

CHAPTER 23

"FIVE- OR SEVEN-CARD STUD, TAYLOR?" STEVE ASKED, LOOKING UP the table to him.

"Either or," he subtly answered.

"Anything wild?" Steve offered, again putting the ball in Taylor's court.

"Dealer's choice," he responded.

"Seven card, nothing wild," Steve replied as he started to deal.

Two cards went facedown to everybody before Steve began to deliver the face-up cards, one player at a time. After the first few rotations, betting continued to be moderate, and all players remained in the game. Taylor had a king and a five of diamonds showing, while Steve's face ups were a jack of spades and a four of clubs. The others had nothing showing to challenge Taylor's king either.

As the third face-up card was dealt, Taylor drew a nine; Steve a seven, and the other players received garbage cards as well. It was Taylor's bet again. He took advantage of his financial edge by opening the round with a fifty-dollar bet. It was pretty shrewd considering fifty was about all Vinnie and Ray had left in front of them, if that. Taylor also knew that it was far too high for conservative Ira, who like the other two would never bet that amount unless he had at least a pair.

Taylor figured that any intelligent gambler would surmise that he didn't have much of a hand either, given that he was clearly trying to drive people out rather than deftly lure them into the game to make more money. However, by the same token, a bet this high so early on wouldn't be worth the price of poker for either Ray, Vinnie, or maybe even Ira. Taylor knew that. And each of his longtime buddies knew he knew that, which was all the more frustrating.

After a series of grunts, sighs, and complaints, which Taylor openly snickered was "whining and moaning," each of the three reluctantly folded, leaving their twenty-five-dollar ante and the other thirty dollars or so they had bet earlier on the table. Taylor's plan of using his money to either flush out a good hand or choke his opponents out of the game had worked, at least for those three.

Though it would have been better form and a lot more gentlemanly to bet a little less and allow his friends some leeway to stay in for the ride a while longer, Taylor's competitive streak got the better of him again, which was putting it mildly.

Attention turned to Steve, who without fanfare placed his fifty dollars in chips into the pot to remain onboard.

"We have a taker," Ray observed.

"Buying his ticket for the next ride." Vinnie chuckled, adding some lightheartedness back into the atmosphere.

Taylor stayed focused, however. Steve also appeared more cautious than usual. He dealt the fourth face-up card, a king for Taylor and a six for himself. Noting Taylor's cards, the former player, now spectator, Vinnie began to playfully prod. "Movin' in for the kill?"

Taylor ignored him. The game was still far from over.

"Pair of kings bets," Steve announced as the dealer, looking at Taylor.

"Twenty-five," Taylor stoically responded, moving in his chips. He pensively viewed his hand, while Steve sized up the exposed cards in front of each of them.

With a shrug, Steve ponied up the twenty-five dollars' worth of chips to stay in. He then dealt the final card, facedown, to Taylor and himself. Without looking up, he invited the next bet. "Pair of kings."

"Twenty-five," Taylor answered in a manner so lackadaisical that it almost seemed like a suggestion rather than a bet as he moved a short stack of chips into the middle.

The maneuver piqued the curiosity of the others who, not fully knowing what their friend was up to, began to watch with intensity. There was now over $300 in the pot, an amount significantly higher than the $200 or so required to enter the game in the first place.

Steve quietly looked again at Taylor's landscape across the table.

"Looks like a potential three kings," Ray commented before mimicking the chorus of the old "We Three Kings" Christmas carol.

"I don't know." Steve smiled, noting with his eyes that a king had already been dealt to Vinnie and was still sitting faceup on his surrendered pile.

"He's counting cards, Taylor," Vinnie playfully warned his friend.

"I know he is," Taylor confidently acknowledged. "He can't count 'em all though."

Steve grinned, though he continued studying his hand.

This caused Ray to loosen up a little with the new guy. "You're a lot different than the other reverend," he said, glancing over at Taylor for confirmation. "Chetman? Was that his name?" he asked Taylor.

"Chetrick," Taylor corrected without looking up. The inquiry was already starting to annoy him.

Ray leaned over to Steve and in a huddled let's-keep-it-between-us-girls tone confided, "He'd call him all the time" as he head-motioned toward their host.

"Couldn't stand it," Ray added, referring to Taylor's reaction to the man.

"Just doin' his job," Steve casually responded without lifting his eyes from his cards.

The comment didn't elude Ira, however, who became protective of Taylor. "Is that your job too, Steve?" he probed in a soft but poignant manner.

A thick silence lulled the room as all eyes went to Steve, who, hearing the concern in Ira's voice, looked up at him and the others. "No, it's not," he answered sincerely.

The reply relieved a quietly attentive Taylor, who looked across the table as Steve took twenty-five dollars' worth of chips and held the short stack in his hand. He didn't place it into the pot yet but seemed to be contemplating the cards on the table again.

"Taking money from a man of the cloth," Ray kiddingly chided Taylor.

"He took your money," Taylor noted, gesturing that Ray had hardly any more chips in front of him.

His old friend just laughed. Taylor knew he wasn't embarrassed. Nor would Ray mind losing a couple hundred bucks for the entertainment he was about to see. In fact, like the others, he seemed kind of intrigued with the kid's poise.

"What happened to Father Chetrick anyway?" Vinnie asked, turning to Steve.

"Retired," Steve answered, still looking at his cards and ignoring that Vinnie had gotten the title wrong again. He put in the twenty-five-dollar stack of chips and in a surprise move quietly pushed his remaining $250 worth of tokens into the pot.

"I'm all in," he stated, looking back at the cards in his hand.

Vinnie not uncharacteristically raised his eyes in a *Whoa!* fashion but didn't say a word. Nor did the others.

Though Taylor was also surprised by the bet, he was more irritated with the obvious attempt to scare him out of the game. It was also a childish and unpretentious insult to his intelligence; he stewed to himself. And he certainly wasn't going to be intimidated by a thirty-two-year-old idealist who probably knew even less about life than he did about cards.

After an unusually long, contemplative pause, Taylor finally spoke. "You're desperate, Steve." The veteran sighed with a mixed tone of offense and disappointment. "Do you really think I'm gonna go for this?" he challenged again with an edge of condescension in his voice.

An emotionless Steve shrugged as if to say it was up to him. Taylor continued to smolder inside, electing not to make a move yet but instead going into a verbal analysis he intended as a well-measured diatribe to both expose the brashness of the newcomer and at the same time firmly establish whom it was he was trying to play around with.

"Okay, my friend," Taylor started. "You have a jack, a four, a seven, and a six showing, with three cards in the hole," he said, pointing to Steve's face-up cards. "You put up your fifty and stayed in the game on the third round when I cleared everyone else out, probably because you have a pair, whether it be jacks or something else. Not a bad idea. I get that.

"On the fourth round, I got my second king showing. You got a six, which left you with no pairs or anything else showing. I kept the next bet low to make it worth your while to stay in and take the last facedown card, which you did. You were undoubtedly hoping it would be the card that gave you your three of a kind, your only hope left. I kind of get that too," Taylor admitted after a pause, glancing at Steve for some kind of acquiescence.

He didn't get it though. Instead, the young man just looked back at him, waiting for his next move. The others, however, began to subtly squirm in their chairs over Taylor's remarks and the tension it was creating. Their reactions graduated to reaching for potato chips and exchanging awkward glances with each other to avoid eye contact with either of the two finalists.

Undistracted, Taylor slowly began to push his chips into the middle in twenty-five-dollar stacks. "It used to be my business, Steve, to know what the other guy was thinking," he said, reaching for his next group of tokens.

However, before he could continue, Ira quietly cut in. "Better think long of it," his old friend cautioned.

Taylor knew what Ira was saying, fully realizing himself that their unfamiliarity with Steve was a big disadvantage. According to Ira, it would be better to fold now and let the kid's ego be massaged a little rather than come out of this thing completely broke and looking like a donkey. However, on the other hand, Taylor thought his colleague was giving Steve a little too much credit and quietly shot him a polite but firm *I got this* look. Ira's return glance wasn't convinced that he did.

Ignoring the advice, Taylor continued placing his stacks into the middle and unfortunately went on with his unwelcome lecture.

"We both know that two jacks and two sixes have already been played, Steve. There are a couple fours and sevens unaccounted for, but you would agree that most of them were either dealt facedown to our friends or are still in the deck where 'reason,' my friend, says they belong," he added.

Taylor then calmly measured out the last three stacks of chips and began sliding them into the pot to meet the full $250 bet. As he was doing so and without looking up, he continued to patronize his guest. "A more understandable bet like fifty dollars or seventy-five dollars, and I probably would have folded," he conceded. "It would've told me you wanted me in because you had the three of a kind to beat me. You don't have that though, so you got a little desperate and tried to scare me out," he said, slowly shaking his head in distain.

"We do better when we cut our losses, my friend," the host continued, putting the last stack in, "when we accept the cards we're dealt rather than betting it all on something that isn't there."

The edgy comment induced a deafening silence throughout the room again. It seemed like everything was fair game now, which left the three men sitting between them extremely uneasy and struggling with the awkwardness of Taylor's implicit challenge to Steve's faith.

Steve, however, appeared more curious than offended by the remarks. He sat back in his chair and looked at Taylor. "You schooled me," he said with a disarming smile, seemingly admitting defeat.

"Just a longtime student of human nature, Steve," Taylor added for good measure.

"But we're playing cards, right?" Steve volleyed back with the same raw honesty Taylor had been dishing out to him.

"We are." Taylor coolly nodded.

"Okay, that's what I thought," Steve confirmed, though he appeared to still be thinking. "But the other stuff you were saying, Taylor. Are you as sure about that too?" he poignantly asked, looking up at the head of the table.

"More than you'll hopefully ever know, Steve," an annoyed Taylor condescended again.

"Okay," Steve answered, nodding that he had indeed heard what Taylor was saying. "But would you ever listen to my side?" he passively challenged.

"Have for the last ten years, Steve," Taylor retorted, while impatiently pointing for him to flip over his cards.

Steve resisted the push, however, and looked back at Taylor. "Well, actually you've been the one preaching, Taylor, not me," he responded, sounding a little annoyed himself.

The room became tense again, and Taylor could tell he had probably taken things too far. He tried to back out. "I don't know what brought this—"

"It's okay, Taylor," Steve interrupted before he could finish. "I wasn't looking to insult you or anyone else. I'm just playin' cards. Sorry if you took it the wrong way," he offered apologetically.

Taylor felt relieved somewhat, but it was apparent that the conversation wasn't finished. Though he regretted opening this can of worms, given that he had, he knew he had no right to stop Steve from saying what he had to say.

Sensing that he still had the floor, Steve continued. "I'm new here. We all know that, and you guys all view me a certain way because of what I do for a living. I get it. It happens all the time when people find that out," he confided, looking around the table. "And Taylor, you don't want to be bugged every week or every time you see me about what your beliefs are or what someone else thinks they should be," Steve added, to which Taylor affirmed with his own independent nod.

"I get that too," Steve acknowledged. "And about this," he added, motioning to the cards on the table, "maybe you're calling my bluff. Maybe you're n—"

"Oh, I'm calling your bluff!" Taylor heckled kiddingly, now fully relieved that the heavy part of the conversation was over and looking to keep it that way.

"Really, Taylor?" Steve laughed, playfully mocking Taylor's confidence.

"Really, Steve," Taylor assured him, smiling but a little more serious again.

"Okay, would you risk coming to church tomorrow?" Steve challenged.

"No thanks," Taylor flatly replied.

"Didn't think so." Steve laughed. "I can see how you'd never be that sure," he needled again as if he had successfully set his host up for that.

All the guys started to chuckle. Taylor didn't though. He had backed down, making even a win sour after that last exchange.

Whether it was real or a product of his own imagination, capitulating to fear always left a dull ache in the pit of Taylor's stomach that took forever to go away. In fact, he felt that nagging feeling already beginning to start.

"All right, all right, Steve, I'll bite," he said, quelling the humor. "If you win, you get the money, and I go to church. But what do I get if I win?"

"You get the money, and I'll never ask you again," Steve answered plainly.

"Ever?" Taylor verified.

"Ever," Steve confirmed.

"That's probably impossible for you guys, but I'll do it," Taylor joked.

All laughed, including Steve.

"You're sure now?" Steve chided with a grin, giving Taylor a last chance to back out.

"What've you got?" a now-irritated Taylor replied, motioning again for the challenger to flip over his cards.

As Steve began to turn his facedown cards, a four popped up first, followed by a king. A cool quietness descended over the table as he began to flip the last card over.

"He's bluffin'!" Vinnie injected, sounding more cocky than confident.

Taylor, however, didn't share the same sentiment after seeing the king, and he started to get a sinking feeling that he might have just been played.

The last card was turned, followed by a hush and Vinnie gasping, "I don't believe—"

CHAPTER 24

FOLLOWING HIS WIFE, A STONE-FACED TAYLOR WHEELED HIMSELF quickly through the lobby of the fairly large theater-type building. It didn't have any of the statues or religious-type symbols he was familiar with, but instead what he saw was a large screen behind the pulpit continually projecting announcements and other events. The place seemed more like a social center than a church to him as he scanned the musical instruments and other equipment lining the simple three-step-high platform in front.

He looked for an area more out of the way and close to an exit. Paula's socializing, however, held up his progress, and though many of her friends came up to greet him, he preferred not to be noticed at all. Meanwhile, more people were filtering in and began to fill the seats.

"Let's go to the back," he murmured in a voice meant only for her to hear.

The tension on his face and in his hands as they tightly gripped the wheels of his chair made plain his extreme discomfort with being there. She of all people ought to be aware of this, he thought, as he impatiently negotiated around the small group and wheeled on, awkwardly leaving her behind. As he passed, out of the corner of his eye he could see her breaking off and dutifully following. He was going to pay for that for sure, but he didn't care.

As he headed toward the back, his mind rehearsed polite but

dismissive one-liners for anyone else who approached. "Hi, I'm here with Paula. Good to see you" would hopefully suffice.

Though Steve had told him he didn't have to go, he was there to keep his word.

Just sit it out, he told himself, which was ironically the same advice he used to give his more belligerent criminal clients, who were being sentenced to jail.

What Taylor feared most, however, was seeing anyone he knew or giving the impression that he now needed some kind of religious crutch to get him through his paralysis. His ego could never handle being seen that way, which further perpetuated his desire to get out of there as quickly as possible.

Looking behind him, he saw Paula still in tow. She probably wished he'd stayed home too, he thought to himself, though by the look on her face, she was trying to make the best of it.

Diverse bunch for sure, he sneered, poking fun at a group of young adults with tattoos and body piercings. Paula's cool returned glance warned him not to be rude.

Taylor wisely decided to keep his comments to himself, turning his head back toward the screen, while more people populated the room. Many were far too chatty for Taylor's comfort, though some appeared more reserved. There didn't seem to be a dress code either, Taylor noticed. Though some wore suits, others had donned colored T-shirts and jeans. Their attire didn't seem to matter to anyone though, since the mood was light.

He contented himself by staying in the back and off to the side.

Just then he spotted a young Irish-looking bodybuilder type with short red hair and tattoos on both of his muscular arms. He was joking with his friends, and though his size and shape were intimidating, the cheerful smile seemed to dispel that image. Taylor couldn't place the name; however, he was sure he'd seen the face before and began to rack his brain over it.

Turning his head away to avoid eye contact, he strained to remember. As he did, he noticed Steve walking up the aisle to the right toward the platform. Seeing Taylor, he gave a welcoming nod. Thankfully he kept walking. His not coming over was a relief, at least for that moment.

Turning back to his left, Taylor met the gaze of the Irish guy, who was now standing next to his wheelchair. He was with a young woman, who appeared to be his wife. She was fairly tall and slender, and had light-brown, shoulder-length hair parted in the middle. Wearing jeans, sandals, and a stylish T-shirt, she offered Taylor a welcoming smile like she was about to be introduced to an old friend of her husband's.

"Hi, Mr. Green." The young man grinned, extending his hand.

"Hello," Taylor answered, searching his face to recognize him.

"Sean Donovan, but I don't think you know me," he said with a laugh. "I saw you in court about three years ago," he added.

There was some slight hesitation as Sean's face reddened while he gave an awkward smile to the young woman with him. He reached out to hold her hand, now seeming a little embarrassed over what he had to remind Taylor of. Though Taylor had an idea of what was coming, his mind continued to grope for specifics of who the kid was.

"I was the guy with all the DWIs who had to go to jail," he said with a pause. "The judge really laid into me that day right before I went upstate."

Taylor remembered.

Justice Wilson Emory Fennorich, whom Taylor knew personally, was about as cantankerous as a judge could be. He also took it personally when people repeatedly broke the law. Though His Honor would never do that with any of Taylor's clients, he was known for making public spectacles of those he considered to be menaces to society, which unfortunately that young man was that morning.

It was brutal, Taylor recalled, his memory starting to become clearer. The judge had taken his time to openly humiliate Sean with the details of each of his prior arrests, calling them "missed second chances" before harshly sentencing him to "the most jail time" he could.

Those were the final words from the judge to Sean Donovan that day, all for a packed courtroom to hear. Taylor remembered feeling bad for him.

"Classic Judge Fennorich," he offered the young man sympathetically.

"Should have had you for a lawyer." Sean sheepishly grinned back.

"I'm glad you didn't," the young woman piped up, though with a warm smile.

"You're probably right." Sean chuckled. He shook Taylor's hand again. "Good to see you, Mr. Green," he said as they went back to their seats.

"You too, Sean." Taylor sighed.

Watching them go, his mind lingered in the memories of those days in the courthouse. He then came back to the present and wheeled himself over to a corner behind the last row of seats. Paula retrieved an extra chair and placed it next to him. Her businesslike approach made clear that she was less than enthusiastic about the situation, given that she knew the real reason he was there. Nevertheless, he felt her warm grasp on his bicep, encouraging them both to stick it out as the music, far too loud for Taylor's liking, began to play.

The last song finally wound down as Steve approached the front and placed a few pages of notes and his Bible on the floor of the platform next to the plexiglass pulpit. It was odd to Taylor that he didn't go up but remained at floor level. He seemed pretty comfortable as he adjusted his headset and greeted everyone. Opening his Bible and beginning to read, Taylor could see the verses up on the screen.

"I'm reading John, chapter eight, starting with verse one," he said, pausing for those who were looking for the passage in either their Bibles or phones. Paula had her own Bible, and Taylor out of respect followed along with the screen as Steve began to read aloud.

Jesus went to the Mount of Olives. At dawn he appeared again in the temple courts where all the people gathered around him and he sat down to teach them. The teachers of the law and the Pharisees brought a woman caught in adultery and made her stand before the group and said to Jesus, "Teacher, this woman was caught in the act of adultery. The Law of Moses commands us to stone such a woman. Now what do you say?" they challenged, using this question as a trap in order to have a basis for accusing him. But Jesus bent down and started to write on the ground with his finger. When they kept on questioning him, he straightened up and said to them, "Let any of you who is without sin be the first to throw a stone at her." Again he stooped down and wrote on the ground. At this, those who heard began to go away, one at a time, the older ones first until only Jesus was left with the woman still standing there.

Jesus straightened up and looked at her and asked, "Woman, where are they? Has no one condemned you?"

"No one sir," she said.

"Neither do I condemn you," Jesus declared. "Now go and leave your life of sin."

Closing his Bible and placing it back on the platform, Steve gazed down at the floor for a moment, appearing to be digesting the story for himself before looking at the congregation again. He spoke conversationally, as if talking to one person.

"The Feast of the Tabernacles was a holiday where most of the

Jewish world, including Jesus and his disciples, went to Jerusalem to celebrate. For those of us who never realized it, Jesus was a Jew, a faithful, law-abiding, practicing Jew who kept the Passover, the holidays, and the feasts. By that time many were calling him Rabbi, or teacher, because they saw he knew the law like no other, and he had a way of making God understandable to anyone who was willing to listen. It didn't matter who you were or what you looked like to Jesus. This included those considered in the lower end of society, either morally or economically; and even tax collectors, who were perceived as actual traitors to the Jewish community.

"Jesus's contact with men and women like that offended a lot of people. Others, however, were amazed by his miracles and continued to follow him closely, hoping he was the Messiah who would finally break Israel free from Roman oppression. Though many questioned that, given his common upbringing, further research would have shown that he was actually from the line of David and had been born in Bethlehem, as it was written their Messiah would be.

"But Jesus had no interest in overthrowing Rome. When he did confront, it was mostly toward a religious establishment or mindset that had become so elite that it had separated itself from the very people it was called to serve. This obviously made him very unpopular with the powers that be but not with everybody else. In fact, at this period in time, crowds were flocking to him, as they did on that fateful morning."

Steve stopped a moment to take a drink of water before looking out into the congregation again. The quiet attention he received in return reminded Taylor of the rapport he himself used to feel with a jury after he had established their trust during a trial. Steve had that with this crowd, Taylor noticed, and the warmth in the room was almost palpable.

"Yes, the adultery thing was a setup." Steve softly smiled. "There was no doubt about that. Though I'm sure it happened, it was really being used to put a wedge between Jesus and his popularity more than it was to bring anyone to justice. And yes, it kind of backfired on the guys who dragged her there.

"But what nobody counted on, my friends, was that it would be an event that would profoundly define the human condition for all of us. That's me," Steve said, pointing to himself. "That's you. And it's everybody in the past and everybody in the future."

"It would also be a moment that would reveal the kind of Messiah God had sent and still sends today, right in here," he added, lightly tapping his chest.

"So what did she see?" Steve quietly challenged, slowly walking down the center aisle. As he did the atmosphere of what happened two thousand years ago started to connect with even Taylor, who though typically skeptical became somewhat intrigued.

"When she looked into the eyes of the only one left who could condemn her, what do you think she saw?" Steve continued. "That she was worthless? A disappointment? A failure?" he asked, gazing into the eyes of his listeners again.

"No," he offered conclusively. "No, my friends, no," he added, slowly shaking his head. "You don't get that look from the one who came to save you, the one who looks past everything else and into the image you were created in, and that image alone," he said. "That was the look she saw, ladies and gentleman. And it changed her life. And quite honestly, I think it's the only thing that can change ours."

A deep quiet saturated the congregation as Steve walked back to the platform and nonchalantly perched himself on the ledge. He looked more like a guy sitting on a curb, confiding in his friends, than a preacher, and for a fleeting moment Taylor wondered whether Jesus was more like that rather than what he'd always imagined him to be. He continued to follow along, if for nothing else than the sake of the story.

"Certainly a lot's been made over the dirt and what Jesus may have been writing in it," Steve said. "Some say that he was memorializing the sins of the guys there so they wouldn't be able to judge the woman. But the Bible says their consciences were already doing that, so that doesn't work for me. Others think Jesus may have been rewriting the woman's future to be very different from the life she obviously struggled with. I can see that, but honestly I think there was way more to what he was doing than just words.

"I see it as deity touching dirt, like God did in the beginning when life was first created. In this story we see his deity touching the soil of the human heart again, but this time to forgive its sins and to fill it with the love it was made for. That's what really happened here, my friends, although it's interesting to see that the grace of God can affect people in different ways, depending on where they're at. To the humble or softhearted, God's grace is like a healing balm of forgiveness that is well received and melts the person in his love and acceptance. To the prideful, however, his grace can harden them even more; just look at the prodigal's older brother. This story is no different, with hearts being touched and having a choice to either harden or soften at the invitation to God's grace given to another."

Steve paused for a moment, and after taking a sip of water, he looked back out at everyone. "Sometimes I ask myself where I would have fit in that crowd. Honestly, I do. Would I be with the prideful guys who felt they could stand apart from sin, like they did with her? And wind up walking away, leaving my true condition deep in the sand of my own heart for God to just know about but not be able to change because I walked away?" he challenged.

"I've certainly been that before," he admitted.

"Or would I stay, like she did, leaving myself open to the look of a loving God? Could I be that humble in a moment like that? Could I actually overcome the fear of being just me?"

Taylor tensed at the poignancy of Steve's transparency. For starters, adultery was never a popular subject for him, given the affair he had, and like most men he still battled temptation, which was just one of a handful of things that would have been in the sand for him. Nor was he ever comfortable around conversations this personal. His fingers quietly gripped the armrests of his chair as he glanced down at his phone, counting down the minutes to when this thing would finally end. As he did so, he felt Paula's hand slide under his elbow as it often did when they were sitting together.

How can she do that? he wondered in a rare moment of vulnerability. He never would've forgiven her.

Steve's voice and another innocuous squeeze of his arm thankfully interrupted that all-too-familiar guilt cycle that occurred whenever his mind went there.

"No stone was thrown that day," he continued. "And it was only a short time later that Jesus would go on to complete the task his father had sent him to do ... for her ... and for everybody else. It certainly wasn't what his disciples had in mind for a Messiah. That's for sure." Steve sighed. "But whether they realized or not, which I'm sure they didn't at the time, it was for them too that he had to sacrifice his life.

"Truth be told, Jesus's death and even the humiliation of it was so that none of us would ever have to die without God or live with the shame of any part of our past. And the whole reason he allowed himself to be ridiculed by the world as weak, powerless, and even a fake was so that I, Steve Woods, wouldn't have to be; because deep down, my friends, that's what I was."

Steve paused reflectively before gazing over the audience with a look that said again, *Yeah, that was me too.* His honesty was met by an engaging stillness in the room and a warmth even Taylor could sense.

"In other words, society looked at him the way it would look at me if it saw my sin out there in the open, if it saw me from the inside," he said, illustrating with his hands on his stomach. "And that's how he took your place and mine. So that would never have to happen.

I guess you could say that he took the place of the me you'll never see: the hypocrite, the failure, the things that were in here," Steve said, tapping his chest, "things that I can't even say publicly so I wouldn't have to."

He stopped for a moment and surveyed the congregation again.

"And that, ladies and gentleman, was the fulfillment of the Jewish law and obviously God's purpose all along—Christ becoming the sacrifice for all people. And in so doing, He gave you and me full rights to forgiveness for the sin we each have.

"'All we like sheep have gone astray; we have turned—every one—to his own way; and the Lord has laid on him the iniquity of us all' is how the prophet Isaiah described it hundreds of years before. John 3:16 and 17 says the same thing: 'For God so loved the world, that he gave his only Son, that whosoever believes in him should not die but have eternal life. For God did not send his Son into the world to condemn the world, but in order that the world might be saved through him.'

"You see, he was our offering," Steve reflected, still sitting against the platform edge. "But it wasn't for the sake of dying that Jesus did it. In fact, it wasn't about dying at all. It was for freedom that all that happened, my friends, for yours and mine. The kind that only God can give. And the kind he wanted us all to have from the very beginning.

"If you're a scholar, you can read about it from the prophets in the Old Testament, where the life of the coming Messiah was described many times over, or in the New Testament, where we see it actually lived out. But I honestly think that the only way to see God the way he really is, is with your own heart, up close and personal, just like that woman did. She represented all of us, you know," Steve added after a pause. "All of what we are inside. And like us, she needed a freedom that was way beyond the rocks that were going to be thrown at her. She needed a freedom from what was in here," he said, tapping his heart again. "Just like we do.

"And if judgment had the last word in her life, she certainly would have died that day, as would eventually the men with the rocks, and as would we. In fact, when judgment has the last say, everything dies: love, relationships, even people. But when mercy has the last word, as it did for her that day, things come alive again. And people I daresay receive a new life as she did.

"You see, her behavior wasn't the central issue here, my friends. Was it painful to others? I have no doubt about that. But as to her, it was really just a symptom of a greater disease we've all had at one time or another, which is not actually believing that we matter to God or to anyone else.

"She was the story of the prodigal son played out in real life. And when she saw that her Messiah was personal and that God was a loving Father that she didn't have to be afraid of anymore, she could walk away with that 'beautiful now' Spirit-breathed life that knew deep within her that God was good and, more importantly, that she belonged, that she mattered.

"That's what made all the difference." Steve softly smiled. "It's the love of God that changes people and only that love," he said, signifying he was about to close.

"Let he who has no sin cast the first stone," he quietly repeated. "Forgive, my friends, from your heart. It's hard, but it's the only way to move forward. Honestly I think it's the only way anyone can look toward God without shame."

Steve paused a moment to let those last words land, knowing they probably touched nerves buried deeply within many who were listening.

"In my case it was forgiveness that made me whole again, not perfection," he confided. "Because my sin never stopped me from seeing God. But my pride certainly did. Truth be told, on that day two thousand years ago, everybody could have gotten what the woman did, even the rock throwers. All they had to do was take their eyes off judging her and instead look toward the one with the power and the grace to change us all. That's what Jesus was looking for that day. And it's all that he's looking for today," Steve gently challenged.

He paused a moment before quietly collecting his notes and Bible. Then, looking back up to everybody, he offered his final thought. "You don't need a perfect heart to look toward God and see him, my friends. Just one that's not afraid to change. Let mercy have the last say in your life. It will never let you down."

CHAPTER 25

Avoiding eye contact, Taylor wheeled himself toward the door to get out to the car. Paula diligently followed, gathering Nathan on the way. The minivan was parked a considerable distance into the packed parking lot. As usual, Taylor never let anyone use the handicapped spaces, preferring end spots instead. He had already opened the passenger side door by the time a jogging Paula reached him to help.

"You got the door, Taylor?"

"Yep," he curtly replied.

Grabbing the inside handle with his right hand and the top of the doorjamb with his left, he pulled himself up as Paula guided his midsection into the seat. She then lifted his heavy legs and turned them into their face-forward position. He finished settling himself while she rolled the wheelchair to the rear of the van, folded it, and placed it in the back. Finally, everybody else piled in, and they began the drive home. All remained silent, however, as Taylor sat motionlessly, continuing to stare blankly out his passenger-seat window. He knew people were curious about what he might say about the morning, and the tension over that anticipated conversation began to percolate within him. He didn't like the sermon. In fact, he didn't like anything about being there.

Finally, Paula broke the silence. Her tone was upbeat but cautious. "So, what did you think?" she asked.

"About what?" Taylor responded, keeping his gaze out the

window at the passing mailboxes and fine-trimmed lawns of Rivermont proper.

"Taylor," Paula pushed again.

"He's a nice guy, Paula. I always thought so," Taylor answered, rebuffing her desire to talk substance.

He was still smoldering inside, however. There wasn't anything wrong with Taylor Green as far as he was concerned, and he resented the implication that there was. Moreover, the inference that he wasn't "free" because he didn't believe the way the rest of the people in that place did was downright offensive and probably the main reason most people didn't like being around Christians like that. Besides, he couldn't be like his wife, even if he wanted to. Far too much had happened in his life, both to him and through him, for him to think he could be any different than what he was. He was free enough though, he angrily reminded himself; free from having his life being controlled by anyone else, that was for sure. He felt he earned at least that.

"That's all, Dad?" Sharon piped up, interrupting his internal tirade.

Wedged between her two, now uncomfortable, brothers while the third, Skip, sat in the far backseat listening to his earphones; his daughter's glare was reflected in the rearview mirror just to Taylor's left. She was poised to defend her mother again.

"Yep, that's all," Taylor sternly replied to his teenager.

He would have none of that right now.

"You don't know as much about life as you think," he muttered condescendingly as he turned his head back toward his window. These were words he wished he could have caught before they left his lips.

"I never said I did, Dad!" she snapped back. "The question was 'What did *you* think?'" she stormed, proving herself to be her father's daughter again.

"Stop!" a fed-up-sounding Paula interjected.

They both did—Taylor because he wanted to, Sharon because she had to.

CHAPTER 26

"So, did he ever say anything to you, Ma?" Sharon asked.

"Nothing yet," Paula answered.

It was warmer than usual that afternoon, which was a welcome change for both of them as they embarked on their routine jog. Donning sweats and running attire, they hustled through the residential streets of the neighborhood. Paula valued the time, given that the two could easily converse while keeping an impressive pace. It helped clear her mind and even stay in shape a little bit. It was also her opportunity to be with her daughter outside the house, where they could relate more as friends.

Though it was Taylor who wisely advocated that this transition be commenced before Sharon went to college, he himself abandoned that process after his accident. Paula wouldn't though, so the road running remained a must, no matter how hard it was on Mom's less resilient knees and hips.

"Pfff, don't hold your breath," Sharon quipped after a moment or two.

"Sharon!" Paula reprimanded.

Undeterred, the teenager went further. "He doesn't talk about anything! How can you take him, Mom?"

"Your father's a very hardheaded man. You know that," Paula affirmed, though feeling a little anxious.

Sharon nodded, cutting her mother a break. She allowed a

pregnant pause while they went single file to let a car pass. A troubled look came over her face as she attempted her next point.

"Mom, Dad's life was Skip and baseball, and now it's pretty much gone," she said as delicately as possible.

"Now you sound like him," Paula sullenly replied.

"Am I being too blunt?" Sharon challenged.

"What are you saying?" Paula snapped back, annoyed with the whole conversation.

Another moment or two passed while the two reestablished their pace and timing. Sharon approached the subject again. "He doesn't believe in God, Ma. He never has," she said, trying to be sensitive but honest as well.

"So, what am I supposed to do, daughter? Give up?" a frustrated Paula offered in between huffs. Keeping up with her thinner, and now taller, daughter was difficult enough.

"No, Ma, I'm not saying that," Sharon answered. "But he's not looking for God or anything else. He doesn't care."

A long silence passed, allowing each some time to regroup.

"I know Dad's not looking for God, Sharon," Paula conceded, sympathetic to how difficult it was for her to say what she said. "But that's okay as long as he's looking for the truth," she added, still looking ahead and apparently thinking aloud.

"The truth?" Sharon questioned, a little puzzled.

"Yeah," Paula answered soberly.

"Because if your father really wants to know if God exists or not, he won't have to look for him," she said, seemingly answering her own soul-searching.

"Why not?" Sharon puffed as the two began to increase speed.

"Because God'll find him," Paula answered resolutely, breaking into a sprint around the last corner and onto the block they lived on.

The swift teen began catching up as the two laughed, striving neck and neck the rest of the way home.

CHAPTER 27

PAULA ORCHESTRATED CLEANUP IMMEDIATELY FOLLOWING DINNER. Though duty bound to remain at the table until he finished his vegetables, Nathan took the opportunity to tease his big brother.

"Tim's got a girlfriend," the boy repeatedly sang while mimicking his brother kissing a girl.

Tim's face reddened as he glanced toward his father in embarrassment before sharply scolding his obnoxious little brother. "Be quiet, you little brat!"

"Enough!" Paula intervened, holding up her hands between the boys. "You finish your vegetables," she said, pointing to Nathan, "and you relax and help clean up," she instructed her oldest.

"Mom—" Tim protested, shaking his head with a moan.

"I don't want to hear it," Paula continued, holding up her hand again. "By the way, are your clothes all picked out?"

"Yup," Tim assured her in a tone that implied no further discussion was needed.

"It's a semiformal," his mother reminded him.

"I know," a defiant Tim responded.

"You have a nice shirt and tie ready?" she pressed.

"Uh-huh," Tim stammered again, careful to avoid eye contact.

"Your suit?" she prodded again.

"No," Nathan revealed.

"Shut up, Nathan!" Tim retorted.

"Tim?" Paula asked again.

"I'll look fine, Ma," he calmly replied.

"I wanna see," she insisted. She wasn't buying it.

"Ma!" he protested again, now with some attitude.

"After we're done, I want to see those clothes, Timothy," she demanded again, undaunted by her son's grossly misplaced righteous indignation.

In a huff, he headed toward the sink with a stack of dirty dishes to complete his post-dinner cleanup.

CHAPTER 28

"Are we agreed, Timothy?" Paula inquired.

It had been an intense and painful negotiation between the two over the last half hour, which Paula was glad she'd gotten the better part of.

"Yes, Mom," he grudgingly answered.

He has no idea what a semiformal is, she said to herself, *and he has to trust me on this.*

Tim and his girlfriend, Alexandra, had been together for the past six months. Alex, as she went by, was very friendly and easy to be around. Paula liked her. However, the two had never been to anything that involved dancing, certainly not formal dancing, and Tim's attire was in need of some parental tweaking. She stood next to him in front of the couch, viewing the laid-out clothes they'd finally agreed on.

While Sharon and Nathan sat in and watched, the generally disinterested Skip was up in his bedroom, listening to his headphones and viewing social media on his phone as he often did. Taylor wasn't present either.

"It looks good, Tim," Sharon encouraged.

His big sister's approval caused him to cheer up a little bit.

"What kind of music are they playing?" Paula asked.

"Ma!" Tim loudly complained, resisting her over intrusiveness.

"I'm serious," she said. "Will there be any ballroom dancing too?"

"Yes," Sharon teasingly reported, escalating the anxiety of an already-exasperated Tim.

She and Nathan started to laugh as their brother tried to downplay the whole thing.

"Ma, don't worry about the dancing. I know how to dance," he assured her, though everyone knew he didn't.

"I've never seen you dance with a girl before, Tim," Paula innocently said.

Her comment was unwittingly augmented by the laughter of his siblings, which in turn caused Paula to irrepressibly smirk herself. This catapulted Tim into a crimson shade of embarrassment.

"Ma! Stop!" he spouted. He struggled to compose himself.

"Proms always have formal dancing," Paula calmly advised him, trying to dial things down and restrain the humor. She held out her hands for him to clasp and begin to practice.

"Ma!" Tim objected, refusing to comply.

"C'mon. You and Alex will be the hit of the evening." She warmly smiled, continuing to hold out her hands. "It's way easier than you think."

Tim reluctantly joined his mom in the middle of the living room.

"Hold on, hold on," Sharon said, locating some big-band-style dance music on her iPhone to put through their sound system.

She found it quickly, and the Glenn Miller Band began echoing for the first time ever through the Green household.

"No posting!" Tim warned his big sister, who pledged not to.

"Mom, I'm no good at this." He groaned.

"Just relax and follow me," she assured him, swaying him along, undeterred by his lack of confidence.

Down the hallway and into the darkened and seemingly unoccupied kitchen, the sounds of fun and merriment could be heard as they all danced, flopped around, and laughed hysterically for the next forty-five minutes or so.

The outline of Taylor in his wheelchair, sitting crouched down and to one side against the wall, faintly shadowed the kitchen opening. Unable to be seen by those in the living room, he remained still as he peered through a crack of light and into the festivities. Though everybody was involved in the frolicking, all Taylor could see was Paula.

Sloppy bun bouncing while lightheartedly chirping their son through each move, she may have been a woman Tim had never saw before, but Taylor certainly had. He rested his chin on the palms of his hands and let his eyes drop to the floor as the voices began to fade in the background.

CHAPTER 29

"You're so full of yourself!" sparked the fiery college freshman. She didn't appreciate the sarcastic grin while she was passing by his aisle seat in the auditorium.

The startled junior tried to appear surprised as his accuser stopped and, with all her 115- pound, five-four frame, remained towering over his seat, daring a response.

"Excuse me?" he retorted with an edge.

"You heard me," she challenged again, not caring about the negative attention she was drawing from the clog of students behind her, trying to exit the crowded lecture hall.

"American Classics" was a course she'd taken because it fit within her otherwise-busy schedule. Taught by the ever-popular Professor David Patterson, he took it because he liked to read. Being an English major was also an easier academic route for him to travel than something like math or biology, and it could just as easily get him into law school if he wanted to, he figured. But that would be his second career choice.

In any event, the book they were reading was *The Scarlet Letter* by Nathaniel Hawthorne. Obviously a classic, the story was set in 1645 Salem, Massachusetts, and involved the societal outrage over an adulterous affair a young woman had while her husband was overseas. After Hester Prynne, the lead character, became pregnant and had her daughter, Pearl, she faced the gallows and potentially capital punishment over what she'd done. She refused, however, to divulge the identity of the man she'd had the affair with, who ironically turned out to be the local minister.

The penalty Ms. Prynne ultimately received was a requirement that she wear an embroidered red (scarlet) letter *A* on her blouse across her chest on a daily basis. Though the author of the story let the letter go undefined, it was implied to be a constant public reminder of what she had done. Professor Patterson, however, sought to test that supposition, challenging the class to consider what the *A* really stood for as well as its cultural significance both then and now.

Looking up at the packed rows of seats that ascended the theater-like auditorium, he scanned for an opinion other than that of the regular participants. A young woman down in the third row mistakenly made eye contact and became his first victim.

"Ms. Defin-ee-on," he attempted, thinking he was correctly pronouncing the French name while glancing down at his seating chart.

"Defin-ee-yoon," the first-year nursing student meekly replied.

She'd taken this class purely as an elective and was clearly apprehensive about the ninety or so pairs of eyes that were undoubtedly staring at her from behind, waiting to hear her voice for the first time.

"Okay, Ms. Definiunē. What are your thoughts?" Dr. Patterson asked, stretching out his hand in warm invitation.

"Well, I think the *A* stood for 'adultery,'" she feebly responded, "which was condemned in the community she was living in."

Easy enough, she thought as she exhaled in relief. However, that wouldn't be the case in a class like this.

"Not an incorrect answer, Ms. Definiunē," the professor dryly acknowledged after a pause. "But could there be more to it?" he challenged, lifting his eyes to the entire group. "Why was Hester Prynne actually the protagonist in this story?" he added as the familiar hands began to raise.

Paula's eyes dropped into the shelter of her notes. Even the soft, comforting elbow bump of her roommate and nursing buddy did little to console the embarrassed freshman. Unfortunately, the professor's subtle inference that she was out of her league was about to get much worse.

"Mr. Green, what are your thoughts?" Patterson bellowed, looking up toward the back of the auditorium.

Paula cringed. Of course, it was that obnoxious upperclassman who'd insulted her in the student union, the one who caught her turning her head as she was leaving, the boy she hated liking. She didn't know whether he'd raised his hand or not but surmised that he probably had.

"Though on one level I would agree with Ms. Definiuñ̃e," Taylor offered with a confident chuckle, "I think the *A* really stands for antinomianism," he answered matter-of-factly.

"Antinomianism," Patterson repeated, reflecting on it positively before affirming again the more sophisticated response and inviting more from Taylor.

"Basically, it stands for one who rejects a socially established morality, as Hester Prynne did here, under a view that God alone is her judge," he continued.

"Very good," the professor applauded, reiterating part of what was said in the hope that it would reverberate with the rest of the class, who were now equally captivated.

He baited his student further. "And your support?"

"Well," Taylor smugly began, "in the story Hester wore the letter proudly rather than with any sense of guilt or shame normally associated with adultery, at least back them. So it had to have meant something else to her, something positive, whether it be a belief that God forgives what society doesn't or simply that no one has the right to impose their views on anyone else—"

That last comment was interrupted by cheers and a round of rowdy applause from the class as a chuckling Taylor became slightly bashful himself. He thoroughly enjoyed the attention though.

"That's antinomianism," he started again, "the popular though controversial theology of the 1640s, which was the time period Hawthorne was writing about."

"Bravo, Mr. Green!" Patterson proudly grinned immediately before the buzzer rang.

A mortified Paula had already packed her books and was trying to exit the side of the auditorium opposite Taylor, but it was too crowded to get through. Turning around, she and her friend began making their way up his aisle as inconspicuously as possible. Thankfully he was buried behind other students, who had congregated around his seat and stopped to talk. Her presence unfortunately didn't escape him though.

"Hey, Paula!" He smirked as she tried to sneak by.

That was it. She turned with a glare before letting him have it.

"Tough talk for a French girl," Taylor barbed back after being publicly put on the spot. "Is it because I used a word that's not in the cliff notes, Paula?" he added for good measure.

"Don't call me 'Paula!'" was all she could say before fleeing up the steps, noticeably humiliated by that last comment.

Taylor went after her. Though the consequences of his overly large ego had never concerned him before, it did now. Truth be told, he'd been smitten with Paula Definiunẽ from the moment he saw her. And though he had no idea how, he knew he needed to fix the damage his big mouth had done before it was too late. He chased the bouncing backpack and ponytail as it furiously traversed the walkway splitting the campus. Taylor did all he could do to catch up to her inconspicuously without breaking into a run. It wasn't easy though, given she was wearing sweats and sneakers, and was moving pretty fast.

He finally got about five yards behind her. "Paula," he called.

"Get away from me!" she stammered through angry tears.

"Paula, stop. Just stop for one minute, please," he implored.

She did and through smudged mascara looked directly at him. At this point, she didn't care what she looked like or that he would see the pain his sarcasm had caused. *Assuming that he has a conscience in the first place*, she thought.

"Okay, you're smart, and I'm stupid. You feel good about yourself?" she coldly replied, not bothering to say his name.

Taylor didn't know what to say as he awkwardly stood stock still before her.

Emotions were never his thing, but the girl standing in front of him certainly was, and that undeniable fact caused him to remain stationary and in a vulnerability that was starting to scare him. He hoped she didn't see that.

"Honestly, I don't think I've ever felt this bad before, Paula," he blurted, half surprised those words were actually being said.

"Well, I guess there's a first for everything." She glared, turning to walk away. "Glad I could help."

He gently grabbed her elbow, hoping she'd hold on a minute. She did and looked back at him again.

"All I can say is, I'm sorry. And I am," he added.

Deep down he wanted a lot more than just to convince her of that. He wanted her to like him, though by her expression, that didn't appear to be in the cards at all. Who was he kidding anyway? he began to sadly realize. A pretty girl like her undoubtedly had a boyfriend at home who was ten times the guy he was. Besides that, she wasn't attracted to him, and all the wittiness in the world could never get a girl like her to like a guy like him. *Who am I kidding?* flooded through his mind again as his insides quavered with both fear and an oncoming crestfallenness for imagining that he'd ever had a chance in the first place.

Paula, however, didn't say anything but instead continued staring into his eyes like she had some kind of x-ray vision. Though this made Taylor extremely uncomfortable, she clearly wasn't. She was reading him like a book and probably figured out by now that he liked her, he nervously thought. He just hoped she couldn't see how much.

After another few seconds went by, which honestly felt like

hours, Taylor realized he could either retreat or go forward; and since he was already committed, he just went for it with the last smidgen of pride he had left. "Can we have coffee later, Paula?" he asked. "And I promise I'll never say 'cawfee,'" he hesitantly added, managing to push out a slight grin.

"No thanks," she curtly replied, not buying into the levity either, though she continued looking at him as if testing his response.

"Okay," Taylor answered.

He remained steady with both the rejection as well as the power shift that had obviously just taken place. *At least she hasn't walked away yet*, he thought.

"Can we have coffee ever, Paula?" he asked again, now calmly looking into her eyes, unafraid that she had the upper hand.

"Why don't you try being nice to me first, Taylor?" she answered; however, this time saying his name like she knew him, like she may have actually been thinking about him. She even allowed a slight glimmer to come into her eye as she now looked into his, causing his insides to jump in elation.

"Absolutely," he blurted.

Though his confidence was beginning to return, Taylor was going to be very careful with it this time. He gave her one last look and offered a soft smile as if to say that.

Paula turned and headed toward the dorm. As she walked away, Taylor couldn't take his eyes off her. He was enamored, and at that moment he honestly felt for the first time that his life would be missing something, missing everything, if she wasn't in it. Even more so, he knew there was something inside him for her, something alive, something he'd never felt for anything or anyone before.

After she got about fifty yards or so down the cement pathway, she glanced back and caught him still standing there, looking. It was as if she had felt his eyes warmly resting on her as she was walking. He didn't care though, smiling at her again.

He saw her smile too.

CHAPTER 30

"Unbelievable!" Charlie punched out of his mouth, slamming back the hung-up shirts in his closet as he looked for his favorite jean jacket. They'd been roommates since freshman year.

"Charlie, c'mon, we—"

"You're with her every second, Taylor," he interrupted. "Eating before class, after class. You walk her to class—classes you're not even in! And where's Taylor Green at night? In the science library. Whadda ya doin', Taylor? This is college. It's been two months!" Charlie blasted.

"Well, I never knew you cared." Taylor smirked.

"It's not funny," Charlie answered, his countenance remaining unchanged.

"Ask me where I'm goin', Taylor," he said, looking at him sternly.

Charlie didn't wait for an answer, though Taylor couldn't give one anyway. He felt unnerved by his friend's upset and started to wonder if he really was "missing college" and other stuff that was important. Worse than that, Charlie was right about his abandoning his longtime buddies. Taylor never wanted to be that guy, but for the first time, he was beginning to feel like he was.

"I'm going to Bubs. Remember that place, Taylor?" Charlie jabbed, breaking the silence. "It's a bar where we used to go and drink and have fun. And some of us still do," he punched out.

"Where's my jacket?" Charlie muttered to himself, scavenging through a pile of clean laundry he'd never fold or put away.

Seeing a quarter on his bureau, he flipped it hard over to Taylor, who was still sitting on his bed. He reflexively caught it.

"Quarters. Remember that game, Taylor. You were the best at it."

I was, Taylor thought. He was the best at beer pong too, though he often had his friends fooled by sneaking in the bathroom and refilling his Budweiser bottle with water while the others got so drunk they could barely keep the ping-pong ball on the table. By night's end none had even a hope of hitting Taylor's bottle or stopping him from hitting theirs, as he laughingly drove each challenger into oblivion and a hefty hangover the next morning. It was all in good fun though, Taylor mused, gently massaging the quarter between his thumb and index finger while drifting back to the popular, though overly played, jukebox tune of "Low Budget" by The Kinks, a song appropriately written for him and his friends.

"Where are you, Taylor Green?" Charlie said, coming over and grabbing his buddy's ears with his catcher's mitt-sized hands and staring into his face from about three inches away.

Taylor let him do it, his glazed-over eyes numbly looking back into his friend's. He still didn't know what to do.

Charlie let go and frustratingly strode back to his closet to find his shoes.

While there probably was a more sensitive way of making his point, that was never Charlie. This was never Taylor either though, which was exactly the problem his roommate was having.

"Paula doesn't think you guys like her," Taylor offered as kind of an excuse, but even his tone gave away that it was a lame one.

"We don't," Charlie stated plainly. "She's a hog."

"A wha—?" Taylor started to snap back.

"Easy, big guy," Charlie replied, putting up his hand without flinching.

The five-nine catcher from Watertown, New York, was about 220 pounds of pure muscle. Besides, he knew better than to be afraid of his best friend. "She's a hog with your time, is all," he said with a little more diplomacy.

Charlie's character and upstate accent always added credence to what he had to say, and beneath his tirade, Taylor could see he was also making a last-ditch effort to extend an olive branch.

"Charlie, it's me. I'm crazy about her," Taylor admitted, now looking up at him for a solution.

"I get that, but you're losing your soul, buddy," Charlie counseled sympathetically.

"I'm not losing my soul," Taylor indignantly answered, though there was a hair of concern in his voice.

"All right, then hang out," Charlie insisted, keeping on the pressure.

CHAPTER 31

"You're really beautiful, Mrs. Green," Paula said as Sheila stood outside the dressing room.

Taylor almost died when he heard it, though his girlfriend's elbow in his side demanded his agreement. "Yeah, ya look great, Mom," he said, causing her to blush a little.

Truth be told, she really did, and Sheila and her daughter, Grace, saw that Paula Definiunê was not only all in with Taylor but also with them too. It likewise became apparent that keeping to yourself or living in any kind of solitude was pretty much impossible with Paula around. Though the chatty girl from Queens had already grown on Taylor's friends at school, this trip home to Columbus to meet his mom and younger sister was a first for him. Of course, nothing stopped Paula's warm and emotional embrace of his little family, and it spurred an intimacy that quickly had Grace lighting up whenever they were together.

Paula indeed had a way of making everything fun and making everybody talk too. Though Taylor was used to this, it was a bit of a challenge to his stoic, usually standoffish mom. Eventually the young Ms. Definiunê's compassion and persistence won out, pulling thoughts, opinions, and even feelings out of Sheila Green that not even her own kids knew of, probably because most of them were sad. It was usually while she was ironing or doing one of the many other chores working moms were routinely behind on that Paula plopped herself down with coffee for both of them and began asking questions about a life Sheila Green had never thought anyone would be interested in. Nor would Paula tolerate Mom being alone for too long either, often dragging her out shopping and on this occasion to the mall to buy a fashionable dress for herself.

Taylor experienced his own piece of culture shock during his indoctrination to the Definiunē clan and New York City. Opposite his life in Columbus, in Paula's community everyone was family, and everybody talked about everything, big or small, usually at the same time—unless of course it was Paula's dad, Joe D., who was speaking. Taylor never knew what it was like to have such a strong and gregarious presence control a family dynamic the way Mr. D. did. He liked it though and admired the man a great deal.

Taylor's first trip down was the summer after he and Paula had met, which followed a spring that was almost magical for him. The Great Danes of Albany had lost only three games that year, and their ace pitched the season of his life, losing only one of them. Now he got to be in New York with his favorite tour guide as they covered Coney Island, the Bronx Zoo, and pretty much every inch of Manhattan. But what he loved most about the city was located on 216th Street in Bayside, a two-story, three-bedroom house with a detached garage, all sitting on a lot that was the size of a postage stamp. Of course, the Definiunēs' was a meticulously kept residence, with flower gardens in the back and a well-manicured lawn and brick walkway leading up to the front porch. Built in the forties, the home was tastefully decorated with paintings, portraits, and a sprinkling of framed family photos, which reflected both their old country heritage as well as life in America.

Unlike the more practical furnishings of the compact and sometimes cluttered two- bedroom apartment Taylor had come from, you knew where you were, both ethnically and historically, when you were in the Definiunē house. And but for their teenagers, it was so well maintained that you could probably eat off her mom's kitchen floor with her father's tools.

Paula's brothers were indeed slobs and liked to argue a lot, which made Taylor way more comfortable and kept some attention off him but not much.

"How ya doin', Taylor?" Paula's mom smiled over a hot cup of coffee she'd just poured for him. The problem was, she meant it, her motherly eyes always looking into his and wanting to know details Taylor honestly never bothered to think about.

"I'm good, Mrs. D," he said back with a grin.

Unlike Paula's brothers, Taylor wouldn't talk about every ache, pain, or annoying situation that presented itself in his life like Mrs. D. was accustomed to listening to. But she cheerfully took whatever she could from her daughter's boyfriend, and truth be told, Taylor was always feeling "good" when he was around the Definiunẽ family.

Mr. Definiunẽ's store was literally three blocks away, and her mom, Dot, worked as a teacher's assistant in the local elementary school. They never had a lot but always enough, and every day her parents worked hard to keep a roof over their heads, food on the table; and even somehow put the kids through Catholic school. That was just the way it was back then, and from an early age their daughter learned the importance of living right, doing well, and making their family proud.

However, like many of her contemporaries, as Paula grew up and started to see outside the bubble of her neighborhood, the conflicts and confusion of life in the bigger world made the concept that God existed in only the way she knew far too difficult to honestly believe or even understand. She couldn't "not believe" in God. That wasn't in her either. So, from a religious standpoint, she was left with the view that if she lived a moral life on the big ones, sent her kids to catechism, and generally stuck with what the church said about faith, everything would hopefully be all right in the end. That was Paula's life when she met Taylor.

As for the young Mr. Green, he saw religion as simply a result of the way a person grew up, a product of their culture or ethnicity, he would argue during the late-evening debates that sporadically broke out in his college dorm rooms from time to time. It wasn't a bad thing necessarily, and though he could never rationally consider such a life for himself, it certainly had its place in helping keep society generally safe and maintained with a moral standard that benefited all.

As a kid, Taylor's mom had to work most of the time, managing to drag him and his sister to church only on Christmas and Easter, where they both sat, constantly shifting themselves around in their uncomfortable formal clothing on the hard, wooden pews while they waited out the forty-five minutes before they could go home for presents or candy.

He also remembered that the austere buildings were always filled with either elderly women or intact families; the former group he obviously never wanted to be, and the latter he couldn't. Besides, religious people had no life as far as Taylor could see, regardless of the denomination. Worse than that, the crazier ones had an annoying agenda to get other people to believe the way they did. It was a power thing, Taylor surmised, and he never wanted anything to do with it.

Who God was was anyone's guess as far as Taylor was concerned. That was his religion, and he was "faithful to it," he would chuckle to Paula whenever the subject came up. However, for Paula's sake, the young Taylor Green didn't mind going to church with her family when he was down there or the once or twice a year he'd always done. She seemed okay with that too.

CHAPTER 32

"THESE ARE RED SOX TICKETS, PAULA. HOW DID YOU GET THEM?" Taylor exclaimed, shocked that she could get box seats to the Yankees against their archrivals.

"My dad got them," she nonchalantly replied.

She doesn't understand what she has, Taylor thought with a smile, though it was no secret how much he loved baseball. Whether it was spring, summer, or fall, Taylor was playing. Nor did it make a difference that he was on scholarship to do so.

His dream was a shot at the pros, and though he wouldn't let himself think of playing there yet, he could set his sights on a tryout, because that was what was possible. This was how Taylor thought, having developed a mindset early on that the key to building anything was one brick at a time. It could be done no other way from where he started in life, and his coined mentality of "positioning before winning" had proved quite successful for the young man, especially in what he wanted most.

Simply put, the immediate goal wasn't to win but to get in a position to win. Once you got yourself into that place, you could win, Taylor believed. As a result of this simple philosophy of breaking things down and mastering only what was directly in front of him, he was rarely discouraged or overwhelmed, and he could always keep his cool on the mound.

It was that perspective, coupled with his ability to throw a baseball, that got him a call from Albany's head coach, Craig

Gorton. Gorton happened to be in Akron, Ohio, scouting another player, when he saw Taylor. It was obvious that the high schooler knew his opposing batters well and had an uncanny ability to peg the ball in the lowest percentage areas of each hitter's respective strike zone. The slugger Gorton had come to watch struck out three times, turning that coach's full attention to the young Mr. Green. After seeing Taylor's complete repertoire of pitches and the heat that came with them, he offered him a full ride.

Albany was by no means a Florida or Arizona, but it was still Division I and a place where Taylor could go to school for free, so the choice was easy.

He worked hard there, in and out of season, and by his junior year his fastball was clocking between eighty-five and eighty-nine miles an hour. It wasn't enough to be drafted but enough to possibly get a tryout, enough to get into a position for the win Taylor yearned for.

Paula knew that too, which made taking her first serious boyfriend to Yankee Stadium all the more special. Even though the Yankees were at the bottom of their division, the "House That Ruth Built" was the pinnacle of all baseball. It was also where Thurman Munson, Taylor's hero from his home state of Ohio, had played his amazing but short career. Munson had been a college all-American in 1968, rookie of the year in 1970, an MVP, golden glove, and the first captain of the New York Yankees since Lou Gehrig. He was bigger than life as far as Taylor was concerned. So was baseball.

"You see, Paula, this game's not just about being an athlete," he excitedly explained. "You have to think. You have to strategize. It's way more," he added, coming alive and unknowingly giving her the window every woman desires into the child her man had once been and sometimes still was. She was beaming.

He loved watching the game, and she loved watching him watch the game.

"You see the field positioning, Paula? That's called a 'shift.' They're shifting left—"

"I know what a shift to the left is, Taylor," she replied with a smile, setting him up.

He looked back at her, impressed that she knew.

"It's when someone has an infection. The lab values shift to the left." She smirked again.

Playfully pushing down on the visor of the Yankee hat he had just bought her, Taylor laughed as she grabbed his hands in resistance. Though he could temporarily fend that off, he couldn't suppress the high-pitched "Taylor!" cry that was as intoxicating as it was piercing. He let go and warmly pulled her in under his arm, briefly catching the familiar shine of her smile and captivating dance in her hazel eyes; the telltale sign that she could never stay mad at him for too long.

"There's a lot going on out there, Paula. Just watch," he offered, trying to coax her back into the game.

The catcher subtly reached down and grabbed a little dirt with his hand, a move that immediately got Taylor's attention.

"Look, Paula, look," he said, almost whispering to her. "They have a man on first with one out. That's Wade Boggs." Taylor pointed to him standing about ten feet off first base. "Probably one of the best players in the game. Unbelievable hitter but not a great base stealer. He's leading a little too far, and I think he missed the signal."

"What signal?" she whispered back.

"Just look at the catcher," Taylor replied, his eyes remaining peeled there himself. "Sometimes when a catcher grabs a piece of dirt, he's signaling the first baseman that he's going to try to pick off the runner. The catcher doesn't look over. It's the first baseman's job to see the sign. Everybody knows about stuff like this, but Boggs and his first-base coach were looking at each other when it happened. I think they missed it."

"Look! He's leading long again."

"They missed it," Taylor said, now scooting up toward the edge of his seat as his eyes darted between the Yankee catcher and Boggs, who continued to inch out. "The pitcher's gonna throw a little high and to the outside so the batter won't swing and the catcher can get off a good throw down to first. Watch."

Sure enough, that's what happened as Boggs was picked off. The stadium erupted. Taylor smiled, proud about impressing his girlfriend while they both observed the frustrated all-star angrily pull off his batting helmet and fling it to the dugout floor.

"What a sore loser," Paula noted, shaking her head in disapproval and looking toward Taylor for his reaction.

He wouldn't condemn the behavior though. "You know they're killing everybody this year," he said, referring to Boggs and the Red Sox.

"So they can act like babies?" she replied.

Taylor just raised his eyes and softly shook his head. "He hates to lose more than he likes to win, Paula." He shrugged. "That's how it should be," he added, trying to defend Boggs again.

"It's a game, Taylor," she soberly reminded him.

"A great game!" he grinned, rapidly changing the subject.

He put his arm around her again and pulled her in. He knew she would never understand what he was saying, but that was okay. Paula's affectionate tickle between his ribs told him she was okay too.

She rested her head on his shoulder. Though they had about six more innings to go, she could put up with it because, regardless of what they were doing, weekends always ended at Coney Island with just the two of them. That was her time, and truth be told, Taylor never minded the constant chatter or endless questions she asked during those walks, even if it meant him having to talk more than he had in his entire life.

"Well?" she would say, stopping to see if he was paying attention.

"Well what?" he'd ask, half daydreaming as he looked out at the water.

"What do you think, Taylor?" she'd say again.

"I think you're so cute I can't take it," he always replied with a smile, much to her annoyance.

He meant it though. Never could anyone make life so full from a boardwalk on Coney Island than Paula Definiunẽ. Taylor had no doubt about that.

CHAPTER 33

FALL CAME QUICKLY, WITH PAULA ENTERING HER SECOND YEAR IN the nursing program, while Taylor became a senior at Albany. It would also be his final season, and in his mind, his make-it-or-break-it chance to get a tryout with the pros.

Coach Gorton was working diligently toward this too, sending films and contacting coaches and agents he knew as well as friends, friends of friends, and anyone else in the baseball world he thought could help. Things were looking good, since he was successful in generating enough interest to ensure at least three tryouts come spring, which left Taylor extremely excited about the opportunity.

Warming up for what would have been his third game of the customarily short fall ball season, Taylor pumped out a fastball, which smacked hard into Charlie's glove. However, before it left his fingers, he felt a snap from deep inside his shoulder, causing his arm to violently retract against his side. Immediately falling to his knees, he clutched his shoulder with his other arm. The pain was excruciating and felt like something deep inside had been cut and was separating from his arm. He'd never had a major injury before, and the last place he wanted it was there. His mind raced. If only he'd laid off that pitch a little bit.

Coach Gorton and the trainer came running over. The concern on their faces was as frightening as the numbness that began to tingle down his pitching arm. The trainer held it and gently moved Taylor's fingers. The feeling was there, but he barely had enough strength to make a fist or lift his arm. Something was seriously wrong. How could his whole dream shatter with one pitch on a cold, dank afternoon?

As his shoulder was being wrapped in a makeshift sling, the team huddled around their wounded veteran. Taylor felt alone though. All he could think about was the horror of his future being over. Worse than that, he may not even get a shot if his shoulder turned out that bad.

About a week later, his fears were confirmed; "torn rotator cuff" was what the upstate surgeon said. Taylor well knew those were three words no pro coach or general manager ever wanted to hear. There were months of recovery following his operation, and Taylor worked tirelessly in physical therapy to regain his strength and mobility. In the end, however, the residual scar tissue inside his shoulder took almost ten miles an hour off his fastball and with that his dream as well.

Taylor was crushed and remained despondent for months. Nor did the long, cold upstate winter help either, though Paula's peppy smile and upbeat disposition kept his depression from getting the best of him. His acceptance into law school, Taylor's second dream, finally started to bring him through it. He was headed to Albany Law of course, but as the spring of his final year in college was approaching, he debated whether he wanted to play at all during his last season.

"You're still good, Taylor," his girlfriend cheerfully prodded. "And the game isn't just for the pros. It's for anyone who loves to play," she added as she began clearing the dinner table at her family's home.

"Oh, c'mon, Paula." Taylor sulked, pushing the last of his food around his plate.

Though it was visible on his face only when the subject came up, inside the struggle was always real for Taylor. Nor was Paula aware that, even after his tryouts were canceled, her boyfriend had continued to secretly train in the gym during the late hours—lifting, stretching, and hoping against hope that by some miracle the tendons in his shoulder would recover enough to deliver the power his arm once had. But that moment didn't come, and Taylor had only just started to accept that it never would.

Sitting at the Definiunē table while down for winter break, Taylor wished the entire subject of him and baseball would never come up again.

"Your shoulder's better, and you can still hold your own, Taylor. And you're also a really good hitter," Paula reminded him, rubbing his shoulders from behind and making eye contact with her father, who was still sitting at the table.

"That's a decision that belongs to Taylor," Joe D. affirmed, giving his daughter a look that he wouldn't be recruited to support her on this.

Taylor always appreciated how her dad never imposed himself and was always willing to be as much of a father as Taylor would let him be.

"What about your coach? Your friends?" Paula snipped at them as she strode into the kitchen with another stack of dishes before either could answer.

Taylor did manage, however, to mimic her serving the men at the table and how her friends at school would have died if they'd seen it. She turned her head to ignore him.

Later on when just Taylor and Joe D. were sitting in the living room, the patriarch took a moment to privately offer some advice.

"You're a hardworking young man, Taylor," he said, proudly looking at him.

"Thanks, Mr. Definiunē," Taylor dutifully responded.

Joe continued to gaze at Taylor like he was looking right through him. *I guess this is where his daughter gets it from*, Taylor thought, feeling a little uncomfortable. He'd also been around the Definiunē family long enough to know that Joe D. wasn't finished talking, and until he was, silence was golden.

"You're not always going to be the best at everything, Taylor,"

Joe said with an understanding look in his eye. "But that's not what's important. What's important is that you be *your* best," he offered with the confidence of a dad who was genuinely standing behind him, and him alone, in this situation.

It felt good. And Taylor knew that Mr. D. had his best interests in mind.

He was telling him that other things, probably having to do with character, were important here.

He was telling him he should play.

Chapter 34

"Taylor, no!" a startled Paula shrieked, stopping to look at him full on.

"What?" Taylor answered. He was confused and looking a little hurt.

The two remained stiffly silent as they stood alone, now facing each other on the boardwalk.

"What do ya think?" he eked out, hoping she'd say something.

"Stop!" she demanded again, shaking her head in disbelief before burying it in his chest.

She struggled with what else to say. So did he.

He knew she loved him, and he certainly loved her. *It would just make sense*, he thought as he wondered why everything had become so awkward.

Far from the hopeless romantic she had imagined as a little girl, the one she loved was "hopelessly unromantic," if anything, and probably one of the most practical people on the face of the earth. Up until that moment, Paula was okay with that, knowing that from a relationship standpoint, flowers, enchantment, or even melodrama were never exactly her boyfriend's strong suit. However, this current stunt took the cake, even for Taylor.

She pushed back to look at him again. "What do I think? Is that what you're asking me?" she charged in disbelief.

Taylor just stood there, blankly looking back as the pupils of her eyes narrowed and pierced into his, searching to find something that wasn't there. He knew enough not to answer her immediate question though. She was about to answer it for him anyway.

"What I think is, that's not how you ask me to marry you, Taylor," she scolded, thankfully with a tone showing that she still loved him. "You don't just say, 'What do you think about getting engaged?' and put it out there like it's an idea," she cried, now waving her arms at him.

Taylor could accept that, he calmly thought, especially since it wasn't a no. He tried to make amends. "Paula, I—"

"Stop," she said, putting her hand out. "Getting engaged is supposed to be a special occasion, Taylor. For both of us," she added, becoming annoyed again the more she talked about it. "You have a ring. We're dressed up someplace. Hopefully at a—"

"I was going to get a ring, Pau—" Taylor injected before she cut him off again.

"No, Taylor. You *have* a ring! You're dressed up. And it's a surprise," she said, becoming animated again. "Though now the surprise will obviously never happen," she muttered in frustration. "It's a moment girls dream about, Taylor."

He felt bad but quite honestly was inspired by the challenge. He would make this up to her, and he would hit all three. "Okay," he conceded, though confident he would prove himself. "It's a suit, a ring, and a surprise. Is that it, Miss Definiunẽ?" he added with an eager smirk.

"I'll be happy with the first two, Taylor," she sighed, hooking her arm in his as they finished their walk, squarely at the Jamaica doorstep of her great-grandparents, Edguard and Marie Definiunẽ.

CHAPTER 35

TAYLOR ENJOYED SEEING "POPPY" DEFINIUNẽ MORE THAN MOST OF the patriarchs' own relatives probably did, and he could sit and listen to him for hours. The old soldier patiently answered pretty much all Taylor's questions as he told his stories about the war, the hard times in Europe, and even the world as he saw it now.

Gleaning from a man who had lived through more life than most would ever know endlessly fascinated Taylor. Paula, on the other hand, had heard the stories before and quite frankly wasn't half as interested in the past as her inquisitive boyfriend was. Raising her eyes when she saw the process starting, she often went into the kitchen with Mimi and had coffee.

To Taylor, Edguard Definiunẽ was a man loaded with first-hand history, and if asked, he could tell it in such a way that you felt like you were right there. He was also the man whose love and French last name rested atop Paula's now-huge Italian family and who Taylor insisted was the only reason she was allowed to date someone outside the tribe.

"It's thanks to Poppy that I'm around!" he joked.

Paula vehemently denied this, though her blush amid his teasing let on that it may have been a little true.

"Taylor, enough," she snapped, pinching his side as they strolled down the Coney Island boardwalk after the visit.

He chuckled again, bringing her in close. "I'm gonna play," he said after a pause, almost as a concession.

"That's good," she answered, squeezing him.

CHAPTER 36

TAYLOR'S LAST SEASON FOR THE PURPLE AND GOLD WAS WELL WORTH the memories. Though the speed on his ball was limited and he couldn't get the movement he used to, he still won more games than he lost. He also got to play other positions when he wasn't pitching, something Coach Gorton had never permitted before to protect his arm.

When Charlie sprained his thumb and had to sit out for two weeks, Taylor even got to catch again like he used to in high school. His pop time was still under two seconds, and he obviously had the arm to pick people off just as well as their starter could, so he got the job. It filled the temporary gap nicely and made for another solid contribution to the team from their former ace.

All in all, it was a positive end to a shortened baseball career. And though there were times when Taylor grieved while watching young pitchers in the pros, he was gearing himself up for law school now and actually looked forward to it.

Spring also ushered in some sad news for Paula's family. Edguard had died. An active and robust workaholic for most of his life, Poppy befit his generation well, having been forced into retirement by his sons when he was well into his eighties. A year or two later, he started to experience some technical difficulties that slowed him down significantly, so the news, though upsetting, was really not a surprise.

Taylor, however, took it harder than he thought. He couldn't imagine not seeing that man again and felt like a living part of history was now gone forever.

As he sat quietly in the funeral parlor, gazing at the pictures frame by frame, he remembered in detail what their humble granddad had described every time he and Paula visited. Dating all the way back to Italy and even the war; Taylor knew the stories behind each one of them.

"And there we were," the elder Definiunẽ would say after telling the tale of any given photo. In the first familiar frame, Taylor viewed the small group of French soldiers, barely beyond their teens, who somehow found a way to dig themselves out of the bloodiest conflict of the century. The next picture was taken at a train station after the smiling twenty-one-year-old entered La Spezia for the first time. That was the one with the old Italian conductor, whom Edguard had always remembered dearly but never knew the name of.

"Gorgeous green country under a pastel-blue sky—La Spezia only three hours away." His eyes twinkled as he started that story, holding up his three fingers the way the conductor did.

Taylor had him tell it probably ten times since he'd known him. Paula probably heard it ten times more than that, insisting she was sick of it. She knew it by heart though, and Taylor pridefully did too.

Another print was an aged black and white of two formally dressed young adults sitting together in a classically decorated parlor. The photo next to it told more of the story of the same two people, previously lost and damaged by the world's chaos, who now found themselves in a small coastal fish market, secretly glimpsing toward the hope of future happiness.

The war stories were Taylor's favorites, though the picture of the small family landing on the streets of Jamaica with literally no place to go but up was a close second.

"So there we were," Edguard would say again after describing another leg of their journey. As long as they had each other, they'd be okay, was what he really meant.

None of the stories, however, compared to the look the tired, old sage gave Taylor at the end of each tale. Both men had grown up fatherless, and though nothing was ever said, it seemed that the warmth in Edguard's gaze all by itself had a way of telling his young listener that he understood and that it was all okay.

"You want some cawfee, T?" Anthony said, pulling him out of his daydream.

"T" was Anthony's short for Taylor, and it pretty much stuck for everybody south of the Tappenzee Bridge, except of course for Paula and her parents.

"No, I'm good, Ant," Taylor replied, politely waving it off.

They both glanced across the room at Paula, who stood out in front, receiving people as they entered to pay their respects. Though Taylor had been next to her for the last hour or so, getting endless kisses on the cheek from both women and men, he needed to sit down for a little bit.

"Madonna's been at it all morning," Anthony quipped, referring to his older sister.

Paula couldn't stand the pop singer nickname he'd given her, which only encouraged him more. Being the princess of the family, coupled with a flawless trip through the teenage years, often made life difficult for her younger brother, who had an overly stubborn mind of his own. She probably told him to do something Taylor figured, which always irritated the seventeen-year-old.

"Ant, c'mere." Taylor motioned, bringing him close to whisper something in his ear. Bending over, Anthony's eyes widened. "Talk to Joe D.?" he asked under his breath.

Taylor casually nodded as Anthony walked away, reaching in his pocket and pulling out some change.

Taylor slumped back on the couch and wondered whether he should have taken that coffee. He was tired from the drive down but thankfully didn't have to get back to school until Monday to make the game on Tuesday. He still couldn't believe it was his last season of organized ball, but he was trying not to think about that as much as he could. Law school was coming too. He had living arrangements and loans to deal with, and on top of that, he recognized that the classes there weren't going to be a walk in the park either.

Yes, Taylor Green had a lot in front of him, though it all seemed to dissipate when his eyes drifted back to Paula across the way and quietly rested on her. Adorned in a tastefully fitting navy-blue dress with matching pumps and eye-catching though stunningly simple jewelry, she wasn't the cute, gum-chewing coed bouncing a loaded backpack across a college campus anymore. What he saw now was the classically elegant young woman she'd probably always been.

Maybe she's both, he thought, remaining captivated by her profile as she so naturally welcomed each guest from what seemed like a never-ending line. By now the number of people had filled both the main room and two overflows, but Paula's love for her family took it's time, exuding in each embrace and in the careful handling of her great-grandmother, Mimi; her grandma, Lillian; and everyone on down. Though she was only twenty, Paula somehow was the one in control, ensuring that everything went smoothly, while the rest of the family either grieved or frustratingly chased the dozens of toddlers and little kids running around the funeral parlor.

That's the way it was in the Definiuñe clan—family breaking out and running "every which way," as the great-granddad would smile and say every time he watched the chaos occur during holidays. A radical expression of dozens of different and unique personalities making up the beautiful fabric of who they were was undoubtedly just the way the once-alone and orphaned Edguard would have wanted it, Taylor reflected as he began to quietly choke up.

CHAPTER 37

"A LOTTA DEAD PEOPLE IN THIS WORLD," THIRTEEN-YEAR-OLD Nicholas said.

My little brother has never been to a funeral before, Paula thought, *at least not one he is old enough to understand.* The family had just exited the limousine and started to walk to the burial site. Watching Nicky curiously scan the peculiar landscape revealed that he'd never seen so many headstones in one place either.

She put her arm around him and gently squeezed. Though the youngest, the oversized adolescent was only a few inches behind Anthony and already significantly taller than she was. He'd inherited their father's husky build, and Mom was doing all she could to keep up with his clumsy and unpredictable growth spurts, sometimes having to squeeze him into suits that were less than four months old. Such was the case that day, and Paula could see it was frustrating both of them.

"Button your jacket, Nicholas."

"I can't, M—"

"Nick?" Dad interjected, raising his eyebrows.

The boy complied.

It was going to be a long wait given the Queens traffic and the size of the crowd coming from the church, where the attendance was even higher than at the wake. The senior Definiunē had been blessed with a very large family in a special kind of way, which made it all the richer and more popular when he was finally put to rest that Sunday afternoon.

Following the graveside service and a fairly solemn limo return to the church, Paula got into her boyfriend's well-used Datsun pickup, a vehicle he'd had since his freshman year and was barely able to keep alive. She was exhausted and wanted to ride home with just him.

"I'm done. How about you?" she said, kicking off her pumps to let her toes breathe. Taylor just nodded.

She gently slid over on the bench seat and rested her head on his shoulder as he pulled out behind her dad and, after traversing a few short streets, merged onto the expressway. From there he adjusted his speed and settled into the relaxed flow of, lighter than normal, weekend traffic. Both were quiet and gazing ahead while the next few moments drifted by.

"What was your father like, Taylor?" Paula asked after a pause, slipping her arm under his.

"You already know what he was like, Paula Marie," Taylor answered, addressing her formally the way he did when she asked questions like that.

"Not from you," she probed.

The remark was followed by a tense silence.

"I have nothing to add, Paula. I was twelve when he left. You already know that," he said.

"Do you ever think about him?"

"Paula," Taylor protested, "one of the greatest guys in the world just died, and you want to talk about *my* father? Really? I mean, those two names don't belong in the same sentence."

"Yeah, they do," she calmly replied, picking up her head and looking at him.

"Why?" Taylor challenged, continuing to look at the cars ahead of him.

It was obvious that he was avoiding eye contact.

"Because he was *your* father," she blurted.

"You have no idea, Paula. And that's a good thing," he answered.

"Then why don't you tell me?"

"Because there's nothing to tell, Paula!" Taylor said, voice rising again.

"Yes, there is," she insisted.

She wasn't backing down. Though this wasn't the first go-round they had had about his father, her timing took Taylor off guard, leaving him a little confused but now angrier.

"All right, here it is!" He bristled. "He was no good, Paula. You already know that, and—" Taylor paused and purposely diverted his attention back to the road again.

"And what, Taylor?" she gently prodded, unconcerned that he was mad.

"And there's really nothing else to say."

She continued to look at him, wanting more. "What *do* you remember about him, Taylor?" she finally said.

"Are you kidding, Paula?"

"You've never told me," she pleaded.

"I just did!" Taylor said, shaking his head dismissively.

Whether he realized it or not, Taylor Green's whole life had been an argument against his father's leaving him, a running from the tombstone he'd let get planted deep within his soul that had the word *unworthy* chiseled on it. Common though it was to kids without fathers, this perspective resulted in an insecurity that often twisted and hid itself in either denial or anger if that's what was necessary to stave off those who sought to uncover the pain and challenge that inscription. This included the people who loved him most.

Of course, Paula hit that nerve every time she went there, and she grew more and more frustrated with her boyfriend's closing her out of a past she knew was still hurting him. In fact, his refusal to talk about it only fueled her suspicion that there was a woundedness there that she undoubtedly had to try to fix.

Taylor obviously would never admit to being that fragile ever. It wasn't in his nature, and regardless of how well intentioned his girlfriend was, her snooping into a childhood he wholeheartedly wanted to forget was absolutely pointless in his book. Quite frankly, he was baffled by why she did this, and she needed to back off and let it go.

But that plainly wasn't Paula's nature. And though she rested her head back against his shoulder, she unfortunately wasn't calling it quits. "It wasn't your fault, you know," she quietly let out, stunning the atmosphere again.

"Paula, please," Taylor replied, rolling his eyes while still looking ahead.

Though it was his best attempt to make her feel ridiculous, she wasn't buying it at all.

"You deserved a good father," she softly added, tiredly snuggling into his shoulder.

Taylor stiffened again. He never understood why she would say things like that or why it made him so mad when she did.

"I love you, Paula Definiunê," he answered, trying to make peace but signaling that he was done for the day.

She gently squeezed his bicep a time or two as if to say without words that though the issue was over for today, it wasn't really over. Taylor subtly shook his head again in disbelief.

Maybe it's a woman thing, he thought to himself as he followed her father's car off the exit toward home.

CHAPTER 38

But for Joe D's Plymouth, the driveway was finally empty after two and a half days of a house packed with family and well-wishers. It was now just the six of them dribbling in, collapsing on any available couch or stuffed chair. Dot was insisting everybody eat, while Joe kicked back and reminisced with Anthony and Taylor about Poppy. All three were far too exhausted to play basketball outside with Nicholas, who persistently beckoned them through the kitchen screen door. His dad had widened the driveway enough to provide for a comfortable game of two on two, which was what the preteen was bugging everybody about. Taylor was usually the first to give in and play, but even he was too tired that afternoon.

"Nicky, I can't, man. I'm beat," he said.

"Knock it off, Nick. We're not playing!" Anthony chimed in.

Joe D. didn't respond but continued to fondly recount some of the memories he had as a kid working at his grandpa's fish market. He wasn't crying anymore, Taylor noticed. He'd already done plenty of that during the last day or two into his drenched and well-wrinkled hanky. Taylor couldn't cry like that, though he didn't know why. He felt just as bad about the loss, however. That was for sure.

Striding through in her sweats, Paula headed to the laundry room to hunt for the warm-up jacket she usually wore when she went jogging. "Will you be here when I get back?" She smiled at Taylor, love-tapping him on the head as a reconciliation for the tiff they'd had in the car.

"Probably. It's not till six thirty," he answered, returning a slight grin.

"What is it again?" she asked.

"Dinner with that recruit and his father. Remember I told you about—"

"Oh, yeah, yeah," she replied from the other room. "That's in Uniondale, right?"

"Yeah," Taylor confirmed.

"You better leave yourself enough time. Uniondale's in Nassau, you know," she said while pushing through the back screen door to start her run.

CHAPTER 39

"TAYLOR, YOU HAVE TO GO!" PAULA BELLOWED FROM THE DINING room. She had just gotten back and was sitting in her mother's chair at the end of the table. It was almost six, and he was definitely going to be late, a fact that annoyed her to no end.

Though busily setting the table, Dot gave her a frown, probably over her appearance and the way she was talking to Taylor. *She's old school*, Paula reminded herself, raising her eyes. Her mom was also not a fan of Paula's remaining in her sweats and leaving the aroma of her workout and kicked-off sneakers ruminating in the place they were all about to have dinner.

"Paula!" she reprimanded, darting her eyes to where her daughter had her foot tucked up and perched on the seat of the chair. Her sock was halfway off while she was scratching the top of it. Dot's glare continued to scold a distracted Paula, who didn't budge but remained steadily barking to Taylor that he had to leave. She wasn't as much concerned with his being on time for the meeting as with his being back as early as possible.

Her mom headed into the kitchen, impatiently stepping over one of Paula's loose sneakers, which had flopped on its side and sat in the middle of the pathway.

"All right, I'm goin', I'm goin'," Taylor said, his feet clapping down the stairs. He was still fixing his tie.

"You look handsome," she said as he strode over to give her a quick kiss. "How long you think you'll be?"

"As long as it takes to convince the kid and his dad to play for Albany," he answered, turning to the front door.

"If he does, Gorton says he'll pay for my trip." Taylor smirked, glancing back with a wink.

"You will." Paula smiled.

After a moment or two, she could hear his truck start up and leave the driveway.

"You need help, Mom?" she called into the kitchen.

"No," Dot responded without coming out.

A few minutes later, Paula heard steps on the front porch and saw the door opening. It was Taylor again. "What'd you forget?" she asked.

He didn't respond at first.

"You want to know what I forgot, Paula Definiune?" he said, now standing in his suit and tie in front of her as she was still itching the top of her sweaty foot.

Paula had no idea what he was talking about, but she wasn't really paying attention either, expecting him to start looking for his wallet or something before heading out again. He didn't though and just remained standing there.

The room suddenly seemed strangely quiet, especially for dinnertime. She looked up and noticed she couldn't see or hear any of her family members; there was no basketball bouncing outside, no rap music upstairs, no mom yelling for people to come down, and no dad sitting at the head of the table, waiting to eat. Only Taylor stood in front of her, reaching into his jacket pocket. Paula's eyes widened.

"Taylor, no!" she screamed, self-consciously looking about herself as if seeing for the first time that she had no makeup on and was actually wearing sweats, while her boyfriend was proposing to her.

"Yes, Paula." He smirked before glancing slightly over her head as if something was behind her.

She turned and saw her dad, mom, and two brothers silently standing behind her chair. Her mother was crying.

Paula turned her head back around in utter shock, only to see Taylor, now on one knee with a small box in his hand.

"Taylor, look at me," she protested, referring to her attire again and almost pleading for him to stop, at least for now.

However, her resistance was weakening by the second the more she received his welcoming gaze.

"I *am* looking at you, Paula." He smiled, though his eyes were now welling while he knelt before her, uncomfortably still.

She had never seen him so vulnerable before, so raw, which only increased the flow that had already begun to stream down her face. The room became solemnly quiet as Taylor put his other hand on top of hers.

"Paula Marie, you're the most beautiful woman in the whole world. And I love you with everything in me," he said. He lifted up the box with his other hand and looked at it. "When I was home a couple of weeks ago, I told my mom what I wanted to do. She was very happy, of course," he said, looking up at Paula's parents.

"And then she went into her bedroom, and after a few minutes she came out with the ring I'm about to present to you, Paula. It's the engagement ring that belonged to my grandmother," Taylor said, now holding it up for her to see. "I'd never seen it before, but my mom was keeping it for that special person I would marry—if I wanted it, she said."

Taylor's voice was now cracking as he began filling up with tears himself.

Though Paula remained respectfully silent for him, she couldn't wait to say yes and found herself feeling both shocked and crying a river at the same time. She turned around briefly to catch a glimpse of her family and noticed that her parents were weeping as well. Her mom, of course, was an intensely relational woman who, no matter how hard she tried, had never been able to get even an ounce of emotion out of Taylor since she met him. She was also extremely sentimental, so Paula could only imagine how the ring, coupled with Taylor's rare display of heartfelt intimacy, was melting her. As for her dad, honor was big to him, and the history behind what his future son-in-law was presenting to his daughter was obviously breaking him up too.

Taylor looked up from the ring and into Paula's eyes, gently squeezing her hand for a second or two. He wasn't able to talk.

"I'm gonna do this." He smiled, wiping his cheeks with his suit-jacketed forearm.

He brought the diamond close for both of them to look at. "The band part is what I bought, because it's gold and because that's what you are, Paula. And I wanted that to be from me," he said. "But the diamond was my grandma's," he said, showing it to her as she looked even closer. "It's pretty beautiful, but if you look real closely, you'll see a little black dot in it, which makes it imperfect.

"Now, you have an awesome family, Paula," Taylor said, softly smiling as he glanced up at them again. "And I can't offer you much more in that area. But when my mom showed me this diamond, I saw for the first time that it was a lot like my little family—not perfect but pretty beautiful. And I wanted you, Paula, hopefully my future wife, to wear it," he stammered.

Without a thought, Paula's chin began gyrating a yes, though an emotional Taylor was at the same time trying to calmly signal that he wasn't finished yet. He quietly took her hand in his and held the ring with the other before starting the words he obviously had practiced and desperately wanted to get out right.

"Paula Definiunē, I don't want to live a single day without you. I want to love you, protect you, and take care of you for the rest of my life. And I can't wait for the time when I can wake up every single morning with you. Paula, would you make me the happiest man in the world and be my wife forever?"

Dot was now sobbing uncontrollably, and her daughter had pretty much lost it too.

Unable to speak but bobbing her head, she finally was able to get the words out. "Yes! Yes! Yes!" she kept repeating before grabbing her new fiancé's head and planting an extra-long kiss.

It had been no secret that Taylor wanted to marry her, but hearing him talk like that completely caught Paula off guard and made her barely able to contain her affections.

He pulled her up with him as they embraced, which after a minute or so turned into a group hug that even her brothers became immersed in.

"Dude" was all Anthony could say, grasping Taylor's neck. "Nice job!"

Nicky's bone-crunching squeeze made Taylor feel like he had just become a big brother again. Following that, Dot did the same, taking the longest time letting her future son-in-law go.

Constantly looking back and forth at her ring, Paula darted toward the stairs. "Taylor, we have to call your mom ... I have to change ... I have to take a shower," she said, starting to stress.

"A lotta people coming in fifteen minutes, Paul." Anthony laughed, adding to her panic.

"Paula, it's okay," Taylor said, looking over at her. "You look beautiful."

Though she disagreed, she could tell he meant it as she charged back over to give him an extended kiss that almost suffocated him. "No, I don't!" she exclaimed, pushing off toward the staircase again.

"Hey, Paula." He smirked. "What do you think?"

"What?" she smiled back, though a little confused.

"C'mon, Paula," he teased again. "A ring, a suit, and a surprise." He couldn't help gloating. "I did it, didn't I?" He grinned.

"You did!" she said, taking another trip down the stairs to kiss him again. She finally departed upstairs for the last time.

Turning around, Taylor saw big Joe D. standing before him, alone. Her dad had patiently awaited his turn to congratulate his son-in-law to be. His soft smile and nod of approval blanketed the moment between them before he brought the lanky pitcher into his grizzly bear chest and squeezed. Though the customary peck on the cheek was something Taylor had long gotten used to, the hug told him Joe D. wasn't giving away his princess as much as adopting a new son.

Paula was indeed special to her father, a feeling Taylor experienced years later on the day Sharon was born. Proudly lifting his little baby up and caressing her into his chest, he would be the greatest father there could ever be, he swore to himself. Joe D. was just that to his daughter. Taylor, on the other hand, was—

"Is Dad still up?" came a voice from the living room.

Jarred by the sound of Nathan's oncoming footsteps scampering toward the kitchen, Taylor abruptly wheeled backward down the dark hallway and into his bedroom without being seen.

CHAPTER 40

"BE BACK IN A LITTLE BIT," PAULA CHIRPED, OPENING THE FRONT door on her way out.

Taylor was sitting in his wheelchair in the middle of the driveway, waiting.

It was warmer than usual as she jogged out to begin their Saturday morning walk, one of the few things she insisted on doing together that he'd actually agreed to. People were generally not out and about that early on a weekend if they started the walk soon enough, which was why he was irritated.

They both had their spring jackets on as they headed to the little park situated on the water down at the end of their block. Taylor pushed hard on the wheels to get exercise while Paula more or less speed-walked to keep up. Once they reached the end, away from all the houses, Taylor slowed down to a coast and eventually rolled to a stop. He kept his glance toward the bay and motioned for Paula to push him from behind. This was a bit awkward for her, given that Taylor had had the rear handles of the chair taken off as soon as they got it. He didn't want people pushing him. In fact, before that moment, her husband had never allowed anyone to do that.

She gingerly placed her hands on the posts of the chair back and slowly propelled him forward. Quietly amazed that he was letting her, she didn't want him to change his mind and was glad there was no eye contact while they rolled into the park and meandered along the tranquil walkways that overlooked the bay.

They were the only ones at the beach that morning, and as always, Paula was upbeat. Taylor, on the other hand, seemed more reserved than usual. After a moment or two, he broke his silence.

"Tim all set for the big night?" he asked.

"Yeah. He's so excited," she answered. "He's picking up Alex's corsage this afternoon."

"He's got two left feet, you know," Taylor said, admitting he was aware of the activity the night before.

"Oh, you saw?" Paula laughed, though appearing slightly embarrassed.

"I heard." He chuckled back. "Doubt any of those kids will know how to dance tonight," he added. "We sure did though, didn't we, Paula?"

"Yes, we did, Taylor," Paula answered.

Her voice sounded a little concerned about where this talk was going, though she continued to push him leisurely along the walkway paralleling the water. They both remained quiet and reflective, looking out on a calm and peaceful bay as the warm wind blew through their hair.

"Taylor?" Paula said, gently reaching out to take his hand to connect with him.

He didn't say anything at first, but after a brief pause, he responded. "Paula, I haven't heard you laugh like that for over a year," he said, still looking out at the water. "Smile like that either," he added with a sigh.

"Yes, you have, Taylor," she softly answered, combing her fingers through his hair.

"No, I haven't, Paula," Taylor retorted, knowing it was his fault. "And why should you?" He motioned with his arms. "Look at me. I'm miserable." He turned and gave a look as if to scold her for not being honest about how painful he was to be around.

"I'm not getting out of this wheelchair, Paula," he added coldly, turning back to the bay again. "And things will never be the same. Not for me. Not for you. Not for anybody."

"Taylor?" she said. He wasn't having any comfort though.

"Let's be honest, Paula. This is not the life we had, and it's definitely not the life we planned. I know I certainly didn't sign up for this. And neither did you," he murmured under his breath, hoping the implication would slide by.

No such luck though. He felt Paula's hands tighten on the back posts of his chair. "What are you saying, Taylor?" she challenged.

"Just tryin' to be honest, Paula." He sighed matter-of-factly.

She gave his chair a firm push. They were obviously heading to the park's exit.

Though he could sense the mercury rising in her, he tried to finish his point as diplomatically as possible.

"Paula, listen, I know it's against your beliefs, but sometimes I wonder whether staying with me would be any good for you in the long—"

The wheelchair suddenly took a violent swing in the opposite direction, and he met a furious Paula face-to-face. Her tightened brow and flaming pupils were fiercely resolute as she crouched down even closer, now eye to eye with him.

He shut his eyes momentarily to avoid the fervent glare. It definitely wasn't meant to go this way, and he was now at a complete loss as to how to handle a side of Paula he'd seen only once or twice in his life but obviously had forgotten how bad it was to be on the other end of. He calmly held up his hands to try to dial things down. "Listen—"

"No. I've heard enough!" she sternly interrupted. "Now *you* listen. I'm here because I love you," she said, voice sizzling.

He could tell she was still utterly insulted by his insinuations and about to upbraid him again. "I know that, Paula, but we have to—"

"We have to what, Taylor? Face reality?" she snapped, cutting him off again. "Really, Taylor? Is that what we have to do?" she further chided.

She continued to stare into his face as he sat there, frustrated, deflated, and uncharacteristically at a loss for words. Though her husband was indeed breaking new ground in feeling sorry for himself, deep down Paula was rattled. She knew from the beginning what he'd been doing on the deck but hoped that over time, and in his time, he'd accept the handicap and be able to move on. Things hadn't worked out that way though. In fact, the person she was hearing was a different Taylor; one that was no longer 'finding the way to win'. Paula had never seen him give up before, and the prospect of that happening was always what she had feared the most.

"No, Taylor," she pounded again. "That's your reality, not mine. I'm not letting you give up," she said, standing back up.

"You're not the one anchored to this chair, Paula," Taylor quietly answered.

"I know I'm not, Taylor." Paula sighed. Realizing she may have gone a little too far, she took a step back to sit on the park bench a foot or two away and turned her head to look out at the water. After a moment or two, she turned back to him. "None of us have had to go through what you have, Taylor. And I honestly can't imagine what it's like for this to happen to a man like you," she said as her eyes began to fill up. "I can't," she compassionately said again.

"And I can't change what happened, no matter what I do or how much I pray," she added, glancing back at the bay to try to contain her emotions. "Believe me, I've tried."

After a moment passed, she quietly turned back to him while reaching into her pocket for a tissue to catch the tears now rolling down her cheeks. "But I can be in the pain with you … if you let me," she said. "And we can get through it, Taylor … we can."

Taylor slumped back in his chair and gazed out at the water, struggling with what he knew his wife needed and the looming reality that he may not have that kind of spirit in him anymore.

"Sometimes I don't know if I can, Paula." He sighed. "I'm sorry," he added after another pause. "I don't know if a person like you would have any idea—"

"Yeah, I would, Taylor," she said, causing him to look over at her.

"Well, that was thanks to me too." He sighed again.

"No, it wasn't thanks to you, Taylor," she answered, slowly shaking her head in disagreement. "When I crashed, it was thanks to me."

"Paula, that was me. It wasn't you, it was me," Taylor repeated a little more indignantly. "And you didn't crash!" He angrily recoiled as an afterthought in her defense.

The memory of his affair still twisted Taylor's insides, and Paula's having to go there mortified him even more.

"I know that, Taylor," she said. "But I got pretty lost. You know that. And I bounced between hating you for hurting me and wondering why I wasn't the woman my mother was, whose husband had been faithful to her for over forty years. 'Where did I go wrong for this to happen?' I would say to myself."

"No, Paula," Taylor said.

"I know, Taylor," she assured him. "But the reality I had to face was that things were missing, even before you left me."

"There was nothing wrong with you, Paula. I would have hated my guts too," Taylor insisted.

"Well, I don't hate your guts, Taylor," she said, moving over and kneeling in front of him to be eye to eye again. "I forgave you a long time ago, and you know that."

"I do," he conceded sympathetically.

"And the truth is, only God could help me do that," she said. "But I don't think it could have happened if I stayed a victim," Paula added after a pause.

"So, you think I'm a victim?" He sighed.

"No, I'm not saying that," she replied, sitting on the bench again and looking out at the water. "Taylor, when you and I met and got married, I lived in a bubble. I really did," she offered candidly. "And I think you kind of did too.

"We both thought we would make each other happy and that we didn't need anything more than that. I loved you, you loved me, and together things would always be good. Then life happened," she added with a knowing smirk at Taylor. "And we found out that that wasn't always gonna be the case.

"And when it all came apart, I came apart. And after the trauma, I realized I couldn't go back to the bubble of thinking life was so simple or that I could control everything. Nor could I continue to believe that I was okay without anybody's help, including God's. Because none of that was true anymore, Taylor, not for me. I needed something else deep in my life to help me make sense of why I was living in the first place. So I went on a search, a real soul search. I was that desperate, Taylor," she said after a pause.

"I couldn't put myself back together, and honestly I didn't want to because I knew that even if I did, there would be something still missing. I know that sounds like a recipe for depression," she said, softly smiling, "but it was actually the turning point of my life when I realized I needed something beyond what anybody, including myself, could give and that only God could help me and that that must have been the reason why Jesus came into the world in the first place.

"It wasn't just about going to heaven, Taylor," she said. "It was really about forgiveness for my, Paula Green's, sin, and about finally getting away from self-centered me to knowing a love-centered God, which I think deep down was a relief for both of us," she said, offering a slight, knowing smile.

"Jesus's life was really about God's love for me and how the Holy Spirit, God's life, could actually come and live inside of me," she added, now looking at him. "But it was from that broken place that I saw he wasn't just a man who died on a cross but God's living Son taking what was in me, putting it in himself, and dying with it so I wouldn't have to. And then God rose him again without it so I could live without it too.

"You see, from that day, sin couldn't separate people from God anymore, Taylor. And the more I learned about who Jesus was and God's love for you and me and everyone else, the more I wanted that in my life.

"I can't say that what happened with us caused me to believe in God or become crazy, as you used to say." She smiled again. "But it did cause me to take an honest look at a lot of issues I should have been looking at way before. And probably the toughest part of that was admitting that there were things in my life and in my heart that needed forgiveness. It didn't matter that other people may have been worse than me or whether I was a pretty good person or even a pretty good Catholic."

"Paula, you *are* a good person," Taylor argued, shaking his head in disbelief. "What did you ever do? Nothing. How in the world could any of this be fair? Honestly. You've got to give me that one."

"Taylor, if you want to think that way, fine, but does it bother you to think that I had sin in my life too?" she shot back. "Even great people need a savior, Taylor. That's what that whole stone-throwing thing was about.

"And as for me, I had to stop pretending that because I was a good person, relatively speaking, I didn't need to be forgiven by God or that there wasn't an emptiness deep inside. Something had to change in my life, Taylor, and I realized that was it."

After a moment or two went by, Paula started to stand up. "And you know what one of the awesome things about forgiveness is, Taylor?" she said, now with a soft smile.

"What?" he said, mockingly raising his eyes.

"It heals our past, regardless of what happened to us," she replied, ignoring his sarcasm. "It's like my finger here," she added, putting her hand in his and pointing to the scar near the tip of it. "You remember that when I was a little girl, one of my friends accidentally closed the car door on it. The cut was deep. The pain was unreal, and I had to go to the hospital, where it was cleaned and stitched.

"It was an absolute horror show for a seven-year-old, and it took a long time before I could move it again. But look, Taylor," Paula said, pressing and pushing against the scar. "It's there and part of my past, but it doesn't hurt me anymore." she added, still moving her skin around.

"I can see what happened … between you and me. But like my finger, even the most difficult parts of my past are not open wounds anymore. I forgave, and God healed me," she said. "It wasn't easy, but with God's help I could actually do it. Don't you want that, Taylor Green?" she asked as she began pushing his chair forward.

He didn't answer. She wasn't expecting him to.

As they proceeded down the winding walkway out of the park, Taylor was at a loss for words. Finally he spoke. "So I don't have to wear the scarlet letter anymore?" he said, safely looking ahead.

"What?" Paula asked.

"English class, Professor Patterson," he said, trying to jar her memory.

"Oh!" She laughed. "You mean, when the cutest guy made me look like the dumbest girl on campus?"

"Oh, I came crawling to you, Paula. You know that."

They both were silent for a moment or two.

Though Taylor wasn't looking for another sermon, he awaited her response.

"Maybe the *A* means 'able,'" she said.

"What?" he answered.

"Able," she said again. "Maybe she was 'able' to let God forgive her, even though nobody else would. Kinda like the woman who was in front of Jesus. And maybe that's why there was so much joy in her life when everybody else was so miserable," Paula added.

"Not bad for a nursing major," Taylor admitted after a pause.

"Maybe it was that simple, smarty," she teased, giving his chair a playful shake.

She'd gotten the best of him again, he realized, as he subtly began to push down on his chair wheels and retake control of the journey home.

CHAPTER 41

"Marge, I don't have all the files," Taylor barked from behind his desk.

"Yes, you do," she affirmed, ignoring the accusation.

Dusk had already settled in the downtown area as the sun set over the streets of Rivermont proper. It was the end of another day.

The last of the attorneys and staffers dribbled out of the converted Victorian law office Taylor had once thrived in. This left only Marge and her old boss, who had come in on Monday evenings after everybody else was gone. Paula had just dropped him off in the parking area behind the building, where a ramp led to his private back-door entrance.

These nights were reserved for client meetings and other tasks that couldn't be done out of Taylor's home. It was also the time he and Marge exchanged files and discussed items necessary to get through the up-and-coming week. Other than some real estate closings and meetings Taylor had to attend, he was rarely in the office during the day. He still hadn't returned to court since his accident but sent an associate, whom he would prepare by telephone beforehand.

Despite his partners' absolute loyalty to Taylor, an increasing client base and the need for him to either come back full-time or have his old position filled were putting a heavy strain on the firm. Taylor stubbornly avoided conversations about this, and his denial of the potential of his being replaced frustrated Marge to no end.

It was enough that her boss had unilaterally reduced his salary and partnership share because he refused to take "handouts." However, his resistance to even try to return to something they both knew he loved was even more painful for his office mom to stand by and idly watch.

Even the Monday nights weren't like the old days. Taylor's zeal was gone, and the obligatory visits he made to the office were just that: necessary to the firm and for the sole purpose of supporting his family. Fun no longer seemed to be in her boss's job description either, and laughter was all but gone as well, no matter how hard Marge tried. Though she'd get a little chuckle out of him once in a while, it was only if her humor was at the top of its game or during one of those rare and isolated moments when the old Taylor bubbled up unawares and seemingly forgot that he was paralyzed. She missed him terribly, hardheadedness and all.

The office doorbell rang unexpectedly. *There are no appointments scheduled*, she thought as she headed toward the front with a quizzical look on her face. Taylor continued to toil through some of the files next to his desk, undisturbed by the muffled discussion taking place in the reception area. Marge would handle it. She always did.

After a few minutes, he was annoyed to hear two sets of footsteps heading down the hallway toward his office. What in the world was his secretary doing? He didn't have time for this. The other voice sounded familiar as the two approached his open door. Marge came through first.

"Taylor, this gentleman says he's a friend of yours," she said, motioning toward the casually dressed, heavyset younger man standing in the doorway.

"How ya doing, Reverend?" Taylor exclaimed, feigning enthusiasm as best he could toward his unexpected visitor, Steve Woods.

Marge looked at Steve and gave a double take, surprised he hadn't introduced himself that way.

"He does that on purpose," he said with a smile back at her. "It's Steve."

"No, he's a real reverend, Marge. Don't let him fool ya." Taylor laughed, having fun keeping his guest on edge.

"Steve Woods. I'm a pastor at the church Paula goes to," he conceded almost apologetically as he extended his hand to Marge.

She raised her eyes and offered a consoling grin, signifying that this was typical Taylor and that he shouldn't be embarrassed.

"I beat him in cards the other night," Steve volleyed back with a grin. "He took it hard, so I just wanted to bring him—"

"Got lucky, my friend!" Taylor interrupted with a smirk, accepting one of the coffees Steve had brought in.

Though losing the game certainly irked him, he couldn't help a slight smile as he reached for a file on the floor next to his desk.

"He's never liked the taste of his own medicine," Marge mumbled under her breath for only Steve's ear as she passed him on the way out.

"I heard that!" Taylor quipped as he unpacked some of the paperwork in front of him. He invited Steve to sit down. "What can I do for you, my friend?" he asked, hoping Steve was there for some kind of business rather than anything personal.

"Nothing. Just dropping by to say hello is all," Steve answered.

"Who told you I was here?" Taylor asked.

"Your wife." Steve chuckled, instigating another quick but candid grin from Taylor. "It was good seeing you last Sunday. I appreciated your coming."

"You won," Taylor answered matter-of-factly, looking again at the file in front of him.

"I did." Steve chuckled. "I'd like to play again."

"I bet you would," Taylor said with a laugh. Sitting back and thinking about the game, he began to relax.

"'The mass of men lead lives of quiet desperation,'" Steve said, noticing Thoreau's *Walden* sitting on one of Taylor's bookshelves and quoting the novel's classic line.

"Nice! English major?" Taylor inquired. He was impressed and a little surprised that a religious man would read such a book.

"No, biology. But I liked the novel." Steve smiled.

"One of my favorites," Taylor remarked.

"Guy went out and lived in the woods. Got away from everybody—" he noted with a pause.

"—but himself, is probably what you're going to say," Taylor added, looking over at Steve and beginning to smirk again.

"I didn't say anything," an embarrassed Steve protested.

"You were thinkin' it though," Taylor playfully charged.

"I was," Steve admitted with a chuckle.

Taylor indeed had him pegged. Steve didn't mind though. There were no pretenses with Taylor Green and something brutally refreshing about his honesty that Steve enjoyed and even found himself attracted to. His eyes moved across the shelf before stopping again. "Who's that?" he asked, pointing to an obviously dated photograph of a young woman.

The picture was well preserved as it sat within a simple but classy silver frame just above eye level. Like everything else in the room, it was dust free and in pristine condition, thanks to Marge.

"That's my sister about twenty years ago," Taylor answered, glancing up at the photo with him. "And that's her and my mom a few years ago," he added, motioning with his eyes to the picture one shelf higher.

"How they doin'?" Steve asked.

"Mom's okay. She's living over in Ridge," Taylor said.

"Retired?"

"Oh no," Taylor replied with a tone denoting that his mother would never agree to that. "She's been waitressing in the same place since I got her to move here." He sighed.

He'd been trying to get his mom to slow down for the last decade or so, but the hard and often stubborn eastern European woman would never accept rest. Figuring she probably feared not knowing what to do with it once she had it, Taylor had eventually given up.

"How 'bout your sister?" Steve continued.

"She's living up in Vermont with her two kids, my niece, and nephew," Taylor said, looking at her in the photograph. "They got divorced a few years ago. She's pretty much doing it on her own."

"What's she do?" Steve asked.

"Works in a medical office," Taylor replied, reaching down to the floor to pick up another file. "I used to be able to help her out a whole lot more than I can now," he murmured to himself while his head was still below the tabletop.

"That's rough," Steve offered sympathetically.

"Whatever," Taylor replied, apparently indifferent to the situation now that he couldn't do as much anymore. "So, you've played cards before?" he asked, changing the subject after resurfacing.

"I did a lot in college. Not so much now," Steve said. "Love to play though." He grinned after a pause.

"No kidding," Taylor grumbled under his breath before looking up at Steve, who was already laughing.

"You thought I was a babe in the woods." Steve chortled.

"And you let me think that!" Taylor joked back.

"I did," Steve acknowledged, still chuckling a little bit.

"Ira caught it, but I didn't until it was too late," Taylor admitted. "So, what turned you?"

"I had a king in the hole, and once the other one dropped to Vinny, I stayed in," Steve said.

"Yeah, I figured that." Taylor sighed.

"And when I got the third four facedown, I went for it," Steve added, still milking the moment.

"And you played me like you were a dumb kid," Taylor said with a sly smile. "And got church too," he added.

"Oh no, Taylor!" Steve laughed. "That was you!"

"Marge! You need to throw him outta here!" Taylor kiddingly yelled to his secretary.

"I think I need to throw *you* out of here," she shouted back, happy her boss was finally having some fun.

"It was the only way to silence him!" Steve bellowed out to her.

"I believe it!" she answered.

"He set me up, Marge!" Taylor yelled again.

"Good!" she yelled back.

"Actually, that's why I came over, Taylor," Steve said on a serious note. "Things got a little hot ... I got a little hot the other night, and I wanted to apologize for that."

"For what?" Taylor protested.

"Well, I—" Steve started.

"It's all good," Taylor quickly assured him.

"I just wanted you to know that I enjoyed the game, and I'd love to play again in the future," Steve said, putting himself out there a little bit. "And as far as church goes, I don't wanna be that guy who—"

"You're not, Steve," Taylor interrupted again. "At least you don't seem that way." He smiled.

"Thanks, Taylor," Steve replied and started to get up, not wanting to overstay.

"So how's the team doin'?" Taylor asked, inviting him to socialize a little more.

Steve seemed easy enough to talk to, and Taylor was curious as to what was going on in a world that used to be such a big part of his life but now felt so distant.

"Not bad," Steve answered, settling back in his seat. "But pretty spotty. Some of the kids can play, but most need a lot of work."

"Make sure the bats aren't too heavy, and recondition the gloves—all of them," Taylor offered.

Steve looked a little puzzled.

"They all come in with new mitts, and glove oil alone doesn't really do it for them," Taylor explained. "You want to know how to break them in?"

"Of course." Steve smiled.

"Okay. Fill a five-gallon construction pail about three-quarters of the way with boiling water. Add one shaker full of salt. Stir it well. Then soak the mitts in it for four to five hours," Taylor instructed. He was focused on describing the process with his hands as he leaned a little closer into their conversation. "After that, you take them out of the water, turn them inside out, and then hang each one individually by a string from a clothesline or something until they sundry completely.

"It takes about a day or so usually. Then you turn them back in and saturate each one well with Vaseline, working it in by hand. Let that dry, and you're done. It'll feel like it's ten years old, and even a baby could flex it open and closed."

"Sounds pretty involved," Steve remarked, looking a little confused.

Taylor could tell the fledgling, new coach was hesitant about messing with the kids' mitts, especially the expensive ones.

"Don't worry about it," Taylor confirmed with an assuring grin, "and your kids will catch."

"So that's your secret." Steve smiled.

"One of 'em." Taylor smirked, fondly remembering it. "It always worked."

"I hear you were pretty good yourself back in the day," Steve said, changing the subject.

His eyes studied Taylor, receptive to as full a story as his host had time to tell.

"Who told you that?" Taylor replied.

"Paula. Your friends." He smiled.

"I guess the older we get, the better we were," Taylor said with a chuckle, downplaying the compliment.

"What did you play?"

"Pitcher. And catcher when I wasn't pitchin.'"

"High eighties?" Steve asked, showing a greater-than-normal understanding of the game, especially for that era.

"Steady eighty-seven. Ninety was the fastest ball I ever threw," Taylor answered as a reward for the baseball savvy.

"Whoa!" Steve noted. "That's impressive."

"It was pretty good," Taylor admitted with a sigh. "I had a shot," he added, reflecting on his past.

Steve remained quiet and appeared comfortable just listening.

"A shot's only a shot though," Taylor added with resign. "I wasn't getting drafted. I could only hope for a tryout, which didn't happen because I tore my rotator cuff right before my last season."

"Wow, that hurts," Steve replied.

"Certainly did at the time," Taylor said stoically. "But that's life."

"Yeah." Steve sighed in agreement.

Changing gears to look over a document to ensure it was in order, Taylor placed it on a short pile and looked up at his guest again. "Steve, let me ask you something," he said earnestly. "Why do you do what you do?"

Though Steve knew Taylor would be closely scrutinizing everything he had to say, he also felt he was being honestly confided in. In fact, he had a sense that the man sitting across the table was exactly whom Jesus was referring to when he talked about the integrity of people who were either cold or hot toward God and that he loved them both.

Taylor was certainly ice cold, but there was a purity about him that Steve found comforting; it was something he could trust.

Honesty is where it all lived for Jesus anyway, Steve thought. Even more so, he felt an interesting shift taking place whereby he was realizing that he needed Taylor's candor just as badly as Taylor needed his. He wished more Christians were like that rather than putting on a show of clichés every time he was around. What bothered him more was that he responded the same way most of the time. There was no room for that here, and quite frankly, Steve was glad about that.

"I didn't always want to do this, Taylor," he admitted while taking a sip of his coffee. "In fact, my father thought I should be a lawyer, the way I argued all the time." He smiled.

"Was he a lawyer?" Taylor asked.

"Naw. Has a plumbing supply place out in Michigan where I grew up," Steve said.

"Midwestern boy," Taylor commented. "Where?"

"Linden. Which I'm sure you've heard of." Steve chuckled sarcastically.

Taylor smiled back.

"Town of Fenton, county of Genessee, population three thousand. How 'bout you?"

"Columbus, Ohio," Taylor answered.

"I guess that's all you have to say." Steve grinned. "Bet you didn't have a racetrack though," he added.

"Probably not like yours," Taylor noted, raising his eyes. "Redneck?" he continued, knowing what the answer was.

"Beer, stock cars, and packed stands on the weekends," Steve answered matter-of-factly.

"I get it." Taylor smiled, shaking his head.

"That's where I grew up." Steve chuckled. "Definitely some rough people out there," he reflected again, gazing out the window. "Some good ones too," he added as his mind seemingly drifted back to his hometown for a minute or two.

"Well, you can get the same thing over at Rivermont Raceway," Taylor said with a grin after a pause. "You'll feel right at home."

"Don't wanna feel that at home." Steve laughed back.

"So, what got you doing this? Was your family religious?" Taylor said, not forgetting his original question.

"We were Methodists, I guess, and we went to church. But for me neither the liturgy nor the ritual comforts seemed to do as much as it did for other people, so I didn't really get it. The truth was, I was never feelin' what they were saying, and I don't think many of them were either, so I would debate my parents over what the point was in going. I think I won most of the arguments, but I had to go anyway."

He smiled. "When I got away to college, University of Michigan, I studied biology and did a lot of things my parents wouldn't approve of besides gambling and not going to church." He smirked.

"But they were none the wiser, and when I was graduating, they looked forward to me either moving on to Exon or some other corporate situation or going into teaching. If not, my dad threatened me with working in his plumbing store, which was a great motivator," he added with another smile. "As the day approached, I honestly wasn't ready for any of those options, and deep down I was still trying to figure out who I was and what in the world my purpose, or anybody's purpose, was here on this planet. As simple or unsophisticated as those questions may sound, they were very real to me back then. I knew I couldn't take that to my parents, given my college debt and need to go into a career. 'Not the time to try to find yourself, Son,' I could hear my father saying." Steve grinned, shaking his head. "So I was set to go back to Linden and teach, at least until I had a better idea of what I wanted to do.

"Then during my last semester, I saw something at school where they were partnering with the peace corps to install a water system somewhere in the Ukraine. I grew up plumbing, and since I'd never been overseas before and was looking to do something good in my life, I went for it. Besides that, it was during the summer, and everything was paid for."

"Interesting," Taylor noted, leaning back in his chair and putting the tip of his reading glasses to his lips.

Seeing that his host wasn't bored and was inviting him to go on, Steve continued. "There were about fifteen of us, mostly guys, and five faculty from the bio and engineering departments. It was a good group, and we left right after graduation. The leaders brought all the tools we needed, but it was definitely labor intensive—a lot of digging, wheelbarrowing dirt, and laying PVC. The place was actually a detention center they put orphans in, which was pretty eye-opening for me."

Steve paused to take another sip of his coffee. "Part of it was like a jail and part like a shelter for homeless children and runaway teens. Basically, their government's version of foster care, and though the physical conditions were pretty rough, we connected with a lot of the kids there," he added.

"Then there was a night toward the end of the trip I'll never forget," Steve said more seriously. "We all finished dinner and were sitting around the courtyard when we heard this screaming coming from inside the facility. Evidently a girl who had just been brought in had been fighting with her cellmate, and she was now being dragged out by the guards into this pen area adjacent to where we were. They were leaving her in there until they could figure out where else to put her. She looked like she was about sixteen, and according to one of the officers, had been in and out of that place since she was twelve. Like many girls over there, either poverty or the abandonment of their parents put them on the streets for an awaiting life of prostitution and the drug addictions that usually came with it.

"This girl was no different, though more on the violent side, as she ranted and cursed at the guards and even our group shortly after she was locked in the holding pen. At first, she seemed curious as she looked over at us, but then she evidently decided that we were like everybody else, and started yelling again after they left. Then I noticed one of the girls from our group named Sheryl tap our interpreter and begin to walk over there. A couple of guys and I got up and went along just in case something happened."

Steve paused for a moment, leaving a thick quietness in the conference room. Not even the sound of Marge's computer or her shuffling papers could be heard from around the corner.

"Hey, Marge. Why don't you just come in and sit at the table?" Taylor joked.

"I can hear fine from here," came her deadpan response.

Taylor smiled and head-motioned for Steve to continue.

"She went to the fence and invited the girl over. Her name was Elena. She wouldn't come, however, but stayed on the other end, turning over and sitting on the bucket she had previously been throwing into the chain link at people who walked by or stood too closely. She uttered something in Ukrainian, causing Sheryl to look at the interpreter. 'Leave now' is what the interpreter reluctantly translated. 'Okay,' Sheryl replied, and we all turned to go. After a few steps, something else was said from behind, obviously directed at Sheryl. 'Tell me what she's saying,' I heard Sheryl ask. 'Everything.' The interpreter seemed embarrassed and then hesitatingly told her, 'You come to see an animal in a cage, American? Well, I'm not an animal,' she said. So Sheryl turned around and went back to the fence, which kind of concerned the rest of us, because although she was the fun-loving type, she was also from Detroit, so it didn't look like this was going to end well."

"Really," Taylor acknowledged. "What'd she look like?"

"Certainly not a fighter. Actually a lot like Whitney Houston, to be honest," Steve admitted with a half smile.

"Didn't think guys like you noticed things like that." Taylor chuckled.

"I wish." Steve chuckled back. "She was dating this big guy from Haiti, who also went to Michigan, which kind of took care of that." Steve chuckled again. "She had a real sense of humor too," he added, now gazing out the window. "Her code name in the group e-mail was Skinny Black Girl. I'll never forget having to type that for the first time."

"In any event, up she went to the fence as me and the other guys reluctantly trailed behind her. We definitely didn't want trouble but were pretty sure we were gonna get it. I saw Sheryl look at the girl and pause a minute until she had eye contact. The girl wasn't afraid of her either, so it was tense to say the least.

"'You're not an animal, and you don't belong in a cage Elena,' Sheryl said, still looking at her as the interpretation was made. 'Tell them that,' the girl replied with a laugh, head motioning toward the guards. She was intrigued, however, and started walking up to us, causing everyone but Sheryl to back off the fence a foot or two. 'So you know about me?' she challenged. 'Just that your name is Elena,'

Sheryl answered back. 'And you came to look at the sad, dirty girl from Ukraine so you could tell your friends in America,' she chided. 'No, Elena, I didn't,' Sheryl answered, still looking into her eyes. 'And your life doesn't have to be this way, you know,' she said again. 'Oh really,' the girl shot back with a shrill laugh. 'Where are your parents, American?' she asked. 'They're back home,' Sheryl replied. 'You ever live on the street?' 'No,' Sheryl answered. 'You have no idea what life is here, American. So please don't talk about how to live it,' the interpreter embarrassingly added while Elena cynically scanned the eyes of all four of us before turning and heading back to where she was sitting.

"Sheryl didn't say anything at first but was kind of looking down, listening to the girl walk away. 'My parents loved me, and your parents should have loved you, Elena,' she said as she watched her words chase to where Elena was.

"The girl turned around and just looked at us. 'And you're right,' Sheryl continued. 'I have no idea what your life is like, and I'll never think that I do,' she added, motioning for Elena to come a little closer, which she surprisingly did. Then, just above a whisper, I heard her say, 'But my God loves you just as much as he loves me, and when you see that, you won't look at yourself the same ever again Elena. I can promise you that.'"

Steve paused and briefly looked away from Taylor. His eyes were starting to well from remembering the experience. He turned back again and continued. "Elena didn't say anything but remained there, looking at Sheryl like she was the only person in the world. Sheryl then put her hand against the chain link and invited Elena to do the same. She then told her she would be leaving her address and e-mail for her. 'Take it before you get out of here,' she said in a sisterly tone. 'But what you need to know now, Elena, is that Jesus loves you and died for you, and that the life you have is not who you are.'"

Steve paused again.

Out of respect Taylor remained silent as well, looking up at

Marge, who was now standing in the doorway, slightly leaning to one side, listening.

"That was the first time Sheryl had said anything about her faith on that trip. And three days later, we were gone," Steve continued. "But that moment was a stunner for me," he said, now looking at Taylor. "The way she looked at that girl—there was a compassion that was almost palpable, and I got the distinct feeling that she wasn't advertising anything she didn't have for herself."

"That's why you like that story you preached about," Taylor noted.

"Because I saw it happen," Steve acknowledged, impressed by how Taylor had caught that. "I learned later that the God Sheryl knew was relational and that the compassion she had was from him. Honestly, I could feel it in everything she said that day, especially the part about the girl's life not being who she was. Because the truth was, my life wasn't either, Taylor. I was in an identity crisis too, and as I sat on the plane trip back, I realized that the only difference between that girl's desperation and mine was that hers was loud and mine was quiet, and nobody knew about it. Except, of course, me," Steve said, glancing over at Thoreau's book, then back at Taylor.

"Suffice it to say, I was in a place where, if God could be known the way Sheryl said, then I wanted that in my life too. So I pursued it. Which is definitely another story that I won't bore you with here." He smiled, about to get up.

"Just give me the short version," Taylor said, motioning that he stay seated.

"I guess the short version is that I started reading the Bible, Old Testament and New, with my mind open to God being real and to Jesus being everything he said he was. Most importantly, I went into it with an honesty that if he was, I would follow him. That's when things started to change in here," he said, touching his chest, "and I felt more alive.

"But the real difference came when I actually embraced all that Jesus did and why he did it. In a nutshell, Taylor, it was God's sacrifice and forgiveness that were the answer to my quiet desperation and what I believe is the answer for everybody else's," Steve said, reaching for another sip of coffee and gesturing that he was finished.

Taylor wasn't, however, and leaned a bit more forward. "And you believe that that goes for all other religions too, including the Jewish faith?" he questioned, skeptically studying Steve's face.

"Taylor, after I left the Ukraine and started my own soul-searching, I encountered an inner-city church, whose minister was a guy named Kaufman. He was Jewish and had been there for over twenty-five years." Steve smiled.

"It rocked my world, as did a lot of things someone with my background would encounter in a multiethnic, multicultural place like that. One-third of the congregation was Jewish, one-third Hispanic, and one-third African American. It was one of the best experiences of my life, and what I learned there was that God wants to touch everybody, which was a big reason why I decided to go into ministry myself.

"And the truth is that Jewish people were actually the first to believe in Jesus, and founded the church. It was anti-Semitism that later pushed them out. Taylor, if I'm Jewish, I'm part of a chosen people whom the son of God came for first and still does."

Without breaking eye contact with his guest, Taylor sat back in his chair and slowly pushed himself an inch or two away from the table.

"You don't think that's even a little offensive, Steve."

"A Messiah wasn't anything new to the Jewish people, Taylor. In fact, he was God's promise to them. King David wrote about him in Psalms. And both Isaiah and Jeremiah were prophets who specifically talked about what the Messiah would look like and the new covenant, or new relationship, God would have with the Jewish people when he came. He would be someone very different than what they'd known, and his coming would mark God's law being placed in their hearts, and that their sins would be forgiven and actually forgotten all by that one act. In other words, he was coming so that they, and also we, could know God personally, by no longer having sin between us.

"Given the state of the human condition, Taylor, there could be no other kind of messiah, for the Jewish people or anybody else. In fact, the Old Testament, which is the Hebrew Bible, all points to how their Messiah's enemy would not be a particular people group, but evil and our own nature, which could only be overcome by his death. But more importantly, it goes on to say that the Jewish people would know God in an intimate sense, as he would know them, which in my opinion, was confirmed by their Messiah himself, whom the disciples called 'Yeshua,' which is Hebrew for 'Jesus.'"

"Not everybody believes the Bible, Steve, and not everybody interprets it that way either," Taylor interjected.

"I know that, Taylor, but I do," Steve replied. "My point is that the disciples were Jewish and the first to recognize that in Christ was the person of God and that, by the Holy Spirit, we can all have a meaningful and forever life with God because of what he did to make that relationship possible."

"And that goes for the Muslims and the others too," Taylor said.

"Oh, you're somethin' else, Mr. Green," Steve replied, smiling and slowly shaking his head.

"No, go ahead and say it, Steve. Say that half the world is wrong," Taylor further challenged, baiting the young man.

"Taylor, I don't believe God judges a person's religion as much as he judges their heart. But if I'm Buddhist or Hindu or anything else, I have to be open to the crucial difference between what I believe and who God and Jesus actually are," Steve said, now looking at Taylor seriously. "All other religions are about people reaching to God with offers of purpose and validation rather than embracing what God already did to establish the same thing. Only God could do it though, and he did it by his own sacrifice, not ours. To me, the fact that all of us have sinned and none of us can earn our salvation or a relationship with God on our own is what true Christianity is all about.

"And what made it personal for me was when I saw that the real reason Jesus died was to make it possible for his Father to become my Father, which was God's plan all along. And it was done because I was worthy of it in his eyes and that I was actually made in his image rather than in anyone else's, including my own.

"It forever changed the way I looked at things," Steve said after a pause. "Even the way I look at my own issues—and we all have issues," he added with a soft smile, "dramatically changed, because instead of feeling condemned over them, I walk through them with God. He's my helper. The more I follow, the better I do." He smiled again.

"But at the bottom of the whole thing, Taylor, is that when I finally gave my heart to the God who gave his Son for all that my sin had done to others and to me, I knew that I had what Sheryl, Elena, and the women two thousand years ago got when they did the same the thing—"

"Which was forgiveness," Taylor interrupted in a flattened tone that showed his dry, though familiar, understanding of the concept.

"Well, that and a Father of my own, whom I would always have too," Steve said, finishing his thought.

Taylor paused, respectfully letting a moment or two pass. Though it was a touching story and he had come to like Steve as a person, life obviously wasn't that way for everybody. He took a contemplative glance out the window and formulated his words as nicely as possible before turning his head back to their conversation. "Steve, there once was a day when I could have agreed that there was a God out there. I couldn't have told you exactly who it was or which religion was right. Maybe they all had a piece of it—I didn't know. And maybe I didn't care enough and should have, you might say—"

"I'm not saying anything," Steve cut in.

"But what I did know," Taylor said, talking over him, "was that all I wanted was a chance to live a good life. That's all. I wasn't asking anything from anybody. But I didn't even get that, and neither have millions of other people in this world. So it's very tough for me to believe the way you do, Steve. I'm sorry."

"I get that, Taylor. I really do," Steve replied.

"But you don't agree," Taylor challenged.

"I don't," Steve answered, "probably because my faith was more driven by a change I wanted inside me and a relationship I wanted with God, if he existed, than it was to have the answers to all those questions."

"Okay, but you can't say that having faith in God makes a difference when you see bad things happen to good people every day of the week, Steve, especially if you haven't lived through much of it yourself," Taylor poignantly added, leaning his head forward to solidify his point.

"That's true, Taylor. But my life, as secure as it was and as limited as it was, didn't make me any less in need of God," Steve answered.

"Well, mine did. I was doing pretty good on my own, Steve. And I didn't have much choice most of the time," Taylor smugly replied.

"You sure about that, Taylor?" Steve challenged.

"You know something I don't?" Taylor shot back.

The anger in his voice shattered the atmosphere, causing his guest to become speechless. Taylor felt a little embarrassed too. He had lost control. That thing in there was talking, and though Steve didn't know what it was, Taylor certainly did. He turned and looked out the window again, seeking to let things calm down.

After a brief pause, Steve broke the silence. "We've all got the same disease, Taylor."

"You mean sin, right, Steve? Like that's the answer to everything," Taylor curtly responded while maintaining his gaze into the dusky night sky.

"No, I mean self-centeredness," Steve answered, causing Taylor to look back at him cynically. "I've got it too," he added disarmingly.

Taylor turned his head back toward the window, shaking it in disappointment.

Steve looked out with him for a moment or two. He rubbed his eyes and looked back at Taylor. "I know you don't believe in the Bible or anything like that. But from the beginning, I think Adam and Eve's disconnection started when they thought they could be like God, which is why we all sin in the first place and are never satisfied. We insist on viewing this world as our own when it's really God's."

"Intelligent design?" Taylor retorted sarcastically, looking back at Steve with his hands inviting him to view his wheelchair. "Was this part of the intelligent design?"

"No," Steve quietly replied. "And I can't say why things like this happen to people."

"At least you admit it." Taylor sighed.

"But I can say that nothing that happens in this world is the end of the story, Taylor. Not for God and not for you either if you don't want it to be."

"But we can agree it's a lot easier for you to say something like that from where you're sitting, isn't Steve?"

"It is," Steve answered. "And we can go back and forth about why the world is the way it is, but my point is that even if you were to one day decide there is a God or that none of this is God's fault, a change of mind could still never bring a change of heart, Taylor."

"And only believing like you does that, right?" Taylor challenged.

"No, only God's love does that," Steve replied.

"Which only comes if people think like you though," Taylor sternly argued.

"You can't think yourself into that viewpoint," Steve replied. "You have to want forgiveness, Taylor. You gotta want what Jesus did and what he has."

"And how do you know you have it, Steve?" Taylor pressed further, looking for a more direct answer.

"Hey, Marge. Am I being grilled or what?" Steve joked, turning back to her.

"Cross-examined." She smiled.

"I guess he hasn't lost his touch." He laughed again.

"Welcome to our world," Marge replied.

"Well, one more question, and I'm taking an offering, Taylor. Welcome to my world," Steve volleyed back. It prompted a chuckle from even his host.

"Probably the biggest part of how I know Jesus is in me is that I don't feel ashamed or afraid of who I am anymore or of anything I've done in the past," Steve said. "That's how I know I'm forgiven, and that's how I know he's the Messiah he said he was."

Taylor sat back in his chair and continued to look at him. "Why don't I feel that way, Steve?" he asked, with eyes riveted on him like he was waiting for a pitch.

"Maybe you're just afraid to trust in something outside of your control, Taylor."

"You might be right about that," Taylor conceded.

"I get it though." Steve nodded.

This was a response that surprised Taylor, though he found it somewhat consoling as well.

"Any pictures of your father?" Steve asked, subtly noticing that there was nothing like those on the shelves.

"No. No father," Taylor replied dismissively as he bent down again to retrieve something out of a file on the floor. "He was a drunk, Steve. He left when I was seven," he said from beneath the table.

"Oh," Steve acknowledged, though he didn't appear surprised.

"It was a good thing," Taylor added matter-of-factly as he poked his head back up with the additional papers. "He was a miserable guy, and when he left, we were all the better for it really," Taylor assured him, anticipating Steve's sympathy but implying that it wasn't necessary.

Steve just nodded, leaving it up to Taylor to talk further about it or not.

"He used to come over drunk and then scream at my mother to get her tip money," Taylor said, looking out his office window into a now-darkening evening. The memory still made him seethe. "Unbelievable," he started to emote before catching himself.

"It's okay," Steve assured him, continuing to listen.

Taylor was a little shocked at himself, talking to someone he hardly knew about an issue he'd spoken about maybe five times in his entire life. Marge appeared taken aback as well as she came in to deliver a file at the tail end of the conversation. Her boss had discussed his father maybe only once before, and it had been just a brief reference to him being a useless deadbeat that Taylor was glad to never have known. She discreetly returned to her desk while Taylor continued on, undistracted as he usually was by her coming and going.

"The next time I heard of him was when I was in college. He was somewhere out in California, living with someone on top of a garage. Not working, just drinking."

"What happened after that?" Steve asked.

Taylor didn't respond right away but sat back in his chair, wondering for a moment about where the man's life had actually gone.

After a reflective pause, he gave a synopsis of his father's final chapter. "I'm afraid that was the best it got for him, my friend," Taylor concluded, speaking as if he were describing a character in a faraway novel rather than his own dad.

"In the end he died in the parking lot of some back-alley bar in Baltimore," he said, now looking at Steve. "That was about fifteen years ago. I was twenty-seven when I found out, out of law school and even married to Paula by then."

A minute or two passed as Steve looked out the window, absorbed in what Taylor had said. "That's some story." He sighed, sympathetically returning eye contact to Taylor.

"Yeah," Taylor acknowledged with a soft chuckle to keep some distance from its sadness.

Steve rubbed his forehead and gazed out the window again, respecting the pain that accompanied an experience like that.

"It's okay, Steve," Taylor assured him. "Long forgotten."

"Really?" Steve asked. "I don't think I could ever forget something like that." He sighed again.

"Yeah, ya could," Taylor replied. "Besides, isn't that part of your business, my friend?" he said with a grin. Though he appreciated Steve's sincerity, Taylor preferred to move on to another topic.

Steve, however, remained quiet in thought as he looked out the window. "I don't think anyone could forget that kind of thing, Taylor," he finally answered, cushioning the challenge with his own vulnerability.

"Well, it's easier than you think with a guy like him," Taylor remarked, half kidding, half not. "Especially since he's dead," he added, returning his eyes to the letter in front of him and signing it.

"He wouldn't be dead to me," Steve reflected like he was thinking aloud.

"Well, he's pretty dead, Steve." Taylor chuckled, still looking at his paperwork.

"I know," Steve answered, gazing over at the pictures again. "I could see he hurt a lot of people though."

"Yes, he did," Taylor answered, pulling another document out of the file.

Still looking at the photos, Steve appeared lost in what life must have been like for the people in them. He shook it off and began to get up from his chair to go. "Not being able to do anything was probably the worst of it," he said almost as an afterthought as he collected his napkin and empty coffee cup off the table.

The remark caught Taylor so off guard that he couldn't seem to lift his eyes from the paper in front of him as he tried to regroup from whatever it was that just happened.

Being a kid without a father made him feel different enough, but the fact that he was trapped and unable to do anything about it had either never been recognized or was so deeply suppressed that it felt like a raw and toxic mixture of fear, pain, and anger was now bubbling up out of nowhere and knocking the wind out of his soul.

He struggled to get his mind on saying goodbye to an awaiting Steve, who was politely standing in front of him.

"I'm sorry I overstayed my welcome, Taylor, but I'm really glad we talked," he said. "You okay?"

"Oh, I'm fine," Taylor said, denying that he really wasn't.

Steve nodded and turned to leave.

"So no advice?" Taylor questioned, raising his eyebrows after getting ahold of himself.

"No. No advice," Steve replied, looking back at him.

"I know what it would be anyway, Steve," Taylor said. "But you can rest assured he didn't want anybody's forgiveness."

"Oh, that's for sure," Steve agreed, turning back toward the door. "But what we don't let go of we carry, Taylor," he said with a sigh, peering out the adjacent window like a man who had seen this before. "I'm here for you, my friend," he added, glancing back at Taylor as he exited the doorway.

"Thank you, Steve," Taylor replied, purposely restoring the formality but giving a wave as he left.

CHAPTER 42

CUTTING CLASS AGAIN, SKIP AND HIS FRIENDS ALL MADE IT BACK to their spot behind the rusted, green dumpster at the end of the alley. A barbwire-topped fence enclosed the area immediately behind them. It was the same place the cops had chased them out of weeks before, so a watchful eye was kept to avoid detection as they took turns looking up the alley to ensure it remained clear.

Skip was concerned. It was far too early in the afternoon for school to be out, and the local police undoubtedly knew that too. They were pretty annoyed to have been outrun by a bunch of fourteen-year-olds the last time around. Being ever mindful of that, Skip made sure the boys watched even more intently. His hope was that the cops had lost interest in them by now, though he wasn't taking any chances.

After about ten minutes or so, the last of his cohorts meandered in, seemingly unnoticed. Multiple joints were lit up, all from the stash they had purchased with the proceeds of stolen electronic devices and other items lifted from local retail stores. Skip was uneasy with the number of people who had become involved and the gravity of what they were doing, but he didn't think there was any turning back at this point. Besides, he didn't know what to turn back to. His mother had nothing to offer him, and his father, for all intents and purposes, had left the family years ago. Everybody was pretty much on their own now was the way he saw it.

He poked his head out from behind the dumpster and up the

shadowy garbage-ridden alley. It still looked clear. Only a taxi and about two or three cars went by. A homeless-looking guy, typical for this neighborhood, and a few pedestrians were the only ones he saw pass by the entrance, but thankfully no one came down. He snuck another quick puff and actually started to relax.

Suddenly, two officers leaped down from the fence behind him and yelled for everybody to put their hands against the dumpster. The boys panicked and instinctively burst out from the corners. They frantically began running up the alley, only to be intercepted by three or four other cops, who popped out from the adjoining sides of the passageway and blocked their exit. Completely trapped, Skip found he and his friends being quickly corralled and taken into custody. Unfortunately, he became more angry than scared, getting extra mouthy as their heads were unceremoniously pushed down into the police vehicles.

Meanwhile, Taylor was at home, about to start his usual walking routine, though he seemed more depressed than usual with his lack of progress. Pulling his canes out from behind a lounge chair, he sluggishly began. He had purposely gotten himself out on the deck a little earlier today to see how he did without Corey.

He pushed himself up. The balance and agility of his upper body was impressive as usual as he steadied himself on the two canes and situated his legs directly beneath him. He struggled to put the first cane forward, which seemed even harder than it was a month ago, adding to his frustration. After jutting the cane about eight inches in front, he tried to adjust and allow his right leg to swing under him but couldn't fully complete the maneuver. He was stuck again as he violently strained to lift the other cane and slowly propel his body forward. Though he made it, he was going no farther than a few inches with each subsequent step. This was maddening to him as he stabbed his cane forward beyond where he could usually keep his balance and began to fall.

Letting go of one cane and desperately clinging to the other with both of his now-white-knuckled hands, he still wound up crashing hard on the deck floor.

Sweat dripped from his overly strained forehead and down his reddened face as he remained flat on his back, exhausted and, maybe for the first time in his life, defeated. He lay on the floor, numb. He couldn't think anymore.

Pulling himself up to a sitting position against the deck railing, he angrily flung the cane next to him across the floor. A slight trace of tears mingled with perspiration slowly gathered momentum and trickled down his face. He wasn't going to walk.

Two or three lifeless moments drifted by before Taylor's silence was interrupted by the slam of Corey's back door across the way. He quickly wiped his eyes and forehead with his sweatshirt sleeve along with some blood on his forearm, which he must have scraped on the way down.

Corey's run over was hindered by his mother, who, with baby against her side and diaper bag hanging on her shoulder, called out to him as he jogged up Taylor's ramp.

"Corey! Mommy's got to run up to the store for a minute. Come on," she said, motioning to the car.

"Mom! Can't I stay?" he pleaded.

Evette looked toward Taylor's deck, seemingly to verify that he was there, though she remained insistent with her son. "Corey," she cautioned.

He glanced back at Taylor for support before responding to his mother. Taylor didn't feel he had much of an alternative given that the kid was now standing right in front of him.

"No problem." Taylor's voice scratched over the hedge as he battled what was probably the second worst day of his life.

Corey grinned and assisted his oversized buddy to his chair, oblivious to the fact that Taylor had fallen. "I can watch him," he yelled again.

"Okay, I'll be back in a few minutes," she replied, giving Corey the mom look that said he better listen to Taylor while she was gone.

He innocently nodded and watched her car disappear down the driveway. He turned to Taylor and spoke close to his ear, just above a whisper. "Can we go to the baseball field, Mr. Green?" he plotted in a conspiratorial tone.

Taylor didn't even remotely consider such a request, sluggishly leaning over to grab his glove for them to begin.

"C'mon! Please, Mr. Green," Corey implored.

"Ya know I don't drive, Corey," Taylor gently scolded, his voice dropping an octave. "Your father will take you to the field," he added to close the subject, tossing him the ball.

"My dad doesn't live here anymore," Corey blurted, looking as if he had just released a deep, dark secret.

Taylor knew that but was nonetheless blindsided by the remark. Robert had unofficially moved out a few weeks before, but the coolness and even hardness of Corey's tone were what surprised Taylor. It was out of character for him and unfortunately sounded more like a kid who was growing up too quickly rather than the little boy he was supposed to be.

Though he hid it well, Taylor remained unnerved by the remark and didn't know what to say in response. Truth be told, he had no answers for his little friend, who was now looking for something that would make sense out of why his parents were letting his whole world fall apart when it clearly didn't have to.

"It'll be okay, Corey," was all Taylor could muster up as he tried to usher them both past the awkwardness of that moment and into their routine. "And he'll take you to the field," he further assured him, turning his wheelchair and starting to roll toward the pitcher's mound.

Corey wasn't buying it, however. His trusted friend was now sounding like all the other adults in his life, whose credibility was falling fast with each empty promise made to him. He darted to the garage.

"Corey!" Taylor yelled as he saw him running.

All he could think of was the kid getting hit by a car. Taylor called to him again as he wheeled as fast as he could over the bumpy grass and headed up to the driveway. His glasses and cell phone had long bounced off his lap and were lying somewhere in the yard far behind him.

Corey, unfortunately, had already begun to exit the garage on his bicycle. He had his mitt dangling loosely from the handlebars the way he'd seen the other kids do it. By the time Taylor made it to the pavement, Corey was up the driveway and turning south, which interestingly was the way to the field. It was also toward the town.

Taylor yelled again, but Corey ignored him.

Scanning his lap and patting down his shirt and the warm-up jacket draped behind him, Taylor searched for his cell phone. He was convinced he still had it with him. Nothing. No phone, no glasses, nothing. He quickly looked back and surveyed the driveway behind him, hoping to see something there. No such luck, and Corey was now almost to the stop sign at the corner of their street. Thankfully he stopped and waited for traffic to pass.

Rather than go back looking for the phone, Taylor turned his wheelchair toward the road and feverishly pumped his wheels. Corey had crossed over by now, though he was still within Taylor's sight.

"Corey!" Taylor commanded again.

"What?" Corey innocently answered. He looked back with an impish grin and appeared entertained by the speed and intensity of Taylor's pace. It became a game, and he pedaled faster whenever Taylor got within forty feet or so.

Seeing that he may not be able to catch Corey and fearful that he might chase him into traffic, Taylor slowed a bit to reassess the situation. Thankfully, Corey slowed down as well, though he kept a healthy distance between him and his frustrated babysitter. Taylor's concern for Corey's safety overrode the self-consciousness he had in the past about being seen in society as a disabled person. He despised the curious looks and sympathetic stares people in his position sometimes received. However, as for now, even wheeling down a public roadway like a crazy man was of little matter to him while he continued to follow Corey along the shoulder of Main Street.

"Corey look ahead, not back at me," Taylor cautioned, now partnering with him. He hoped he'd at least listen to that.

"Are you going to get me?" Corey timidly inquired.

Taylor could hear in his voice that he was a little scared of the traffic and speed of the cars buzzing by them on the busy thoroughfare. "No, Corey," he gently assured him. "I won't get you. Just go up on the sidewalk," Taylor said as he motioned him that way.

Corey did, which gave Taylor some relief that he was taking himself out of imminent danger.

It was hard for Taylor to stay mad at Corey for too long, especially considering the enormous changes that were going on in his little life. Whether his parents were going to get divorced or not, Taylor didn't know. He knew why Corey was running though, and he knew how good it felt sometimes to just be someplace else. Forty years later, Taylor was doing the same thing, though he wished he knew of a better way for his little friend.

As the two simultaneously turned the next corner, Taylor found himself wondering why things were falling apart for Corey and why things fell apart for people in general, including him. He usually resolved those issues by pinpointing who was at fault and simply blaming that person either outwardly or in his mind.

It was a philosophy that worked best when looking at other people, but it never really squared with the affair he'd had midway through his marriage and how it had almost destroyed Paula.

Sharon was eleven, Tim eight, and Skip about five when it happened; a time when life was packed, responsibilities were high, and communication was at a dead low, at least from Taylor's end. He struggled with the needs of his then-fledgling career and the financial stresses that came with it. Lurking beneath were the childhood wounds of inadequacy that surfaced every time he faced either a real or imagined failure.

Pain coming out "sideways," is what Paula would say. He abhorred when she said that, consistently denying that any such fears or feelings existed. Of course, having an oversized ego that violently repelled weakness came in handy during these arguments. It allowed the unresolved issues that had become his kryptonite to remain deeply submerged so he could deny the need for recovery with a straight face. It was also a recipe for disaster, he realized, as he continued to roll after Corey.

His wife's belief that she could fix him and her subtle insistence on doing so only thickened his walls. In fact, Paula's demands for more time and emotional attentiveness always felt like "nagging" rather than need to him, and the more she pressed, the more he became withdrawn until an unhealthy admiration he had allowed to develop from someone else gave way to the unthinkable.

Taylor winced as he remembered Paula's face again. Though he had always viewed himself to be either as good or better than the next guy at staying on the right side of temptation, he didn't that time around. He became another loser to what's commonly known, though seldom admitted, as every man's battle.

The moral hangover of what he'd done eventually forced him to come clean. However, considering how deeply the news hurt Paula, he honestly wondered whether he should have told her at all. Nor was he prepared for the swiftness of her response. She wanted a divorce and him out of the house as soon as she could get the kids adjusted to the idea.

She was right, and he knew it, and her steadfast refusal to take him back left him sitting in a one-room apartment for what would become the darkest five months of his life. It was a tortuous time for both of them, though it was during that hiatus that Paula had the spiritual epiphany Taylor later credited for saving their marriage—"for better or worse," he'd mumble to himself.

Though Taylor never thought much about how she did it, Paula really did forgive him "as if it never happened" like she said during their final counseling session about it. Truth be told, she never threw it at him again. How a tough girl like Paula could ever let anything like that go was beyond Taylor.

He winced again as the flimsy excuses he'd always told himself to justify what he did began to cave into the pain he was now imagining she must have felt from the betrayal.

It had to be unreal, he thought as tears now welled up in his eyes while he continued to pump the wheels of his chair.

CHAPTER 43

THE UNIFORMED OFFICERS ESCORTED SKIP AND HIS FRIENDS DOWN the corridor toward the booking and processing room of the Rivermont Police Station. Skip was last in line as the jean-jacketed pre-gang-looking adolescents followed the desk officer in single file. Suddenly, a large brown hand at the end of a suit jacket jutted out from an adjoining doorway and grabbed Skip from behind by the back of his collar. He didn't see it coming and was terrified as he got unceremoniously pulled sideways into the office. He looked up. It was Detective Robert Johnson, his neighbor.

Johnson sternly guided him into the chair that abutted the side of his desk, landing him in a heap as he sat motionlessly amid the stench of the pot he'd just smoked. Though relieved to be in the hands of a friend, he was unfortunately still high enough to sport the hint of arrogance that remained pasted on his face. The detective's countenance, however, wasn't conducive to it, and his quickly emerging glare forewarned Skip of the coming scolding session. Thankfully he was making a phone call first.

"Hey, Tony. Rob Johnson here. Listen, I've got the Green kid with me," he said. "Okay. I'll take care of all that," he added after a pause. "Righto," he said again into the receiver before hanging up.

Scribbling a short note, he directed his full attention back at Skip. "What are you doing?" he demanded.

"Nothin'. I was just—" Skip defiantly retorted before Robert's angry pointed finger cut him off.

"Your mother doesn't need this aggravation right now," he sternly declared as his cell phone started to ring. Johnson's eyes darted to the number as he put the phone to his ear.

"I'm not playin'!" he continued, looking at Skip again, who was a little surprised that Robert had any idea what was going on with his family. "Hello?" Robert spoke into his cell, still with a look of frustration.

Skip could see it was his wife. Judging by the detective's reaction, she was beside herself. He tried to calm her down. "They're gone? What you mean?" he said into the phone. "They're probably at Taylor's house having a snack or something, Evette. Did you check by the horses?" he said, glancing down at the paperwork on his desk.

As the conversation continued, Robert's concern began to elevate. Skip also started listening attentively to the detective's side of the call.

"Where did you find the wallet and cell phone?" Robert asked.

Evette's voice was raised and sounded hysterical now as Robert struggled to rein her in and get more information. "Where's Paula?" he asked as calmly as he could.

"Okay. You have her cell number?" he said, looking to Skip for it and writing something else on a little piece of paper. With his phone still to his ear, Robert hurriedly began gathering his keys and jacket. He motioned to Skip that they were both leaving immediately.

"Okay, okay, I'm on my way home right now," he assured her, sounding more intense than before. "We'll find them. Don't worry. Tell Paula I've got Skip, and we're on our way."

He stopped to listen for a second or two. "If anything happens, call me," were his final words before hanging up. "Come on," he said to Skip. "Your father and Corey are gone."

Having already let go of the attitude, Skip followed as best he could behind Mr. Johnson's quick and deliberate pace through the corridors of the station house. The two jogged to the detective's unmarked car and screeched out of the parking lot. Robert's eyes were peeled for Taylor and Corey along the way. He radioed for the patrol cars to keep an eye out for a kid walking with a forty-five-year-old man in a wheelchair.

Skip's eyes dropped to the floor at hearing the comment. Though Robert probably meant nothing by it, it reminded Skip of how much his father hated being looked at that way. Still scanning as he drove, Robert filled him in on the situation.

"Evette left Corey with your dad in the backyard while she ran up to the store. When she came back, they were both gone. That was over an hour ago. Your father's glasses and phone were on the ground by the driveway. Where do you think they went?"

"He doesn't even drive," Skip responded, confused.

"The cars are still there," Robert answered. "What does your dad like to do?"

"Nothin'," Skip responded, aloofly staring out his side window.

Robert ignored the tone and refocused Skip on the task at hand. "Come on now," he prodded.

"I'm telling you, he doesn't do anything," Skip insisted defiantly, now staring straight ahead through the windshield. *They're fine*, he thought. There was no way his old man would have gone far. He probably took the kid to the bay at the end of the street.

Returning his concern to what was inevitably going to happen to him once they were found, Skip debated whether to volunteer that information to the detective.

CHAPTER 44

COREY GLANCED BACK AND MADE ANOTHER TURN AS TAYLOR quickly wiped his eyes with his forearm. Raw honesty had taken ahold of him, but it actually felt good, like he was taking a shower on the inside. Taylor had never fully understood why he wasn't comfortable in his own skin, but he didn't care to know either. It was always easier to keep others and even himself at a safe distance.

This drove Paula crazy. She could never reach him. But love was never enough for Taylor Green anyway, he painfully admitted to himself. So he lived through the dreams he had for his own life and later on for his kids, especially Skip. Though his wife was able to rescue most of them from that pressure, she couldn't save the one who idolized him the most.

Taylor winced. That was rough to think about, especially considering how much time had gone by, including the casualties and the missed opportunities. If love had been enough, like it was with Paula, what would his life have looked like over the last ten years? Over the last twenty? What would Skip's life look like now? *Definitely not like this.* He sighed to himself.

Wheeling on, Taylor started taking inventory of areas he had never looked at before. *What was it that drove his insatiable need for recognition, for attention?* he asked himself. *What was in him that did that?*

He had always been a fierce protector of his independence and was sincerely proud of it. In fact, Taylor honestly believed it was essential to his survival, especially given the place he started from. Though growing up without a father certainly fueled that perspective, in the end it was his own ego that was at the bottom of where he wound up as an adult. It was also what fed the unquenchable right he felt he had to judge other people.

The story about the guys with the woman in front of Jesus began to run through his mind. Finding somebody worse so he could look okay was what Taylor had done his whole life too. Those guys weren't okay though, and neither was he. No one was okay, which Taylor figured was the point of the story. But no one was judged that day either, at least not by God.

Skimming the right wheel with his well-calloused hand to slow it down, Taylor made the final turn to the field. Corey was still about fifty yards ahead but now moving faster, obviously excited that he was on the last leg of the journey. Their destination would be at the end of the block.

Taylor sped up to keep him in sight, and a short moment later he was up to where Corey had been. The ex-coach's eyes began to fill as he traveled down the same quiet streets he had driven through literally hundreds of times before. Neither the storybook homes nor the aged and masterfully cracked sidewalks had changed, and he found himself welcoming the sight of it all again. He couldn't remember crying so much in one day either. It never felt so good though.

The ball field was now in view as Taylor gingerly rolled himself onto the pathway of the place he had avoided most since his accident years before.

It was tranquil and freshly prepared for opening day, and he couldn't help but take a detailed scan of the real estate that had always been so wondrous to him. The outfield glistened in the afternoon sun. It caught him unawares for a brief moment, taking him out of his wheelchair and back to a time he had never realized he missed so much.

Corey had already raced ahead, dismounted his bike, and was

standing by third base, curiously observing everything around him. The deep-green grass, perfectly trimmed and hedged within the infield, probably enchanted the little boy as much as it once did Taylor. Bright white lines also popped for attention off the deep brown and beautifully crafted base paths. Chalked with precision and artistry, they seemed to be inviting Taylor back like an old friend as the years he and the boys played on them began to flood his memory. The catches, the hits, the moments that had become too painful to remember now warmly flowed through his mind, unobstructed by the usual upset over what happened later. Other locked closets of the past were being opened as well, causing Taylor to pause a moment while he sat atop the grassy slope leading down to the playing area.

As pictures of his own childhood began to surface, it reminded him of how, no matter what else was going on in his seemingly unimportant and ancillary existence, he was always at home here. He had a name. He had a number, and he had a place. And he wasn't the boy without the father, at least not for the ninety minutes or so while he was on the field.

"Strange how kids can do that," Taylor said to himself, glancing over at Corey frolicking around home plate.

"Probably a good thing," he said again as he cautiously rolled his chair down the slope before pausing a few inches behind the left-field foul line.

From there he caught a view of the advertising signs, which had been newly painted and reflected their messages proudly along the outfield fence, foul pole to foul pole. Beyond that the forest of oak and maple trees stood freshly in bloom, awaiting the upcoming flood of little kids, who would wander through, too bored to watch the games of their older siblings.

Turning his head to make sure no one was watching, Taylor leaned forward and untied his shoes, popping off each one before relaxing back in his chair again. The gentle breeze brushed against his stocking feet and continued its whisper across the plain and into the woods to provide soft but enticing background music for a squadron of Canadian geese passing overhead. The birds filled the sky with a symphony of their own as Taylor's eyes quietly followed them as they disappeared beyond the treetops, leaving their sweet chorus echoing behind.

It was beautiful, Taylor thought to himself, still engulfed in its serenity. *Too beautiful not to have something behind it*, he thought again.

CHAPTER 45

THOUGH THE GAS GAUGE WAS TOUCHING THE RED, IT LOOKED LIKE there was still about an eighth of a tank left as Paula sped west on Route 25 in search of Corey and her husband. Evette had already checked the park by the water and combed the neighborhood; she was now heading east on 25.

Corey's not abducted. No, not abducted, a voice screamed inside Paula's head as she frantically scanned both sides of the road and as far down each side street as she could before passing by.

"Why don't you have your phone?" she cried out at her husband, wanting to speed-dial it again for about the twentieth time.

Paula's cell was blowing up with calls from her colleagues and Taylor's friends, reaching out to help. Her eyes darted to the screen as it sat faceup on the passenger seat where she could see it. She anxiously looked for that unknown number that could be Taylor using somebody else's phone. *He hasn't called yet, but it's okay.* He definitely would've borrowed a phone and called if he was separated from Corey, so he's probably with him, and they're okay.

That makes sense, she thought. *Unless something else happened to them.* She panicked again.

Think, Paula! Think! her mind screamed.

Though trained in the ER, she was never good when people weren't in front of her, when she couldn't see or touch them. "Oh God, please!" was all she could say.

It was all she could pray as she picked up speed down the highway.

Glancing at the phone again, she saw it was two o'clock now. Kids would get out of school in half an hour. *They'll be off the bus by three.* Her mind whirled.

"Skip …"

He was with Robert at the police station, Evette had said.

Can't deal with that now, Paula thought.

The phone flashed again. It was Ira. She hit the speaker button.

"Paula?" came the expected calm voice of her husband's close friend.

"Taylor's gone," she blurted, waiting to see how much he knew.

"Marge called me. He's not picking up his phone," Ira acknowledged, looking for more information.

"It was left on the lawn. So were his glasses," Paula answered, a little calmer and more businesslike. "They were in different parts of the neighbor's yard near the driveway," she added to see what Ira would make of that. "He never would have left them," she said nervously as her eyes flicked to the rearview mirror while she changed lanes.

"The police are already looking, Paula," Ira assured her. "I'm in the car now, heading toward your house. You think they could have went to a ball field or something?"

"The fields are on the other side of town," she replied, highly doubtful of that possibility.

"Okay," he answered tentatively. "Where are you headed?"

"I'm going west on Twenty-Five, and then I'm gonna circle back on Roanoke."

"Okay, I'll check in in a little bit, Paula," Ira assured her again.

"Thanks, Ira," Paula said, though she didn't yet hang up the phone. "Ira?" she said after a brief pause to see whether he was still out there.

"Yes, Paula," he responded.

"Could you please pray?" she asked, thinking the worst again.

"I will," he replied seriously.

"Thank you," was all she could manage as tears began to stream down her face again. Moments later her eyes caught sight of a mom and her toddler to her left, heading into Baskin-Robbins.

Ice cream! Ice cream! rang the voice in her head. *There's a Carvel about a mile from the neighborhood. It's a little far but doable.*

"Yeah, it's doable," she said to herself, abruptly doing a U-turn and going in that direction.

CHAPTER 46

TAYLOR SLUMPED BACK IN HIS CHAIR AND ALLOWED HIMSELF A rare moment of candor. The reality that God fit into life and was even its creator was resting all around him, and he didn't want to fight it anymore.

He still couldn't fully understand his accident or any other tragedies people suffered throughout history, but it didn't seem that the unfairness or even the evil of those events were being challenged. Instead, what was unearthing in Taylor was the distinct sense that whoever was behind whatever was going on inside him was alive and loved all of humanity, including him.

Sitting in a wheelchair while at the same time feeling complete and at peace was way beyond what Taylor had ever imagined life could be for him. Did he want to walk again? Absolutely. But there was a fullness inside him, a compassion that was eclipsing even the life he'd had before he became paralyzed.

He started thinking again about the woman who had been thrown in front of Jesus for committing adultery. *What a scene*, he mused, now feeling himself what it must have been like to be caught in the gaze of someone who knew everything about you but loved you more than you loved yourself.

Why wouldn't a God who created the universe have a Son like that? His chest quietly heaved as his mind gave way to the thought of it.

What other purpose could a God who loved the world have? And what other point to life could there be other than to know there is a

God who loves you? he found himself concluding, though now with a presence touching inside him that was deeper than his intellect.

There was something cleansing about that possibility, that belief that seemed to be surfacing simultaneously in Taylor with the truth about himself as well. This time, however, those issues of the past that he was always either too afraid or too ashamed to face were now peacefully unloading as a relief rather than pounding down on top of him the way his conscience was used to.

So Taylor went with it, letting this long-known but newly found God have the full, unadulterated view of everything Taylor wanted to let go of, namely the fears and insecurities he had about the man who lived inside him, the one who didn't look anything like the guy on the cover. This was the man in whom sin was still very much alive, but Taylor was finally able to let it be seen.

Finding himself open about the thoughts, temptations, and even the pride that ruled him from the prison of his own self-centeredness, Taylor began to let out words to the effect that he wanted out of his old life and into the new one Jesus was promising to anyone who believed in him.

"God help me," was all he could say, honestly desiring a life he knew in his gut would be free to touch God and where God would now be free to touch him.

Far from an artful prayer, it was probably God's favorite nonetheless, as issues Taylor had once thought were far too shameful for anyone to see, let alone accept, began to collide with the comfort of a God Taylor now felt actually loved him more than what he'd done.

Whether it was a stroke of humility or the utter desperation of his soul that got him there, Taylor didn't know. But what he couldn't deny was that he was a man who was catching a full view of God's heart that day, and like the woman two thousand years ago, he wasn't being condemned when he saw it but forgiven and let go by the only one who could.

That was the reason he had given his life, Taylor's soul recognized for the first time. But the sacrifice was never designed to bring people to guilt but to God.

The war the Jewish Messiah had come to win was the one inside him, Taylor realized, rubbing his tired and overly drained eyes with his hands. It couldn't be won with success, piety, or even acts of goodwill. Though noble, they could never take away what was embedded in the sand of Taylor's heart. He knew that.

Nor could pointing at others do it either, as the men in front of Jesus had tried to do that day. Like them, Taylor also needed to throw rocks at those whose lives happened to publicly reflect what was deep inside him too. The fact that his judgment remained subtle and internal was no less devastating to others, nor less toxic to himself. Truth be told, what everyone needed on that day two thousand years ago was forgiveness, which obviously was what Jesus was after all along.

Ironically, this brought Taylor to his own father, Robert Green.

CHAPTER 47

ALWAYS AN UNWELCOMED MEMORY, ROBERT GREEN NEVERTHELESS remained there despite his adult son's best efforts to push him out. If Taylor had his way, the man would have been forgotten long before he died and forced to live out the rest of his life in the fractured state he'd left his family in. Unfortunately, it didn't work out that way, and the black dot of Taylor's past had never fully disappeared. Nor did its haunting whisper that Taylor wasn't good enough ever silence either, no matter how loud his achievements had become. Taylor hated his father for that, and he hated not being able to forget him even more. In the end it left him poisoned with a bitterness that had grown bigger than the man himself.

Unforgiveness, and its flip side, self-pity, had become old friends to Taylor Green, and it would be very difficult to kill them. They comforted him and for decades had subtly walled off his pain, and in a contorted sort of way medicated it with an angry motivation to prove his father wrong. It had never worked though, and unbeknownst to Taylor, it had a numbing effect on his soul that skewed even the relationships he wanted, namely his marriage.

In retrospect Taylor could see why his father was still alive in him the way he was. He hadn't been forgiven. And though it still felt better to leave him judged, it wasn't mixing well with what he had just experienced moments before.

Robert Green, for whatever the man he was, belonged just as much to God as Taylor did. And where his dad's life went was between them, Taylor realized, though he was still having difficulty with that.

"Easier said than done," Taylor said to himself as his conscience began to spar with any rights to forgiveness a man like his father should have from the people he'd hurt the most. Other than a smashed trophy when he was twelve and some unwelcome visits before that, Taylor had only scant memories of his father, and none of them were very good. Little League dinners were the worst, however. Taylor would sit next to his mom and his uncle Jimmy, her socially inept brother, who always consumed the uneaten fruit cups at the table and really had no interest in being there. Sheila brought him along so her son would have a male figure with him, but Uncle Jimmy unfortunately didn't come close to fitting the bill. However, what hurt Taylor the most was the empty seat his mom always bought for his father. She denied it every time, but Taylor knew she implored and probably offered money for him to go, but he never went.

Taylor didn't want him to go anyway for fear that his father would be drunk and embarrass him, though his conspicuous absence in the face of tons of boys with their fathers was always awkward for him to explain. He really couldn't, which made the notion that his friends with dads were better than he obviously true and unavoidably painful, no matter how you sliced it.

By the time Taylor hit junior high, the man who was his father was gone for good, leaving his mom still alone and his sister still a mess from the abandonment. As for Taylor, Robert Green wasn't there for anything that would make a healthy father proud or a son secure. Nor did the man ever witness the long walks home his boy took alone, unwilling to accept a ride or anything else that would bring attention to the fact that his dad had left. Truth be told, Taylor spent a lifetime feeling like he had to answer for why he didn't have a father who loved him like everybody else did. Seeing later on that he wasn't the only kid in that position may have brought some solace, but it didn't completely fix the problem. Even his dad's death left

Taylor mixed with feelings of resentment and relief that he could never fully reconcile.

Good riddance, was all he remembered thinking when he first heard the news. And he was thankful it was after any funeral or memorial services could be arranged.

Paula's father certainly wasn't like that, Taylor thought as he let his mind run a little bit in that direction. Joseph Definiunĕ had indeed been a man who was a father to Taylor, filling that gap as much as his son-in-law would let him. He was the quiet but strong backbone of the family.

Always happy to be anywhere he was, Joe D. especially loved being with his kids and grandkids. He was a big man and a hugger, which usually made Taylor uncomfortable, though deep down there weren't many things better than being received by Joe D. Equally attractive was the type of father he was to his own boys and how quickly he could impart a deep sense of identity, security, and belonging with one swat to the back of the head for coming in late and worrying their mother. Like most old-school parents, Joe D. had a knack for being able to deliver that complete message without ever having taken a psychology class. Such was often the case with Anthony, who took it as well as could be expected from a father he knew loved him.

During his courtship with Paula, Taylor had quickly discovered that come easy, come hard, he was gonna be loved in that house. For Paula's brothers, however, it was usually come hard.

Taylor often felt the same meaty hand but thankfully only when it was warmly resting on his shoulder while he was receiving sound advice. It was a comfort no words could express, especially during the weekend of his wedding when he found himself captive on an unartfully planned fishing trip the morning after his bachelor party.

Charlie, Taylor's best man, lived in Rochester and admittedly had no idea what to do in New York, so Anthony stepped in and commandeered the entire schedule. His repertoire started with a phenomenal bar tour of the city, which everybody enjoyed way too much. From there they were limoed out to the Hamptons, where a charter boat, leaving at six a.m., was waiting for them. The father of the bride had made a customary and respectful cameo appearance during the tavern excursion but wisely went home to get some sleep before the next day's outing.

"Pace yourselves, boys!" he heartily cautioned before departing that night, though he wasn't banking on them listening.

They didn't, and the thirty-five-mile off-shore tuna voyage turned into a $1,500 boat ride, with everybody but Dad dreadfully hungover and throwing up the whole time. Joe D. insisted on paying for the trip and kept the group as watered up as they could stand to be on the way in. Taylor and Anthony felt terrible about it, though seeing the upstaters experience seasickness for the first time and feverishly lunge toward the side of the boat drew a few sadistic chuckles between them. Taylor, however, later found that he wouldn't escape the revenge for the night before either.

Though the nausea visited him after everybody else was either huddled in a deck chair or passed out in the cabin, it hit harder than expected, causing the groom to make an abrupt beeline to the two-foot-by-two-foot bathroom, where he spent the next twenty minutes upchucking literally every ounce in him. Finally, after it seemed that the last of the dry heaves had passed, he heard a subtle tapping at the door.

"You okay, Son?" came the comforting voice of his future father-in-law.

The reference was new and inexplicably riveted Taylor as he sat speechlessly only inches away behind the locked door.

"I'm good," was all he could get out, still recoiling from being called "Son" for the first time from a man who actually meant it.

Though he and Joe D. went on to become even closer as the years passed, Taylor's guilt over his affair hopelessly compromised his ability to talk to or even look his father-in-law in the eye the way he used to.

Thankfully Paula spared her parents the details of their marital strife, but her father would probably never have understood what happened, and Taylor quite frankly wouldn't have blamed him. In fact, betraying a good man's daughter was something Taylor could never fully reckon even within himself, so he avoided anything deep with Joe D. from then on, leaving his father-in-law frustrated, and Taylor, as usual, distant from the healthy intimacy that could have been shared with a person who loved him.

Wiping the perspiration from his forehead with the back of his forearm, Taylor sighed again. The comparison he just orchestrated between Joe D. and his own father had obviously boomeranged back to issues of his own doing, which interestingly left him again face-to-face with the need that he forgive his dad. It was a decision he still didn't want to make, and for good reason he believed.

The vulnerability of this kind of forgiveness meant returning to a place Taylor thought he'd escaped decades ago. He never fully got out though, which was probably why he had to go back. Taylor knew it would take another humbling and quiet decision on his part to make that happen. However, he also had seen a bigger God that afternoon, and more importantly, he knew his pain would now have a place to land.

He glanced over at Corey, who was busily exploring the dugouts, and then out at the distant sky over left field. Nothing was right about Robert Green. But avenging the pain never worked either, and deep down Taylor knew it never would. He had to forgive both the man and his memory if he ever expected to move forward. The mercy of God seemed to be requiring that, and why wouldn't it? he reasoned. It was that same mercy that had saved his marriage, and it would be the same mercy he'd want from his father-in-law and even his own children if the whole truth about him ever came out. Thankfully, it didn't, but the issue Taylor had to face was that on the inside he wasn't much different from his dad, and truth be told, it was his own self-righteousness, not Robert Green's abandonment, that led Taylor to be the very thing he never wanted to be, both in his marriage and now with his kids.

This moment was about letting his father go in the same way he would want others to let him go. But it would have to be without a yardstick to measure who was better or who was worse or who caused more pain versus who caused less. *That's probably what the death for all sin is about*, Taylor thought.

Better to stay on the forgiveness side of things. He sighed, his voice quietly cracking as he let it go and felt the forty years of pain that were unknowingly stored in caverns deep within his soul begin to funnel out through the gland it was supposed to. Not knowing exactly what was behind the flow of tears was perhaps the beauty of it. He didn't need to see what it was to know it was leaving, he thought as he wiped his eyes, hopefully for the last time.

Finally, it was done.

Robert Green was let go for good. And so was Taylor.

Resting a moment, he gave the mural of the outfield another look, turned his wheels toward Corey, gingerly pushed himself over the foul line, and headed toward the pitcher's mound.

He could move on now. The past didn't change, but the shame of its secrets did, which made all the difference.

CHAPTER 48

COREY HAD LONG TAKEN THE FIELD AND ALREADY PLACED THE BALL on the mound as Taylor was approaching. Practice swinging inside the newly lined batter's box, he appeared extra careful not to smudge anything. Taylor was concerned with that as well, looking around and hoping no one else was there.

Coming back was hard enough, and he certainly didn't want to get kicked off the field on top of that. He motioned for Corey to throw him the mitt he had sitting in his bike basket. As he was doing that, Taylor spotted to his right a slightly ajar door to the small storage unit abutting the dugout.

"Corey, go in that room over there and look in the corner behind the door. There may be a bucket of balls. Bring the whole thing out to me."

Corey hesitated with a look that he shouldn't do that.

"Go ahead. It's okay," Taylor reassured him.

Corey sauntered into the room and brought the bucket to the mound before resetting himself up at the plate.

Meanwhile, on top of a hill a few hundred yards away, an older gentleman and his younger assistant were putting away the rakes and chalk liners into the maintenance garage. They'd just finished preparing all the fields for opening day and were both pretty bushed. As the older man wheeled the spreader through the open garage door, his associate noticed Taylor and Corey in the distance down on the main field. Specific attention was given to Corey, who was about to ruin the beautifully laid lines of the batter's box. Annoyed, he called over his senior partner.

"Rick, a guy in a wheelchair and some kid are on the field."

The tired vet calmly walked over to see what was going on. Patting off the dust from his well-worn custodial pants, he casually looked over.

"I'll get 'em off," the young man anxiously volunteered, starting to leave.

However, before he could take the next step, his supervisor gently placed his ruddy but powerful hand on the young man's bicep and held him back a moment while he cupped his other hand over his eyebrows to further study who was on the field.

"Hold on, hold on," he softly requested.

"What's wrong?" the young man inquired.

The old man didn't respond right away, his eyes remaining fixed on the person in the wheelchair. After a brief moment a slight smile emerged as he recognized who it was. He continued to watch him, unfazed that Corey was now completely messing up the box lines while pretending to be a big-league hitter.

"Well, look at that," the groundskeeper wondered aloud.

The young man turned back toward the field, curious as to what could be so captivating to his boss.

"That's Taylor Green," the old man responded as if reading his thoughts.

Given the apparent kinship he seemed to have with the man in the wheelchair, it was clear that the unscheduled practice wouldn't be disturbed. The two men quietly remained at the top of the hill overlooking the ball field, unnoticed by either Taylor or Corey, who still believed they were alone.

"Okay, lemme see your stance," Taylor declared, keenly looking at the boy's hip and knee positioning before moving his eyes up to Corey's shoulders.

"It's rough with your dad living someplace else, isn't it Cor?"

Taylor offered without breaking his concentration on the boy's bat angle.

Corey was taken aback by the comment. His coach never talked like that before. Taylor stayed focused, however, intentionally ignoring Corey's surprised look.

"The same thing happened to me, Corey. I was your age too," he added nonchalantly.

This seemed to relieve Corey a little, but Taylor could imagine how unsteady he was with what was going on. Like many kids, he undoubtedly thought it was a safely kept secret, unnoticeable to the outside world and therefore not embarrassing. Taylor also well knew that because he had never brought it up, Corey didn't think he knew until he told him.

"It's not your fault, Corey," Taylor broke in again, still holding the ball, "and I'm never going to bug you about this stuff because I know how much it stinks when you're just a little guy. I was too," he said, motioning with his arm for him to back his shoulders off the plate a little bit.

"But there's nothing wrong with you, Corey. It's got nothin' to do with you at all," he added. "Never forget that, okay?" Taylor confirmed, returning eye contact with his little friend.

The boy's look made clear that he was comforted with what his coach was saying.

"Your dad loves you, Corey. Don't forget that either."

Though such a comment was extremely uncharacteristic for Taylor, he felt good making it. "And you know I'm always here for you, right?" he grinned, lightening things up as he held the ball high, signifying that the first pitch was coming.

Corey reared the bat back immediately before the ball was released. He swung heavily and connected, sending it hard on the ground down the left-field line.

CHAPTER 49

DETECTIVE JOHNSON DROVE BY A SCHOOL PLAYGROUND, SLOWING down and searching for any activity. "You see him in there?" he said to Skip, pointing toward the apparatus.

"No," Skip responded while he was looking.

He then made a left where he should've gone straight. This got Skip's attention. "Where you goin'?" he questioned.

"Just want to check the ball fields."

"He's definitely not there," Skip quipped dismissively.

Robert ignored the comment, turning into the parking lot to carefully scan the empty fields. After a moment he squinted toward the one farthest away, where he could make out the outline of a man in a wheelchair with a boy. The tension on his face broke into relief as he gently elbowed Skip while still looking at them.

"Whadya know." He smiled.

Taylor was still on the mound with Corey at bat. The bucket was near empty as the remainder of the white baseballs generously sprinkled the outfield, shining brightly as trophies to both Corey's success and Taylor's instruction. Johnson's inquisitive gaze toward the backstop spotted only two or three balls that had gotten by the little hitter he hardly knew.

Not aware that they were being watched, Taylor and Corey were still working. The kid had his game face on and remained in his stance, awaiting the next pitch. Taylor studied the strike zone, contemplating what next to throw. He was pushing Corey a little bit, adding heat to the pitches.

Meanwhile, a flustered Skip remained in the car, staring in disbelief at his father, who was sitting in the middle of the same field the two had regularly played on years before. He didn't say a word but continued to look over Robert's shoulder, mesmerized by a sight he had long given up on and even become hardened to.

Robert pulled out his phone to call Evette. Before dialing, he looked at Skip. "Why don't you head down there while I call everybody off?" he offered with a touch of compassion in his eyes.

The young man exited the vehicle, still looking at his father, almost three fields away, and began to jog toward them. All the while he was half wondering what he was doing, but he kept running.

Taylor was about to deliver his last pitch. "Okay, you're gonna run on this one!" he yelled to Corey.

This was a familiar drill, though it had never been done on a real field before. Taylor could see that for Corey it was like being at the big show. He took a beautiful swing, which sent the ball up the middle, slightly to Taylor's right. He managed a back-handed grab, however, and, tucking his mitt in his lap, he hastily rolled toward first base to head Corey off.

"I'm closin' in!" he playfully chided.

Corey was too fast though and safely ran through the base, excitedly turning to his left to determine whether he should go for second. Thanks to Taylor, the kid was way ahead of his age at base running too.

Anticipating that Corey would go for it, Taylor had already turned his wheels enough to keep his momentum while heading for the next base. Corey looked back and let out a cheerful giggle. He was about six feet or so ahead, though his coach had picked up speed and made it a real horse race. Taylor stayed just to the left of Corey as he always did to allow for a slide.

Skip was now about fifty yards beyond the center field fence but still out of sight, thanks to the billboards hiding him from view.

He slowed as he reached the field. Taylor speedily but cautiously closed in on Corey, who desperately tried to keep ahead. Both were totally oblivious to Skip, who was now gliding along the back of the billboard fence, keeping his head low enough to avoid being seen. He maintained a soft jog but kept a keen eye on his father while turning the right-field corner and heading down the line toward the dugout.

Corey safely slid into second, just under Taylor's outreached tag from behind. Signaling "safe" with his arms, Taylor coasted beyond the bag and announced it to the imaginary crowd before a beaming Corey. Skip was now secreted behind the dugout immediately adjacent to the passageway to the infield. Remaining tight against the wall, he peeked his head around the corner to spy out the situation as Corey proudly stood up on the bag and dusted himself off. Both he and Taylor were huffing and puffing but appeared happy with the accomplishment.

"Okay, kid!" Taylor cheered, giving Corey a high five. "Nice job."

Skip quickly turned around and pressed the back of his head against the dugout wall. That was a voice he hadn't heard in over two years, and it felt almost magical. His emotions began to swirl as the sound of his father's conversation came in like a warm salve, medicating his insides in places that had long crusted over. He'd seen too much to be Corey again though. And he'd never trust going back there with his father anyway.

He slid down to a squat against the back of the dugout wall, debating how to sneak back to the detective's car unnoticed.

Taylor gave Corey another thumbs-up before seeing the kid's eyes lift to something behind him toward the stands. He turned his head and saw Robert Johnson in a slow jog, cell phone in hand and looking like he was just finishing a call. Corey remained at second, his face frozen with a fear that he was in serious trouble.

Turning his chair, Taylor tried to think of something to stave off the inevitable trouble his little friend was in. "It's okay, Robert. It's my fault," he bellowed over as a preemptive consolation.

Robert slowed down to a walk and entered the field. Thankfully he didn't appear angry, but he wasn't buying what Taylor had to say either.

"I know what happened, Taylor, and I'm sorry to you," he said, calmly shaking his head and looking toward his now-cowering son. "Why did you do that, Corey?" he sternly inquired.

Corey didn't say anything.

"It's all good, Robert," Taylor offered again. "Honestly it is."

"All right," Robert conceded skeptically. "C'mere, Corey," he said, extending his hand.

Corey dutifully took his dad's hand, and as the two headed back toward the dugout, Robert briefly turned back to Taylor and head-motioned toward the area where Skip was hiding. Taylor looked and saw his son, who now stood in the doorway, looking back at him. Taylor's eyes winced as he tried to gather his thoughts. His day was obviously not over.

Viewing an outfield littered with baseballs he hadn't hit was a bit confusing to Skip. Made him angry too. *Why doesn't he just live someplace else?* his mind silently raged as he continued to survey the moment he'd awkwardly just stepped into. His initial embarrassment about getting arrested was being overridden by a fury that couldn't wait to tell his lawyer father that he did. He even hoped his name was going in the newspaper.

Taylor struggled with what to say.

Truth be told, it wasn't the accident that had driven him into seclusion and separated him from the people who loved him most. It was him.

He had no good excuse as to why, after so much time, life hadn't gone forward for either himself or the young man standing in front of him. Nor had he done anything to stop the downward spiral in his son's life when he was probably the only one who could. There was no getting around that either. The only thing Skip could have heard amid his father's deafening two-year silence was that he wasn't worth it anymore; a message Taylor obviously never intended but nonetheless gave to anyone living close enough to feel the spray of his own self-pity.

"Pretty ironic." Taylor sighed under his breath.

Finding himself on the other side of an abandonment he wouldn't have wished on his worst enemy, he struggled again with what to say. *He probably hates me*, he surmised, *I would.*

If anyone understood how much easier it was to despise someone rather than letting yourself get hurt again, it was Taylor Green. He had done it all his life. The question he couldn't answer was, what should he do now?

He rubbed his eyes to give himself a little respite.

"What's goin' on?" Skip interrupted, looking at the baseballs.

It wasn't really a question, but Taylor tried to explain himself anyway.

"It's kind of a long story, Skip," he sheepishly let out, joining in his son's perusal of the field. "I kinda made a deal with him," Taylor continued, looking over at Skip.

"What kind of deal?" Skip challenged.

"I was trying to teach myself to walk, Skip. I didn't want anybody to know until Corey saw me fall on the deck one afternoon. He helped me walk as best he could, and I helped him play. I guess it was our secret."

"Oh" was all Skip could say, a little taken aback by his father's rare display of vulnerability, though he still felt more and more unsettled by what he was seeing.

He glanced at the field and then back at Taylor with the eyes his mother had when she was catching on to something that wasn't quite kosher. It was a dangerous look that Taylor knew only complete honesty could satisfy, though there was only a small chance at that.

"I didn't want anyone to know," Taylor fumbled again, "because I wanted to walk first, believe it or not. Pretty stupid, isn't it?" he added with a sigh, hoping Skip would at least say something.

He didn't though but instead looked back over the field.

"That's what the canes were for," he quietly let out after a pause.

His voice trailed off to the tone of a boy who wanted to be part of his father's life but obviously wasn't.

Though it was Taylor's pride and only that pride that kept Skip and everyone else out of what he was doing, that excuse wasn't good enough even for him anymore.

The sound of car doors closing and other vehicles pulling up in the distant parking lot distracted Skip, who caught his mother striding down the pathway toward them. She was still wearing her blue nursing scrubs, an outfit he hated seeing because it usually meant she had to leave work early, which was never good for him these days. *She probably knows I got arrested*, he figured. But he was too spent to be scared and too tired to fight today. His father, however, seemed surprisingly calm, even with all the attention coming their way.

"I think we gotta go," Skip said dismissively as he took a step or two toward his dad to offer an assisting push.

"It's okay, Skip," Taylor responded, politely declining the gesture and pivoting his chair toward the outfield to begin picking up the baseballs. "I think I'll stay a little bit."

Skip was taken off guard, especially given the number of people trickling down toward the field. *His father wouldn't want to be around this in a million years*, he thought. He himself certainly didn't.

"Okay, fine." An offended Skip shrugged, raising his hands as if he were taking them off the chair posts he was about to grab. "I'll see you later," he quipped, turning to head off the field.

He can suit himself. He always has, Skip fumed inside as he strode away, unable to fully contain the rejection he was sick of being sick of. Even with that, he still couldn't get his mind around what his father was doing down there without him. He felt betrayed and, even moreso, was upset that it still mattered to him.

Taylor sensed this, and his usually razor-sharp wit scrambled for words that would stop his son from rapidly walking away. *It isn't finished*, he said to himself. He owed his boy something, but he had no idea what to say or even how to start.

"If you need a lawyer, I know a good one, Skip," he blurted out of nowhere, hoping the teen would hear it and at least be curious as he neared the dugout.

Skip held up and turned around. He had no idea how Mr. Johnson could have said something to his father that quickly. It wasn't that he cared that much, especially in that moment, but he did want to know what his dad knew. The two were now looking at each other. It was Skip's turn to talk.

"I got arrested," he said, pretty much point blank. He didn't know how else to say it.

"You okay?" Taylor answered, ignoring the part Skip thought was important.

"I'm good." He stiffened, returning to his protective posture. "How'd you know?" he asked.

Taylor just shrugged, downplaying its significance.

"Guess you found the right detective," he added with a smirk to lighten things up.

Skip didn't respond but still appeared concerned as to what his father knew.

"It's been that kind of a day, Skip." Taylor chuckled as he gazed back out at the field and the fences beyond.

Though his son had no idea what he was talking about, Taylor was happy he at least had his attention. The two were quiet again.

"I think things have been pretty rough for both of us, haven't they?" Taylor said, gently tapping the armrests of his chair with his palms.

Having never heard his father talk about his accident before, Skip didn't know how to react. Across the field he could see family and friends approaching the slope that bottomed out to the left-field line. He noticed his mother was slowing down. She was walking with Sharon and holding fast to Nathan's hand; he was desperately trying to get free and run to them. Mom wasn't letting him go though, and Taylor and Skip were both relieved.

Paula stopped about halfway down. Though she continued to

look inquisitively in their direction, with her hand on her forehead to block the sun, she was leaving them alone. Everybody else was staying in that area too, now talking among themselves.

Skip wasn't sure what to do at that point. He turned toward his father and noticed him rolling into the outfield just beyond second base, taking his time picking up the baseballs. Remaining where he was, Skip shot each of his parents another quick glance.

To see his mother backing off, his father oblivious to the dozens of people watching him, and he himself just standing in the middle of it after being arrested felt almost surreal.

He couldn't understand how things could be so out of control yet so peaceful at the same time. It didn't seem that anybody else knew either or cared.

Taylor picked up the last of the baseballs, turned his chair around, and from the middle of the outfield started casually tossing them toward the pail sitting on the pitcher's mound. Skip watched as they either fell in the bucket or bounced close by. His father sported a slight grin as he tried to sink the last of them, actually making three or four. Skip hadn't seen that smile for years.

"Guess you kept your end," Skip said, referring to all the balls Corey had hit out versus the few that were against the backstop.

"He did too," Taylor affirmed as he started to wheel back into the infield.

"Really," Skip jealously sniped.

"He got me here," Taylor noted, ignoring the sarcasm.

Coasting through the shortstop area a few feet away from second base, Taylor paused a moment as his eyes caught the bag and unexpectedly settled there for a little bit.

He turned his chair to look at it some more as the memory began coming back.

"What?" Skip inquired, wanting to leave.

"This is where we were," Taylor reflected, still looking at the base. "This is where we all were the day I had my accident," he continued, a little surprised as he looked over at Skip. "We were

247

playing that game with Nathan … your mother's game," he added, looking for some help from Skip, who apathetically shrugged in the negative.

Skip remembered, but Taylor could see by the look on his face that he's wasn't going there.

"It's okay. You got that from me." Taylor sighed.

"I didn't get anything from you!" Skip snapped almost before his father could finish.

Taylor sat back in his chair and calmly looked over at him, absorbing what he had said while the next moment or two drifted by. Truth be told, Skip got a lot from him, and as Taylor beheld the ragged hair, tired eyes, and smell of stale marijuana now sitting on the enraged young man who used to be his little champ, he saw that Skip's appearance was in actuality a painful reflection of what he believed his father thought about him.

"You got that too, Skip," Taylor offered apologetically. "But that's not your fault either," he added.

Though it may have looked dramatically different, his son had the same disease Taylor's father had given to him. Taylor knew he had to own all of it if Skip was ever going to have a way out. He took a deep breath and looked at his son again.

"Skip, after I got paralyzed two years ago, I gave up on everything except the possibility of one day walking again. And that's all I cared about," Taylor painfully admitted. "It was a bad decision, and it cost everybody. And it didn't have to."

He paused and took a moment to pick up an errant ball buried in the grass next to him, studying it in his hand while thinking to himself. He looked back over at Skip. "It went that way because your father is a hardheaded, egotistical man who felt the world owed him something. And the truth is, Son, I was like that even before I got hurt."

Taylor looked out toward the left-field fence and collected his thoughts again. "But I think that changed today, Skip," he offered as mildly as he could, realizing how much of a hypocrite he probably sounded like.

Skip didn't respond but continued to stare into his father's eyes, like he was searching for something he'd never seen before. It made Taylor uncomfortable, but he just waited.

After another moment, Taylor gazed into the outfield again, wondering if there was anything he could say that would matter at this point. He struggled to regain the focus and clarity of mind he used to have as a lawyer just before giving a summation to the jury. What he was facing now would be the argument of his life, but something inside him said he'd be okay if he was as honest as he could be. He quietly turned to Skip.

"I used to hate when people would talk about God," he candidly stated. "It made no sense to me that anything or anybody like that would exist in a world like this, at least not the one your mother was talking about.

"But if believing that made her a happier and better person, that was fine. But I wasn't going to ignore reality and think that way. I couldn't," he added, looking into the distance and talking like he was thinking aloud again. "That was something I think I decided a long time ago, Son, even before I met your mom."

Taylor paused a moment and looked back over at Skip. "You did have another grandfather, you know. And he shouldn't have been such a secret," Taylor said with a sigh. "I was probably close to your age when he left," Taylor added. "He was a troubled man who had a terrible drinking problem. He did a lot of stupid things ... made a lot of bad decisions. When he was gone, I was actually relieved." Taylor sighed again.

Skip didn't say anything; however, Taylor could see that hearing something about his other granddad for the first time captivated him.

"But not having a dad hurt your father a lot more than I ever could admit to, Skip, even to myself," Taylor added as he threw the ball toward the bucket. "And I went on to believe that the only thing I could depend on in this world was me. Which I thought I did because I had no choice. But I really did have a choice. I could have trusted people if I wanted to and even God. But I didn't because I was afraid that what had happened back then might happen again," Taylor said, tossing another ball. "And nothing was worth that."

Skip watched his father's eyes focus on the bucket with his usual concentration before throwing the next one. The ball hit the rim and bounced to the side. Taylor looked back over at him and shrugged. This eased the intensity a little bit and allowed them to continue eye contact this time.

"I got the independence I was looking for, Son, but the truth was, I was still pretty lonely on the inside. Pretty empty."

"When I met your mom, a lot of that changed but not everything," he admitted.

"What do you mean?" Skip asked, still guarded but inquisitive for the first time.

Taylor didn't know how to answer that. He certainly wasn't going to bare his soul to his fourteen-year-old or attempt to explain how he had loved the boys' mother on the one hand but had an affair on the other, something that until today he hadn't been able to make sense of himself.

"That's a good question," Taylor bluffed with a soft grin. He needed to buy some time. "I guess you could say I was still living with something I insisted I didn't have," he said.

Skip gave a look that he wanted the full answer.

"I think they call it 'sin,'" Taylor finished, knowing how awkward that must have sounded coming from him.

Skip glanced toward the outfield, apathetically shaking his head in both disbelief and even a trace of disappointment. Though he could respect his father's newfound transparency, he wasn't going to be so naive as to buy into God or religion this time around. He really had become his father's son, Taylor noticed with regret.

"So you're gonna be like Mom now," Skip tersely remarked after a long silence, his hands now stoically resting on his hips.

"If you mean forgiving people who were rotten to you like I was, I doubt it," Taylor remarked. "But I'm going to try."

"What about this?" Skip challenged, cynically pointing to his father's wheelchair.

An awkward quiet filled the space between them as Taylor took in what his son just said. Though he knew it was intended to silence anymore discussion like this, Taylor couldn't let it do that.

He sat back and thought about how to respond. He wasn't mad, and he certainly wasn't going to argue with a young man who, as a boy, had probably prayed a thousand times for his father to walk again without it ever happening. In fact, things only got worse.

After a moment or two Taylor spoke. "I agree with you, Skip. I don't completely know what this is about either," he admitted candidly. "But I think life is really about this," he said, tapping on his heart. "But that's something you find on your own. I don't think there's any other way."

Skip didn't say anything but remained looking at his father. His disillusionment needed more than that, and so did his pain. Taylor did his best to reach out to both.

"Skip, there's something a man faces every morning when he opens his eyes," Taylor reflected, talking to himself as much as to his son. "We can't see it because it's in here," he added, pointing to his heart again. "And I think it's the root of the quiet struggle we face every time we try to hold onto things we were never meant to hold onto. It's probably sin and unforgiveness," Taylor reflected again, glancing around the diamond before looking back at Skip, whose eyes now appeared a little softer and less accusatory toward him.

"Two words that always annoyed me." Taylor chuckled after a pause. Studying the ball in his hand and collecting his thoughts, he looked back at Skip. "It had to be hard seeing me here without you knowing about it. Believe me, it wasn't my idea." Taylor sighed, looking at the imprint of Corey's slide.

"But I had to come back and face a lot of things that went way beyond baseball or even this wheelchair, Skip. And I did that today," Taylor said after a pause. "But it couldn't happen until I put away the facade that I was a good man on my own and admit that there were things in me that were pretty ugly that I could never change by myself," he said, motioning to his chest again.

"Things that hurt me and a few very important people in my life, you being one of them. But I don't think God created us for that stuff, Skip. And I honestly think that's what Jesus died to change. And this is why he had to," Taylor added, touching his own heart again. "That's what the whole Messiah thing was about. It was bigger than anyone wanted, because it was about what's in here," Taylor said, referring to his heart again. "It was bigger than what I wanted, that's for sure. But it's what I needed."

Feeling filleted but relieved it was all out in the open, Taylor looked out at the field again. "I didn't get what I know both of us asked for, but maybe that miracle was too small for what I needed, Skip," Taylor said after a reflective pause. "Isn't that what the story of Jesus and the paralyzed guy was really all about?" He winked, looking to surprise his son that he was actually familiar with it.

Clearly unconvinced, Skip continued to look at his dad, unafraid of the silence now lingering between them. Taylor wasn't intimidated by the quiet either, and though he wasn't looking for a response from Skip, he got one anyway.

"God's supposed to heal people," Skip challenged, though his tone now had a sensitivity about it that exposed his anguish.

Taylor relaxed back in his chair again, choosing to absorb what was being said rather than react to it. Unlike his father, Skip had been raised on this stuff, Taylor realized. But like his dad, it had severely let him down; at least in his mind it had.

He looked back at Skip, loving him with everything he had. Though Taylor recognized that the issue was certainly complicated, he equally understood that just being honest and not playing God were his only options. So he took them.

"I think he has, Skip," Taylor quietly answered, knowing it probably wouldn't satisfy him.

Turning his head away, Skip confirmed that, but Taylor noticed he wasn't angry anymore as he glanced back at him. "This is something I think you have to come to on your own, Son," Taylor offered again, breaking the uneasiness. "And that's okay."

Skip didn't respond.

Taking a final scan for loose balls around the area, Taylor turned toward third base en route to home to get the rest of them. He invited Skip to come as the young man caught up and grabbed the back rests of the chair to help push him along. The mood relaxed, thankfully for both of them.

"So I guess you're religious now," Skip said; the comment sounding more like an observation than a criticism.

Taylor chuckled, continuing to look straight ahead. *He's got his father's candor, that's for sure*, he thought. *And he's certainly entitled to his own journey*, Taylor said to himself as he reached down for another ball.

"You mean religion is gonna be my crutch because I got no other place to go?" he said, gently calling his son out.

Skip was embarrassed to even hear his father talk about himself like that. He didn't know what to say.

"It's okay, Skip. I get it," Taylor consoled. "But I hope you give your old man more credit than that," he added, turning around with a slight grin.

As the two quietly reached third base, Taylor changed the subject to lighten things up again. "So humor me, Skip. What was third?"

"I told you. I don't know," he answered dismissively.

"C'mon," Taylor protested.

"Faith that moves mountains," he reluctantly admitted after a pause. He hoped it would end the silly game.

"Oh," Taylor acknowledged. "That's pretty good," he added, briefly glancing in the distance toward Paula.

"I see your shoes," Skip interrupted, pointing down the left-field line.

He was a little friendlier but not totally.

"Yeah," Taylor answered.

Skip gently tipped up the chair so he could roll over a portion of the bag while making the turn. "What changed?" he asked his father.

"I did," Taylor admitted.

"When?" Skip pressed further.

"Well, it started after I collapsed on the deck for about the eightieth time this afternoon and realized I wasn't gonna walk again," Taylor answered plainly.

"Oh." Skip sighed, slightly startled by his father's response.

"It's okay, Skip," Taylor comforted. "It got me into some soul-searching I needed to do. And the more I did, the more I realized that even if I walked again, I would still have the problem I had before I got paralyzed."

"What—"

"The one in here," Taylor politely cut in, tapping his chest again.

"Oh," was all Skip could say.

"And I didn't want to go back to that either, believe it or not," Taylor said after a pause.

Skip was no longer pushing, though his hands remained resting where they were as Taylor gently brought the chair to a stop. They were only about a foot or two down the third baseline toward home.

"Sounds pretty weird to hear your father talking like this, huh, Skip?" Taylor offered, patting his son on the hand.

"You believed in God," Skip challenged, ironically reminiscent of the way he had defended him the last time they were on this field.

"I did a little bit, Skip, but not because I knew he existed or that he really loved me. Jesus didn't die because anybody killed him, Skip," Taylor said as an afterthought. "It was so we could be forgiven and have a new heart. Because we all need one. Your father didn't get that part until today, but I think that's where it all lives," Taylor added, putting his big hand on top of his son's again and lightly squeezing it.

Both were still facing forward, comfortably not having to make eye contact.

"You didn't do anything wrong, Dad," Skip replied, sympathetic to his father but clearly hardened to what he was saying.

"I get where you're coming from, Skip, but the truth is, your old man was hiding from a lot of things, stuff I don't have to hide from anymore."

"What stuff?" Skip interrupted.

"You're too young!" Taylor laughed, cutting off the inquiry. "You're going to have to trust me on that one." He chuckled again.

Looking at home plate straight ahead of them, Skip anticipated the next question.

"All right—" Taylor started, beginning to roll forward.

"No!" Skip shouted, but he's wasn't mad.

"C'mon! You know I don't know it!" Taylor kiddingly yelled back.

"Forgive others, and you'll find your way home," Skip blurted out but with the giggle of the boy he used to be, the one his father had forgotten he'd even lost.

The laugh so blindsided Taylor that he reflexively placed his hands on the wheels of his chair and brought it to a stop. It was as if Skip's guard had unconsciously slipped for a brief second, opening a window into his soul, where Taylor could hear both the pain of where his son was but also, deep beneath it, the joy of who he had been made to be.

"You okay, Dad?" a startled Skip asked, sounding a little embarrassed he had let the laugh out.

"I'm good, I'm good," Taylor assured him, downplaying it as much as he could while biding some time to gather himself again. He remained still for a moment and gazed down the line at home plate. He knew where Skip's pain was coming from. It was from him.

"Dad?" Skip interrupted again, gently shrugging Taylor's shoulder.

"Yes, Son," he responded, still looking forward but placing his hand on top of Skip's again. "I'm okay," he added, though still slightly shaken.

He wondered if what he had just experienced was the same type of window Jesus looked through at the woman that day two thousand years ago, or the one the college girl was looking through when she saw the women in the Ukrainian jail or even the window God may have been seeing Taylor through earlier that afternoon. Was it a gift to see the pain people were in and want to heal it?

That answer was easy for Taylor, and it was clear what he needed to do for both his son's sake as well as his own. He motioned for Skip to lean over so he could whisper something in his ear, and as he did, he put his arm around his son's head, hugging it against his. Having his cheek pressed against his father's now-moist, unshaven face was far from comfortable for the teen, especially since his slight resistance only caused Taylor to pull him closer.

Looking at home plate with Skip's still-boyish face pressed against his, Taylor spoke in a voice that came straight from the depth of his soul. "Skip, I need you to know something," he softly confided. "I blew it as your father. There's no other way to say it," he said, leaving pause to allow his son a moment to digest his confession, as painful as it was to hear himself say it.

"I would like a second chance though. Do you think you could give it to me?"

Skip was speechless but silently processed what his father just said. "I don't know," he quietly answered, his head still slightly resistant to his dad's pull.

"I get that," Taylor comforted after a pause. "Will you try?" he whispered again, not caring about the tears now beginning to flow between their compressed cheeks.

Skip wasn't talking, but after a second or two, Taylor felt the pulling stop and the grip of both his son's arms squeezing around his shoulders like he'd just gotten something back that he'd never want to lose again. Taylor tightened his hold too.

"I love you, Son" was all he could say, exhaling what felt like a world of hurt that had once been between them.

That was all the forgiveness Taylor Green needed that day as he slid his hands down and clutched Skip's forearms, which were still crisscrossed over his chest. After a few moments, he gave him another squeeze. "Ready to take your old man home?"

"Yeah," Skip said, giving a last hug back and turning his father's chair around.

The field and parking lot were now empty, except for Paula and their family, who were still sitting on the adjoining slope down by the left-field line. They all stood up and looked over when they saw the two were heading toward them.

"So when we goin' to court, Son?" Taylor asked while they were still out of earshot from everybody.

"I don't know." Skip sighed, embarrassed by the reminder.

"Hey," Taylor consoled, tapping his son's hand. "We're going to get through it. May be a little rusty, but your dad's still a pretty good lawyer, you know," he added as Nathan swiftly approached them with the others walking behind.

"I can't help you with your mother though. I lose every time." Taylor chuckled.

"Uh," Skip moaned. He wasn't ready for the confrontation.

"You'll live." Taylor chuckled again. "But just barely," he added, turning and winking at Skip before Nathan jumped on his lap.

"What happened?" Paula inquired, looking at both of them.

"Oh, you're so cute. I can't take it," Taylor interjected, purposely deflecting the question.

Paula raised her eyes and briefly shook her head as she took over pushing her husband. "You're bleeding," she said, glancing down at the scrape on Taylor's arm as they proceeded through the gate and onto the walkway.

"Long story, my dear," he responded, knowing that wouldn't be enough.

"How long?" she said, leaning over the top of his head and kissing it.

"Probably the rest of my life." Taylor chuckled.

"I can do that," she answered, managing a smile for the first time that afternoon.

"Good to see you, Mr. Green!" came a voice from behind.

It was Ed Goodale, the older maintenance man. He was now standing by the other field entrance with chalk liner in tow. He had a mess to clean up, and Taylor felt a little bad. Ed's smile relieved that, however, as Taylor returned a grin.

"Good to see you, Mr. Goodale," he replied.

"Are you coming back?" Ed asked.

It was more of an invitation than a question.

"Is it still a thinking man's game, Mr. Goodale?" Taylor responded in the mock formality of longtime friends.

"It is, Mr. Green. That it is," Ed said.

"Then I guess I'm coming back," Taylor answered. "Just don't tell anyone yet," he offered a with a sly smile.

"I won't." Ed smiled back, tipping his old weathered cap as he headed through the opening.

Taylor's last comment left everyone, including Skip, in shock.

"Taylor?" Paula asked, her eyebrows furrowed.

"Yes, Paula," he answered, acting as if nothing had changed.

"What's going on?"

"I'm coming back, that's all." He chuckled, squeezing her hand.

Neither Paula nor anyone else said anything as the silhouette of the tired but relieved Green family quietly retreated down the path toward the parking lot. Taylor sat back and rested his eyes. He could feel his arms and shoulders starting to ache from the marathon he was on earlier that afternoon, but it was a good hurt.

Not everything in life can be put back together the same way it was or even the way we might like it to be, he reflected as he took in the last of the warm spring breezes blowing through the trees that day. But through love and forgiveness, at least the kind he knew now, all things can be healed.

God was his, and the quiet desperation was over.

Mercy had the last say.

EPILOGUE

"You gotta hang that one a little further down Paula," Taylor said, referring to the mitt she was carrying with the string and clothespin attached. "Are those done?" he added.

"One is. The others are still a little damp," she said after checking the series of gloves that had been hanging in the sun throughout that afternoon.

"Throw it over," Taylor answered, reaching for the oil.

Paula walked toward him with it as well as with a few others she was picking off the line that had sundried from the day before. The balance of the mitts had been soaking in his five-gallon pail of hot water for the last few hours while Taylor was at work. Feeling the temperature with his hand, he was about to pull them out.

"It was boiling when you put them in, right, Paula?" he questioned.

"Yes, Taylor," she wearily answered.

"Full cup of salt?" he inquired again.

"Full cup," she echoed.

Taylor adjusted the towel covering his lap as he reinverted the inside-out glove Paula had just tossed him and began to work in the oil. He still had his suit pants, shirt sleeves, and loosened tie on. It was about six o'clock in the evening, and the two of them were out by the horse fence, hanging the last of the gloves he had reconditioned for Nathan's team.

After tying each newly oiled mitt around a baseball he'd inserted in the pocket, Taylor reached for his own glove and the oversized jar of Vaseline he had nearby.

"So Nathan's catching this year," Paula observed while clothes-pinning the remaining batch on the fence line. She had worked her way back down to where Taylor was sitting.

"We'll see," he acknowledged, cautiously optimistic.

"You're letting him use your mitt?" she said, somewhat surprised, referring to the beloved Nokona he'd caught with since high school.

"Until I see it laying in the dirt." Taylor chuckled. "May be a little heavy for him," he added, working in another layer of Vaseline for the tired, old glove. "But he really wants to wear it."

A few moments passed as the two continued working.

"Heard you went to court with Ira today," Paula said. She remained looking at what she was doing to avoid eye contact.

"How'd you hear that?" Taylor said with a slight smile.

"Marge told me," Paula answered.

"Some things never change." He chuckled again.

"How was it, Taylor?" she quietly asked after a pause.

"Well, one day at a time. Isn't that what they say?" Taylor replied, still studying the mitt.

Paula shook her head though with a soft smile. Taylor knew she was waiting for more.

"It was good, Paula," he added, looking out at the horse farm and into the distance. "It was good," he said again.